The Benefactor

The Benefactor

Erin Fry

Published by Skyscape, New York

www.apub.com

ISBN-13: 9781477817421
ISBN-10: 1477817425

Library of Congress Cataloging-in-Publication Data available upon request.

Printed in the United States of America
First edition

To Zachary:

Your cleverness amazes me;
your heart makes me proud.

You made writing a book in two months
not only possible but fun.

Now, about those clothes in your room . . .

EPISODE 1
THE CONTESTANTS

"[N]othing should be left undone to afford all ranks of people the means of obtaining a proper degree of it, at a cheap and easy rate."

—John Jay, first Chief Justice of the United States, 1785

May 13, 1:45 p.m.
Boston, Massachusetts
The Benefactor

He nearly collided with a tiny, bleary-eyed Asian girl whose earbuds were mostly hidden by the bright yellow beanie she'd pulled low on her head.

"Yo," she said, her look scathing as she pivoted gracefully, her crimson backpack swaying with her.

He watched as she continued down the wide, high-arched hall outside the chancellor's office, not so much because he was distracted by her tight jeans and slouching walk, but more because he was still numb from the shock of what had just happened.

He'd done it.

He'd gotten them all. Every last one of them. No one thought he could. They'd said these fine institutions couldn't be bought; weren't to be compromised; their standards were too high. His investors were convinced that there was no feasible way that the presidents and deans and chancellors of these top universities—the best schools in the world—would agree to be a part of his game—a reality show!

But they had. *All* of them. For the right price.

For some of them, it was about money. Plain and simple. They needed the endowments. Tough times and all that. For others, it was about power. As soon as he'd mentioned that a rival school was participating, they jumped. For others still, it was exposure, air time, being associated with other top-notch schools.

But this one? He looked around at the hallowed, dimly lit hall in which he stood. This was the Big One. He'd been convinced this one would be a hard sell. There was something so prestigious about this school—some of the brightest minds in history, in politics, in medicine had come from this campus. Why would they agree to be a part of his game?

But the chancellor had been surprisingly willing. Once he'd heard the intent of the competition, how thoroughly the final eight contestants would be vetted, he'd nodded slowly and reached for his Mont Blanc pen. Of course, an endowment would be appreciated. But yes, he would agree to be placed on the list among the other fine universities that had already signed on.

The girl in the yellow beanie stopped to hug a kid whose immediate needs (from the look of him) included a steak dinner and a haircut. He leaned in close and she laughed, throwing back her head. If he'd had all day, he would have stayed to watch them. He loved the mystical language of young adults, their subtle but purposeful movements. Underfed kid handed beanie girl a notebook and together they disappeared around a corner, shoulders and hips knocking each other lightly.

He wondered what they'd had to do to get into this school. Their test scores had to have been nearly perfect, their high school grades off the charts. They must have been captains, leaders, volunteers, award-winners. Ass-kissers. Had they even enjoyed high school? He had to wonder if they thought it was worth it now.

He lifted the strap of his messenger bag over his head and started walking toward his car. A few kids turned to stare at him, racking their brains for why he looked so familiar. He nodded at them. Kept walking. They'd Google it sooner or later and he'd be a topic of conversation over more than one study session that night.

He pushed open the heavy wooden door and weaved around clusters of kids. Funny thing was, he'd been on this campus before. Fourteen years ago. A lifetime.

They hadn't wanted him then.

He grinned.

But they sure wanted him now.

July 8, 10:13 a.m.
Manhattan, New York
The Benefactor

Today was *the* day. After months of prep work and interviews and negotiating, today was it. Today, cameras would roll; heroes and villains would be made. He hoped very much to find himself as one of the former.

He reached for his favorite pen. Popped the cap off. Snapped it back on. He needed to get out of this damn office and on a bike, where he could pound away the nervous energy pulsing painfully through every cell in his body. Making him twitchy. He hated feeling twitchy.

Today, he was—no, he *became*—the Benefactor.

He laughed out loud in his empty office. Pictured himself as Trump, pointing. Firing. He had way better hair than Trump. And he was about to become as famous.

"The Benefactor."

He tried to say it in a deep announcer's voice, imagine the way others would hear it. He reached for his empty coffee cup. Put it back down. Twitchy. *Dammit.*

He'd spent way too much time in the past months debating what the kids—or the world, really—would call him.

The Godfather still held such appeal. He leaned back in his plush leather chair, surveying his office—which overlooked Central Park—with its sharp edges and bold but simple furniture. The lights would dim. He would teepee his fingers under a stubble-rough chin, cast a penetrating but somehow sexy gaze into a camera, and say, with just the right blend of swagger and bullshit, "I'm gonna make him an offer he can't refuse."

Aw, man. Who was he kidding? He weighed a buck fifty sopping wet, sported dark wavy hair that was anything but sexy, and screamed *tech-nerd* without even opening his mouth. Bradley Cooper he was not.

He'd tossed around the Broker (too commercial). The Patron (too condescending). The Donor (too morbid—sounded like he was giving up a kidney).

He'd settled on the Benefactor. His secretary—picture a graying Chihuahua in knee-high boots and a skirt so tight she had to shuffle—had nodded enthusiastically and rushed to agree that it was perfect, absolutely perfect. His five board members had laced their fingers across bulging bellies, dipped pairs of fuzzy, caterpillar eyebrows together, and nodded solemnly, though their throat-clearing and sideways glances were hardly subtle. He knew what they thought about this latest project of his.

Screw them. His savvy brain and marketing brilliance had given them those bellies. They could suck this one up.

"Perfect," announced Yaz when the name was settled. Yaz was his director—a buzz-haired, spray-tanned guy who had flown in from L.A. to finalize the details of the show. "The Benefactor. I like."

Yaz, short for Jonathon (he'd made the mistake once of asking about that and got a mind-numbing explanation that involved a grandmother, a motorcycle, and dentures), had the annoying habit of speaking in two-word sentences and gnawing on the outside of his thumb.

"I eat." (*Gnaw.*)

"We go." (*Gnash.*)

"Too darling." (*Chomp.*)

But minimalist Yaz had turned out to be rather efficient, culling through the potential candidates with surprising speed, narrowing down the enormous field of applicants to a few dozen. Together, he and Yaz had found their Ultimate Eight—eight ideal teens all about to enter their senior year of high school; eight desperate kids who needed this one last chance at redemption, a hope for a future.

And he, *the Benefactor*, could give it to them. (Cue theme music and opening montage.)

He stretched his jean-clad legs out before him and clasped his hands behind his head to combat the twitchiness. Purposefully, he propped his black, worn-through

Chuck Taylors on his spotless mahogany desk and reached for a button on his intercom.

"Millie," he said, running a finger over his upper lip. Thirty-three and still barely a hair poking through. "When's my plane leave?"

"Two fifteen, sir," she answered crisply.

"And the kids?"

"They're all on their way, sir. Camera crews arrived this morning."

He nodded, satisfaction spreading through his veins like the heat of a fine Scotch. He spun in his chair to face a huge black screen and reached for the small remote. Even though the show wouldn't air for a week or so (they were rushing production through to get it into the summer lineup), Yaz had promised him access to live footage of the kids around the clock. If he wanted to, he could watch them right now. He could see them as they said their good-byes—trembling with anxiety or maybe bolstering a fake confidence for the camera. He could study their faces—faces he'd memorized down to each freckle—to see if they were reacting as he was convinced they would.

Not yet, though. He wasn't ready. He wanted to savor these last moments. Tomorrow, life changed. Obscurity would be gone. The tabs were already picking up that he was involved in something. They were sniffing around; wouldn't be long before news of this little show of his got out. Which was good. Teasers were going to start airing tomorrow anyway.

His image would be transformed. From multimillionaire technology geek to producer of the hottest new reality show. Maybe he'd get a date. Finally.

But it wasn't really his love life that he was hoping to kick-start. (Though if that were a by-product, he wouldn't complain.) Americans needed to *wake up.* The quality of education was declining. The United States was ranked seventeenth in the world. Behind countries like Finland and South Korea. Finland! A country slightly smaller than the state of Montana. And that wasn't the worst of it. Kids were busting their asses to get into college, only to find that: a) they couldn't get accepted because kids from other countries were filling their slots; b) it was too damn expensive; c) they didn't have a clue what they wanted to do with their lives; or d) they could make just as much money doing what he did—creating and investing in a start-up, working hard, and skipping the degree.

Still, he'd found eight kids—out of thousands of applicants—who thought college was the end-all, be-all. Who were willing to jump through his hoops to get there.

He grabbed for his tablet and quickly called up the file. There were eight folders in that file. He knew every detail of every one. Birth dates and weights. Siblings and boyfriends. Deepest fears, greatest dreams. He knew it all. He'd watched their interview tapes dozens of times, studying the nuanced way that this one held her head; how that one paused; how the last one jiggled his foot, even as he tried to appear cool, calm, unfazed.

He had just closed the last file when Millie's knock came.

"Your ride's here, sir," she said, her eyes darting around his office, as they often did, as if she expected—or maybe hoped—to find something incriminating, like underwear or empty booze bottles.

"Thanks, Millie."

He stood and stretched, quickly dropping his tablet in his messenger bag and tucking his phone in his pocket. He, too, glanced around the office, but finding neither underwear nor anything else that needed to make its way to L.A. with him, he snapped his bag closed.

His plane was scheduled to land in Santa Monica at five p.m. West Coast time. Unfortunately he had dinner reservations with a few of the other producers in Beverly Hills at seven. What he really wanted to do was meet the kids.

The kids. Who were being put up in separate hotels so they wouldn't see each other until morning. Who were being schlepped around in limos and treated like mini movie stars—all on his dime. Who were no doubt ordering room service and enjoying this brief interlude of independence. Who had no clue what awaited them tomorrow.

He hit the down arrow on the elevator that would take him to his waiting car.

Tomorrow they were his.

July 8, 9:48 a.m.
Chicago, Illinois
Cassidy McGowan

"You better know what you're doing, Cass."

Her mom stood at the sink, dwarfed by her faded Bears sweatshirt, scrubbing furiously at the scrambled egg residue clinging to the skillet. Their dishwasher was broken again, flooding the faded linoleum floor with sudsy water when anyone turned it on. And their landlord was MIA. *Shocker.*

"I do, Mom." Cassidy sighed, weaving together the final strands of Faith's hair and fastening it with Faith's favorite pink bow. She planted a kiss on the crown of Faith's head, and breathed her in: strawberry shampoo, baby lotion, and that ever-present tanginess that little kids just seemed to emanate.

No one else could braid Faith's hair like Cassidy could. No one else ever took time to read her to sleep, either. Cassidy swallowed the sadness inching up her throat. She couldn't back out now. She had to do this. It was her only chance of getting out of here. So it was not a choice at all, really.

"Faith, go brush your teeth, girly," Mom said.

Faith's pudgy legs kicked out once as she plopped off Cassidy's lap. She skip-hopped off toward the bathroom, humming.

Cassidy watched her go, her chest brick-heavy. She would miss that little girl so much.

"You won't be stupid, right, Cass?" Mom said, drying her hands on a towel. She spun around. "There'll be boys there. And even though I signed a bunch of stuff about rules . . . and they told me you'd be supervised . . . well, you're teenagers. Just please, *please* promise me you won't be stupid."

The anger always started in her belly. Then, like wildfire, it would lick its way up into her chest and throat, claw at her tongue, squeeze her jaw. Dart behind her eyes. But as much as she wanted to retort, *Shut up, Mom. I'm a freakin' straight-A student. You think I'm gonna do something dumb?* her mouth never opened. Instead, she seethed in stony silence, a wall of resentment and indignation.

Cassidy dropped her chin and traced a finger along a crack in the yellowed Formica countertop, as the anger seeped through her. She was one of the top students at her high school. She was class vice president, co-captain of the volleyball team, and she volunteered at the hospital once a week. She had done everything . . . *everything* possible to erase that one "stupid" choice. But there was no erasing in her mom's book. Stuff in that book got put in ink. Sharpie permanent.

Cassidy's younger brother, Justin, yawned his way into the kitchen and plopped onto a nearby chair.

"You ready, Sis?" he asked, folding his arms and flopping his head down on them, his unruly mop of curls masking his face. "You're gonna kick some ass, right? Not embarrass the family?"

"Language, Justin," their mother admonished, already turned away to dry more dishes.

Cassidy bumped her shoulder into his and felt some of her anger slip away. She could count on Justin to root for her. He was three years younger, but somehow in the last year he'd become her ally in this house. He'd have her back.

"You better not . . ." she started, just as the dull buzz that was their doorbell filled the small house they rented southwest of the city.

Justin's head popped up. Cassidy's mom froze, the towel clenched between two rough, chapped hands. Faith's uneven footsteps bounced down the hall.

"Me got it!" she screamed, her bare toes skimming the floor as she flew toward the living room.

Their mom shot a look at Justin and Cassidy as she left, a look they were accustomed to. A look that said, *This is so your fault.* They'd long ago quit asking what *this* was. Since Dad had bailed out, and Mom had lost her job as a manager when the drugstore closed and was forced to wait tables, they'd learned that somehow everything was *their* fault. No money? It's because you kids need too many clothes. Car broken down again? You two always needin' to be taken this place or that, it's no wonder. Faith got the flu? One of you must have brought the germs in.

Cassidy's eyes dropped to her lap as she heard her mom open the front door. She'd carefully planned this outfit: a white cotton skirt with scalloped edges that showed off her lean, tan legs; a baby blue, sleeveless V-neck sweater that magnified her eyes and hugged her curves; and her favorite brown sandals. Her nails were shiny pink. Her makeup was flawless. Her hair hung in soft waves around her face.

This was her best defense. Sure, she was a straight-A student, but she worked her ass off for those grades. She wasn't naturally bright like she pretended, or like the BFFs she tried to keep up with. She wasn't the best volleyball player, either. She'd gotten to be captain because of *this.*

Her . . . look. It was the one thing she could do without thinking. Smile and make the entire room turn toward her. It was how she was going to have to win this stupid competition. Because she had nothing else.

"Cassidy!"

Her mom. From the front room. A command.

She smoothed her skirt. Took a long, slow breath. Then she rose gracefully from the chair and glanced down at

Justin. He held out a closed fist. Silently, she tapped her fist to his.

Then she turned and walked into the living room, where the camera was already rolling.

Showtime.

July 8, 10:13 a.m.
Kansas City, Missouri
Tyrell Young

He didn't like the camera. Wasn't sure what he was supposed to be doing for it. Talking? About what? How much he'd miss his family? Hell no. He wasn't going to cry in front of millions of people just so he could get in good with whatever Big-Time was running this pimp show. He'd win it. Without the pity vote.

So he stared out the window. Watched his 'hood go by. Tried to see what that circular unblinking eye next to him was seeing. Small houses lined up, some droopy and neglected, some just "gettin' by," as Gram liked to say. Chain-link fences that sagged like the spirits of the owners. And mamas on front porch steps, sweating through thin T-shirts, yapping on cell phones while their kids darted happily from one yard to the next.

"Tyrell." The voice behind the camera was deep, measured, bored. "What are you feeling right now?"

Tyrell didn't turn away from the window. "Cold. Air's on too high."

The cameraman sighed long and deep—not for the first time since they'd left Tyrell's house. Tyrell heard the rustle of equipment being shut off and set aside. There would be no footage of the inner-city boy all nervous, excited. Tyrell felt some measure of satisfaction in that.

"Kid, you're gonna have to talk to the camera at some point," the guy said. "It's part of the deal, right?"

Tyrell shrugged. He felt bad for the guy. He'd shown up at their house, no doubt hoping for a touching farewell scene. Instead, he got Tyrell's mostly-deaf, half-wacked grandma yelling at both of them to shut the door so she could watch *The View*—didn't we see she was trying to hear Whoopi?

Tyrell's eyes followed one of the long, gray MAX "rapid" buses that hauled people around Kansas City. He wondered if his dad was driving that one. Probably not, since his dad didn't usually work the route near the airport.

His mom and dad had wanted to be there. But it was a Monday morning. His dad's alarm went off at 4:30 so he could get to the station by 5:15 and start off on his line by 5:30. His mom, who worked a twelve-hour shift at Children's Mercy Hospital, wouldn't be home until late that afternoon. And his sister, Shaina, hadn't been feeling good again, so he'd just kissed her damp forehead and told her to stay in bed, he'd see her in a couple weeks, but not to worry, he was gonna win.

When the camera guy had shown up, Tyrell had kept him on the porch while he grabbed his duffel bag and pecked his grandma on the cheek, then practically shoved him back out to the waiting car and driver.

So how was he feeling?

As if that first challenge couldn't come soon enough. There was a fire in his belly like before a big game, a building of adrenaline and tension that made him want to pound his body into something or someone until his brain went numb. Until everything hurt. If he'd had a football in his hands, he would've crushed it under one arm until his muscles didn't ache anymore. Until his heart didn't either.

But his hands were empty. Football had failed him.

So how did he feel?

He saw the airport come into view. His gut hardened. He was a warrior. He would do this.

How did he feel? Like it was third down with less than ten seconds on the clock and he needed a touchdown or his season was over. Make that his career. His life.

July 8, 12:03 p.m.
Near Portland, Oregon
Henry Stone IV

"Henry," his dad said, laying a heavy hand on his shoulder in what was meant to be a reassuring gesture but mostly felt awkward and staged for the camera. "We know you're going to make us proud, son. You always do."

Which was total garbage.

The two Drs. Stone stood there, eyes just barely brimming with forced tears, like this was some kind of Hallmark movie of the week and he was going off to fight in Iraq instead of heading to L.A. to compete against seven other desperate losers who must need the scholarship just as much as he did.

Except he didn't. That was the thing. The thing that made this moment so incredibly laughable, if it weren't so absolutely, pitifully, off-the-charts uncomfortable.

Henry reached for his rolling suitcase—swatting irritably at Brandy, the stupid Siamese who was napping on it. The suitcase had been neatly packed by his mother, who insisted that he have new underwear and socks, a sweatshirt (despite his insistence that they'd be in Los Angeles in July and God, Mom, was he, like, six?), a "modest" pair of pajamas, and a suitable bathing suit. That's what she called it, too. A bathing suit. Not board shorts or swim trunks. A *bathing suit.*

"I'm good, guys," Henry said stiffly, leaning to dutifully peck his mom and shake his dad's hand. "Thanks. I'll . . . see you in a few weeks, then, I guess."

Tristan, a basset hound they'd inherited last week when someone brought her into the clinic and decided not to come back, took that moment to start baying from the kitchen. This was the signal for Flip—their parrot—to begin mumbling, "Hate that damn dog. Hate that damn dog." (Which he'd picked up from Henry, who did, in fact, hate that damn dog.)

A train wreck. That's what it was. At some point, people would watch this and be unable to turn away—caught between laughter and horror.

He could sense the cameraman's amusement. Jeez, he'd have been amused watching this nightmare unfold, too. If only he'd been here two weeks ago, he would have gotten a whole different scene on that little camera of his. *Dr. Stone Flips Out When Son Announces He Doesn't Want to Be a Veterinarian.*

God. You'd think he'd told him he was a heroin addict or that he was joining a commune or something. Instead, he'd broken the news that he'd applied for this reality show, been chosen, and oh, by the way, he *didn't* want to attend Iowa State's vet school where every other loyal Henry Stone has gone since like the early 1900s.

His dad, the reputable Dr. Henry Stone III, did what he always did when he heard news he didn't like. He ran a hand through his graying hair and pretended he hadn't heard it.

"Henry," he'd said, "seventeen is a rough age. I remember when I was seventeen. You're wondering what to do with your life. Of course, you're going to have some moments where you're uncertain. You'll make a great vet someday."

But his dad was wrong. That love of animals and biology and smelling like dog piss every day, no matter how many times you washed your hands? It wasn't in his blood. He wanted to be a writer. He wanted to go to USC, bask in the southern California sun, and then get as far away from dreary Portland as geography allowed, where he would live in a house in which cats didn't shed on the couch, dogs didn't scratch to be let outside, and parrots didn't mimic every inane thing you said.

So Henry had explained all of this. Firmly. Unequivocally.

His mom, Dr. Ruth Stone—his father's partner at their family vet clinic and in life—had hurried to clear the dinner dishes and bring out dessert, because things tended not to get as messy over pineapple upside-down cake.

"Henry." His dad's voice lost its jovial edge. "This isn't really up for discussion. There's a place for you at Iowa State. We've made sure of it. And the clinic will be yours when your mom and I retire."

Henry toyed with his cake, pushing crumbs around with his fork. A sheaf of sandy brown hair fell into his eyes.

"I don't want to run the clinic, Dad," he'd said softly, dropping his fork to his plate with a louder *clang* than he'd anticipated. He felt the anger rising, as it sometimes did unexpectedly. "I close my eyes when I see a needle. The smell . . . ,"—he stood up now, his hands shaking—"it makes me sick. This isn't what I want to do. I'm going to do this reality show and see about getting that scholarship. And then I'm getting a degree in literature."

He grabbed his plate and headed toward the kitchen, wanting to have the final word, wanting his dad to know he meant what he'd said. But his dad wouldn't let that happen.

"Do your little competition, Henry," he said. "It'll be good for you to see what's out there. And once you've gotten that out of your system, your mom and I—and the clinic—will be waiting here for you."

It wasn't until later that Henry realized the implication of his dad's statement. Later, when he lay in bed, wondering who the other seven kids would be, where they would come from, why they would be doing this crazy thing—that's when his dad's words came back to him, and he felt something build in his chest. Something he'd never felt before. Something he was pretty sure was determination.

His dad expected Henry to lose.

Henry would do everything in his power to prove him wrong.

July 8, 6:15 a.m.
Brooklyn Chinatown, New York
Mei Zhang

Mei moved quietly around her small room, trying not to wake her sisters, who were tucked head-to-feet in the narrow bed against the wall. Her bag was mostly packed; her *māma* had come in yesterday and silently handed her things to put inside the small, worn suitcase that had once been her grandmother's. She had little to do but wait for the driver they'd been told was coming to take her to the airport.

Furtively, though she knew there was no one to see her, she reached between her thin mattress and the board it rested on and pulled out the soft, cracked red leather book that held the thoughts she never voiced, never shared, never acknowledged—except for here. Her beloved Po Po had given this to her. No one but her grandmother knew it existed—and Po Po was gone now.

In these pages, she could let her letters spill out the way her brain saw them, since there was no one to chastise her when the words made no sense. She could fill the blank pages with sketches—penciled drawings of her sisters as they bent furiously to their violins; her dad, master of his kitchen, with his prized knives a blur as he scissored them skillfully from shoulder to shoulder; her *māma,* all warm, gentle smiles as she greeted each new diner to their downstairs restaurant.

Mei toyed with the idea of tucking this book in her suitcase, knowing it could bring her comfort in the rocky weeks ahead. But what if it was found? She couldn't risk that.

She gazed at a drawing of Po Po, tracing a light finger over her harsh features and the severe bun she always wore. The first rays of morning sun were just rising above the tall buildings that lined her crowded street and finding their way into her window. Like her grandmother, Mei had learned not to let her face betray her emotions; so even though her heart was heavy with dread and her stomach coated with a greasy lining of regret and uncertainty, Mei's face showed nothing. It would be her best weapon in the coming weeks. Maybe her only weapon.

So many things she should have done differently, could have done differently, to avoid this moment. Studied more. Practiced harder. Spent less time drawing and more time with other high school girls—in clubs and sports and things that colleges wanted to see on applications. Instead, she'd come home every day, bowed her head to her homework; but when the numbers and words started to swim as they always did, she'd reached for this book to sketch.

Po Po would have understood. But Po Po was dead.

And her mother and father had different dreams for her. Dreams that would take her out of this neighborhood of immigrants. Dreams that would have her studying medicine or law or engineering or physics. Those dreams did not include drawing or sketching.

Her little sister Li stirred in her bed, rolling toward Mei and revealing her guileless face, the sweet, unworried look of a nine-year-old sleeping. Mei felt a rush of affection for both her and Xia, twins who couldn't wait to see their older sister on TV. Who had told all their friends that Mei was going to be famous. Was going to Hollywood. Was going to win some competition and go to Columbia University like the President.

Mei's eyes burned, but she would not shed tears. Her face was a mask. She would control her emotions and reveal nothing. She would stay quiet and watch. And she would win.

Because she had to. To come home without that scholarship was to disgrace her family. And that was something her father would never allow her to do.

July 8, 8:23 a.m.
On the ferry en route from Winslow, Bainbridge Island, to Seattle, Washington
Sam Michaels

"You can still back out, you know," Rachel said. Her knees were tucked up under her chin, arms wrapped around them tightly, so that she was a tiny, indigo-haired ball on one of the many white benches that lined the top deck of the ferry.

It was still morning-cool and the wind off the bay made it even cooler.

"Not if I want to go to college." Sam's legs were stretched out, resting on his guitar case. He wore one of his only two pairs of jeans—this one with the hole in the knee—and his favorite Bob Marley T-shirt. His striped knitted cap—Rasta colors—was pulled firmly down over his ears, though tufts of his sandy blond hair poked out. Several days' worth of coarse blond hair coated his chin and upper lip.

"You could do what everyone else does," Rachel said, moving toward that nipping, biting tone that Sam found annoying. "You could apply for a scholarship or a loan. Come on, Sam, you live with your *grandma.* You fix bikes and sit around on the ferry strumming your guitar with a can out, just so you can eat. You're telling me you can't qualify for financial aid?"

Sam shrugged and let his gaze follow a couple of suits filing into the main cabin. Suits like that always made him uneasy. The way they held their espressos in one hand and their iPhones in the other, with their Italian leather briefcases shoved under their armpits. Just seeing them made him feel claustrophobic—like they were going to grab him, wrap a tie around his neck, and make him sit behind a desk all day for the rest of his life.

"And what?" he said now, forcing his eyes back to Rachel. "End up at U-Dub? Seattle U?" he scoffed.

"What's wrong with those schools, Sam?" she asked.

He hadn't meant to hurt her. He knew that Seattle University was her top choice. He also knew she wasn't likely to get in. Rachel's future held community college while she continued being a barista for the suits he despised. And then, if she was lucky, she might get a job teaching preschool or as a receptionist somewhere.

"Nothing's wrong with them, Rache," he said, drawing his legs up and bending forward to lean his elbows on his knees. "But I'm not cut out for a business or engineering degree."

She pursed her lips into a tight O and slid her eyes sideways. Classic Rachel look of disapproval. There were a few moments when he thought that maybe he could love her. There were many others when he was pretty sure he didn't. And never really would.

"So Berklee College of Music then." She let each word fall from her lips as if it physically hurt her to say them. "That's all there is for you?" she asked. Her eyes were a soft gray, almost lavender. And though the outside of her was all points and edges, piercings and spiked hair, her eyes were warm and liquid—those of a lost puppy.

Sam shrugged. They'd had this discussion countless times already, and it always ended with him shrugging and her sulking.

The skyline of Seattle was one of the only things he'd miss, if he ever actually got out of here. If he won that scholarship. He wouldn't really miss Rachel, though she was a cool girl when she wasn't acting all pissy about his future. Or his grandma, who didn't notice where he was or *if* he was, even. She'd been more than happy to see him off this morning. Good riddance and don't let the door slam you in the fanny. She'd done her parenting duties long ago—and done a crappy job the first go-around.

No, Sam wouldn't miss much about the island he'd grown up on. An island filled with sprawling estates and suits. Where he and Grams eked out an existence in their crumbling downtown rental.

The Space Needle was rising up in front of them. The suits were tossing their white cups into the recycling bins and dusting imaginary lint off shoulders as they readied for a day at the office. Rachel was pleading with him through her eyes. *Stay*, she said. *Don't do this.*

She knew he'd win. She knew once he stepped off this boat and met whoever had been sent to fetch him that it was all over. He had it in the bag.

Sam Michaels had learned from a very early age what it took to survive. He knew how to read every situation. He knew when to stay quiet or turn on the charm. He knew when to lead and when to follow. He knew which groups to join and which to avoid. He was bright, alert, calculating, talented, and driven. And he wanted this. More than anything. He wanted this.

The boat slid into the dock with a gentle bump. Rachel's hand reached for his arm.

"Sam."

Ever so gently, he pulled away from her so that her hand dropped heavily to her leg.

"Root for me, Rache. Or don't. But I'm not coming back without that scholarship money."

He stood up, grabbed his backpack and guitar case, and held out a hand to her. She unfolded from the bench and took it with a resigned sigh. And they walked down the gangway to meet the camera that was already filming them.

July 8, 2:23 p.m.
On the 5 Freeway northbound,
leaving San Diego, California
Hiroshi Yamamura

Hiroshi blinked uncertainly at the camera before answering. Was he saying too much? Too little? He knew he'd have to do this—talk to a camera—but he'd had no idea how tough it would be.

"I swim. Varsity. Butterfly, mostly. IMs sometimes, but Coach likes me doing butterfly."

Trish, a heavyset woman with short gray hair, kind eyes, and sweat stains under her armpits, poked her head around the camera.

"You're doing fine, okay?" she said, showing him her coffee-stained teeth. "Just talk to me like you would your grandma."

His grandma was in Okinawa. Talking with her was like having a conversation with an unsmiling, stony-eyed wall. She thought he should play the violin, not swim. The red light on the camera was blinking again. Trish's voice floated back to him over the sound of the air conditioning and the cars rushing by on the freeway.

"Tell me a little about your family. You have brothers and sisters?"

"One. Brother. Uh, he's younger than me."

The red light blinked ominously. He wanted to look away, out the window, toward the ocean that stretched endlessly. The ocean. Where he and Maggie used to . . .

"He goes to the same school as you?"

Hiroshi blinked and Maggie's playful eyes vanished.

"Shin just finished eighth grade. He goes to a private school. With me."

Hiroshi swallowed. This was horrible. *He* was horrible. People would be watching this. Maggie, maybe. Judging him. His parents would see this. They would frown, their hands clasped tightly in their laps. They would say nothing, but Hiroshi would know. Their silences always screamed loudly.

They hadn't wanted him to do this. They told him there was another way—a more honorable way. He was a solid student, in nearly all AP classes. His SAT scores were practically perfect—2320 at the last scoring in April. He was a varsity swimmer, almost made it to State last year, chosen as All-League MVP, and already pegged as a captain by Coach McChristian. He'd been courted by D-II schools already for his swimming alone—UC San Diego and Indianapolis. Even UNLV, a Division I school, had shown some interest. Good schools. Not Stanford, though.

And Hiroshi had one blemish on his near-perfect record. Junior year. A lapse in judgment—that's how his family still referred to Maggie. Maggie, whose laugh was more like a hiccup. Maggie, whose mouth twitched upward when she listened to him. Maggie, whose kiss could make him forget about chemistry and algebra. Who was unquestionably to blame for his plummeting grades.

"Your parents," said Trish, "they must be so proud."

His parents had stood stiffly at the door, two identical sentries nodding mechanically and wishing him well. They knew how it would look not to be there to support their eldest son, so they stayed home from work that morning—his dad, a biology professor at San Diego State, allowing his morning class to be taught by his TA; his mom, a cardiologist, cancelling her morning patients. But their mouths were tight. Their eyes expressionless.

"Ah, yes," Hiroshi said to the red-blinking light. "I am fortunate to have such supportive parents."

And then Hiroshi did look away. But instead of seeing the ocean, he saw his reflection in the car's window. His narrow face with its high, defined cheekbones. His wide, muscular shoulders, built hard and firm from hours in the pool. His eyes—serious, dark, and brooding. Only Maggie made his eyes shine. But he hadn't seen Maggie in more than two months. She would never forgive him.

Hiroshi knew there was no going back for him. His parents didn't understand his desire to be here. But that didn't matter now. For them, there was only one outcome: winning.

July 8, 3:02 p.m.
On a plane en route from Houston, Texas,
to Los Angeles, California
Lucy del Castillo

She was sick of the damn camera already. God, the guy had that thing in her face like every other minute! It had been bad enough that he'd kept it practically trained on her for the entire ride from her condo to the airport, asking her stuff like "What are you most nervous about?" and "What was it about this competition that appealed to you?"

Like she didn't know this was all part of the game. She watched reality shows like *The Bachelor* and *Biggest Loser*. And she'd always wondered how those people could be so stupid and say stuff as if nobody else was watching. Did they not get that those cozy one-on-ones with the camera guy were really one-on-millions?

Well, she wasn't a fool. She was already playing the game. She knew that the people watching this at home were gonna be forming opinions of her based on these little "chats" she had up close and personal with the camera operator. So she talked it up sweet.

"I'm nervous the other girls won't, you know, like me," she'd said, dropping her eyes sideways, demure and nervous. Complete fiction—she didn't care if *anyone* liked her. She was here to win the money, not make friends.

"I want to see if I can, like, do it. Compete, I mean. It's one thing to get decent grades and be considered a leader and everything at your own high school. But it's another to see if you have what it takes in the real world, you know?" Lucy tried to open her eyes wide, look sincere and eager. Inside, she was gagging. Of course she had what it took. She was gonna leave boot marks on these seven losers. And not even blink an eye while she did it.

She thought that when they got on the plane, he'd leave her alone. That she could put on her iPod and gel. But it turned out that whoever was funding this little adventure had bought up a whole row of plane seats, just so Lucy could sit by her new BFF and continue to be interviewed all the way to L.A.

Woot—freakin'—woot.

By the time they landed at LAX, she was pretty close to punching him in the throat. He'd asked about her mom: "Oh, my gosh! She's, like, so supportive. I can't imagine what I'd do without her." (It was actually "moms"—plural—since shortly after her dad dumped her mom when Lucy was four, Mom met a massage therapist named Sage who moved in three months later. This was the worst-kept secret in their small, ultra-conservative Texas town just outside of Houston. Lucy told everyone Sage was a family friend. But she knew what they all thought of her family: freaks.)

And her dad: "He's really an amazing guy. I don't get to see him as much as I'd like to, but we stay in contact through texts and Facebook and stuff. He told me not to worry about this competition, that no matter what, he was super proud of me." (Since he'd divorced her mom, he'd remarried a twenty-something who worked in his Houston law office, had another kid, Zoe, who pretty much occupied him 24/7, and Lucy was lucky if she got a phone call once a month. His last words to her had been "What the hell are you thinking, Luce?")

And her friends: "I honestly don't know what I would do without them. Kayla and Lauren, if you're watching, you guys are the best." (The only truthful thing she'd said into the camera since he'd turned it on.)

She strode off the plane, her large, neon-pink purse flung over her shoulder, leaving Eric (or whatever his name was) to lug his camera and fend for himself. Maybe he'd get lost and she'd have a moment to herself. Except that, as she exited the Jetway and found herself in the crowded airport terminal, she was met by a tall, stately woman, her oversized sunglasses holding back her stick-straight blond hair, her red lipstick highlighting gorgeous lips, and her sign clearly reading LUCY DEL CASTILLO.

Before Lucy could paste on a fake smile and drop into the wide-eyed, Texas-girl role she hoped to play for the remainder of this game, the woman was lifting an eyebrow and stepping forward to claim her. Quickly, Lucy tossed her thick, wavy black hair over one shoulder and dipped her chin in fake uncertainty.

"I'm Lucy," she said hesitantly. "Nice to meet y'all."

She stuck out her hand and smiled wide, eyes blinking demurely. But instead of seeing the woman's face soften and relax, amusement blared in her blue eyes.

"Lucy," she said, holding the girl's gaze a second longer than necessary, "I'm Kelly. I'll be hanging out with you tonight and making sure you get to your first meeting tomorrow. And answering any questions you might have, of course."

Lucy hugged her pink bag tightly and gulped.

"Oh, ain't that sweet!" she gushed. "I'm so glad I don't have to do this all alone."

Kelly raised one perfectly plucked eyebrow.

"Oh, don't worry, sweetheart. You're still on your own. I'm just here to make sure you don't get lost."

Then she turned and strode off toward the sign that read BAGGAGE CLAIM, leaving Lucy, who was suddenly glad for the cameraman's huffing presence, to traipse along behind her.

July 8, 5:23 p.m.
Marriott Suites somewhere in
Los Angeles, California
Allyson Murphy

Allyson absently fingered the cross around her neck as her eyes followed two boys at the pool below. From her balcony, she could feel the light breeze wafting by, carrying smells of seawater and Coppertone and the slightest hint of exhaust. One boy shoved the other in the pool and then plopped in after him with a hearty splash.

She should have been nervous. Or excited. Or overwhelmed with the idea that she was going to be on television in front of millions of people, competing for a prize that she desperately wanted—no, *needed.* Instead, she felt numb.

Allyson stepped off the tiny balcony into her room. Her very own hotel room. If she hadn't felt so deflated and tired—so, so tired—she might have laughed at the absurdity of it. A preacher's kid from Ovid, Colorado—population 317—standing in the middle of a suite in Los Angeles, with room service on the way. No one at her high school would have believed it.

She dropped heavily onto the edge of the bed. This was the opportunity she'd been praying for. That her whole family had been praying for. That had made Melanie—her dear, wonderful sister with her swollen belly and exhausted eyes—light candles at the church for three weeks, twice a day, ever since Allyson had filled out that application, sent in her video, and decided that this was her only chance. Allyson's eyes filled. Melanie. Who would be giving birth soon. And Allyson was here—a thousand miles away.

She closed her eyes. "Dearest heavenly Father, my heart is heavy and yet I know this is the path You've chosen for me. Please help me find the strength I need to finish the journey. To let Your will be done. Watch over my family back home. Melanie and Jack and their little baby. The church and my friends. Be with Papa and . . . Mama." Her voice caught. "Amen."

She opened her eyes to a sudden wave of restlessness. The woman who had been her chaperone since she was picked up in her tiny hometown of Ovid had deposited her at this door with clear instructions not to wander—and the threat that she could be dropped from the competition if she did. There was a television with more channels than they got from their ancient rabbit-eared antenna in Ovid, but Allyson wasn't all that interested in the news of L.A. or reality shows. She had her Bible, tucked into the front pocket of her brother-in-law's suitcase, and that's what she should have been doing: reading it. But somehow it wasn't His words that would fill the ache that was gnawing at her heart.

She clutched instead at something her dad had said to her just before she left, hoping to find strength in it.

"You're the smartest person I know, Ally-girl," he'd said, as they'd coasted up on their bikes to the white double doors of her dad's church. "You have loyalty like your mama; confidence like your sister. You have the love of the Lord in your heart. Be true to who you are, kid, and then, no matter what the outcome, you've won."

It had sounded so reassuring at the time. She'd walked off to teach her Bible class feeling confident and loved. Now, replaying in her memory, her dad's words rang hollow. Was she really any of those things? Would it be enough?

And if not, then what? She had no other options. Her mom's disease was moving so, so fast. The doctors said *months.* There was no money for college, and even with loans and scholarships, it would be months before they knew if she'd qualified. Mama could be . . . gone. No, this was the best option. The right way to go.

A light knock at the door pulled her from her thoughts.

"Room service!"

Allyson rose to her feet as if the weight of ten lifetimes rested on her shoulders. She ran a hand through the gentle waves of her brown hair and straightened her pale-blue, button-down shirt.

She could do this. God willing, she would do this.

July 9, 10:01 a.m.
Disneyland Resort Plaza

Visitors were swarming into Disneyland—bug-eyed, jumpy children weighed down with Mickey gear; parents hoping they'd brought enough sunscreen, cash, and energy. They passed by, mildly curious about the eight teenage kids who milled about uncertainly near a deserted kiosk in the plaza, cameramen circling them like predators, one extremely attractive, vaguely familiar-looking woman smiling benignly in their midst.

The kids had been dropped off by their chaperones earlier with no instructions other than to dress comfortably and take nothing with them. They'd been patted down by Disneyland security and then again by someone from the show, making sure that no one had snuck in a contraband cell phone or iPod or credit card.

They were clean.

And eyeing each other like caged animals.

Lucy del Castillo did *not* like the looks of Cassidy McGowan. She was pretty sure Cassidy had all the makings of uptown trash. Girl like that could be trouble. She had to go home. But until then, Lucy decided she was keeping Cassidy close.

Tyrell Young jostled from one leg to another like he was amped up on Red Bulls—though all he'd consumed that morning was a muffin. His only urgent thought was that he needed an ally—someone he could trust until he could figure out this game. He dismissed the curly-haired Rastamahn immediately—too laid back—but the Asian dude with the biceps might work. And he couldn't help notice that the chick in the short-shorts was hot.

Cassidy had dressed for success: Daisy Duke jean shorts, red tank top layered over a white one, and white Converse. All four guys gave her the once-over. Her most pressing question was, who should she make a move on? Who was gonna take her to the end? She bit her thumbnail and tried to look helpless.

Mei found herself gravitating toward the girl who kept fingering her necklace and not looking at the rest of the contestants. She felt there was something about her modest button-up shirt and long khaki shorts that would allow them to do well together.

Henry tried to play it cool in his ironed tan shorts and light blue IZOD polo, hands stuffed in his pockets. He sidled closer to Cassidy, smiling his most charming smile.

"I'm guessing we don't get to ride the Teacups?"

Cassidy laughed nervously. "So that's your motivation?"

A serious look came over Henry's face. "Only if I get to turn the wheel." With feigned disappointment, he added, "I mean, I guess you could turn the wheel, too, if you want."

Cassidy flashed a brilliant grin. "You're such a giver."

Lucy scowled and pushed one hand hard into the knuckles of her other.

Sam shuffled around the edges of the group casually, eyeing his competition. He instinctively started sizing them up: the Hispanic girl, cracking her knuckles but trying to look like she wasn't out for blood, was going to be a loose cannon; the chick in the short-shorts was bad news; the tough, athletic-looking jock seemed ready to kick butt—too ready, maybe. Sam's mind was scrolling through how to play each of them when the woman in the hip-hugging black skirt and heels stepped forward. Cameras swung toward her, and red lights began to blink.

"So," she said, her face wearing a tight smile that didn't quite reach her eyes. "Welcome to Los Angeles. I'm Molly Granger, and I'll be your host through this competition. The Benefactor hopes very much that your journey was pleasant and that you are ready for today's adventure. Because, my friends, the competition . . . starts . . . *now.*"

She paused dramatically. The cameras volleyed from her to the kids. A small crowd had gathered to watch—passersby attracted by the cameras and the possibility of being on TV. "You've all been brought here for one purpose: to win the opportunity to bypass all the college applications, the SATs, the loans, the scholarships—and get accepted to pretty much the school of your choice with a *full* scholarship for four years. A full ride. It's the dream of any high school senior. But to get it, you're going to have to prove yourself to your Benefactor. Starting now."

Molly made a sweeping gesture toward the gates of Disneyland.

"Disneyland is a southern California icon. You'll find throughout this competition that the Benefactor has different ideas about what it takes to survive in this world. And it's not essays or SAT questions that ask you to match analogous words or calculate the hypotenuse of a triangle. No, he thinks you should have more, well, practical skills. Skills he's had to hone himself on his way from being a working-class kid to earning a rank this past year on the Forbes 400 list for the first time."

Sam raised an eyebrow and felt a drop of excitement plunk deep in his belly. Mei swallowed uneasily. Cassidy tried to maintain her wide smile. Lucy felt like cracking her knuckles again.

"Hidden inside the park that Walt Disney opened in 1955 is an address to your new home. You've got to find it. Working together with another contestant, figure out how to get inside Disneyland, find your address, and make your way to your new house, where your luggage is waiting for you. The last two contestants to arrive at the house will sit in judgment by the Benefactor. One of them will be sent home. Back to SATs and essays and loan applications."

Hiroshi quickly glanced again at Tyrell. His nod was firm in return. Mei inched closer to Allyson. She didn't want to be paired with either of the other girls, who'd been glaring at each other as if the claws might come out at any moment. Lucy sidled nearer to Cassidy, figuring her short-shorts might be worth something in this little task. Sam folded his arms across his chest and decided to see how things played out.

"One last thing before you go," offered their host, lifting her chin attractively for the camera. "The Benefactor asks me to offer you"—she smiled conspiratorially—"the best of luck, and 'the hope for a peaceful and unified world.'"

Molly surveyed all eight teenagers. Then she turned slightly as if welcoming them into the Happiest Place on Earth and lifted her arm. "Go!"

For the length it took them to suck in a collective breath, no one moved. Then Tyrell and Hiroshi simultaneously reached forward to shake hands.

"Yo, bro," Tyrell said, grasping the Asian boy's hand, gratified that the kid's grip was firm. "Tyrell Young."

"Hiroshi."

Tyrell nodded his chin away from the park entrance. "Follow me, man, but don't let any of the others tag along. Cool?"

The two jogged off in unison, a cameraman huffing behind.

Mei stood nervously, waiting for the other girl to look up or acknowledge her. When Allyson continued to keep her head low, Mei cleared her throat. "Would you like to work together? I mean, she said we have to have a partner, right?"

Allyson wanted only to run. Find someone who would give her a plane ticket back to Ovid. But somehow she managed to lift her head and meet Mei's eyes. To nod. To whisper her name to this tiny Asian wisp of a girl. And then they were walking toward the gates and the crowds, a camera bopping along next to them. Allyson closed her eyes and offered up a prayer. She had to do this. Even if it felt so wrong.

Lucy cornered Cassidy. "So, hey. You and me, we could do this thing. You look smart. Like you want to win. And I want to win, too. I'm Lucy, by the way. Texas." She thrust out her hand.

Like she'd been hoping they'd be friends, Cassidy grasped it with the widest smile she could muster. Inwardly, she groaned. She did much better with guys than girls. She'd been counting on the guy with khaki shorts to make his way closer again so she could snag him.

"Right on! Cassidy McGowan. From Chicago. Let's do this."

Henry quickly looked around. Just him and the guy with the peace-sign shirt. Not his first choice. But since the guy was standing in front of Henry with his hand out, there was no choosing, really.

"So, looks like we got to be partnered up. I'm Sam."

Henry tried to plaster on a smile. "Henry."

"Any thoughts?" Sam tipped his head toward the park.

"Start asking for money, I guess." He motioned toward Lucy and Cassidy, who were already holding court with a group of college guys. Within seconds, two were reaching into their pockets, grinning goofily. Henry guessed it wasn't going to be that easy for him and his new best friend. Sam rubbed his hands together.

"This Benefactor guy," Sam said, watching Cassidy and Lucy work their magic, "sounds like maybe he has different ideas about what's important."

Henry swung his eyes toward Sam. "What're you getting at?"

"I'm just thinking that maybe our Benefactor . . ." Sam said, choosing his words carefully since there was a camera right over his shoulder and no doubt the Benefactor was listening. "He might have expected us to go that route, right? Start begging for money, I mean. But what if there's a different way in? What if he just wants us to find it?"

Henry's eyebrows dipped together. "You have an idea?" he asked.

Sam grinned. "I might," he said. "Come on."

Together, they trotted off in a different direction, back toward the parking lot. If Sam's hunch was right, they'd be in the park in less than an hour.

July 9, 11:07 a.m.
Malibu, California
The Benefactor

The Benefactor reached for his water bottle. He'd spent the morning pounding on his pedals, climbing the hilly roads that weaved through the Santa Monica Mountains. His quads ached; his butt was tender. He was still in his padded bike shorts and jersey, his hair matted from sweat and hours of having a helmet mashed onto it.

But there was no time to shower. Yaz promised a live, unedited video feed as soon as the kids hit the Magic Kingdom. Lifting his bike onto its rack in the garage, he'd barreled up the steps of his beachside home, two at a time, to the viewing room he'd recently had installed. A whole wall of nothing but flat screens—twelve of them—all showing live views from the cameras assigned to the kids.

He leaned forward on the black leather couch, like a guy in a sports bar with every game imaginable at his fingertips. Only this was better.

Because he knew these kids like they were his own.

There were Cassidy and Lucy, who in only an hour had collected nearly $172, only $12 short of the $184 they needed for two tickets. They made a good team, those two, though there was already a building distrust and thriving competition to see who could bring in the biggest dollar amount. Cassidy was doing well—she'd pulled in nearly two-thirds of the pot with those killer eyelashes and look-twice legs. Guys were going to salivate when they saw that one on their television screens. But it was Lucy who was calling the shots—the brains behind that operation. An interesting combination.

Hiroshi and Tyrell were an equally formidable duo. They'd gone the same route, collecting money, but had headed farther away from the main gates. They'd beelined for Downtown Disney, a family-friendly thoroughfare nearby with shops and restaurants. They hit up businessmen, appealing to them with their "I'm a struggling kid who has a chance at a scholarship if . . ." speech. It was working. They were about to grab the last few bucks they needed and head for the entrance to buy their two tickets. The Benefactor smirked.

Mei and Allyson were not doing well. Their shyness was a huge obstacle, as was whatever was going on in Allyson's head. Their approach to strangers was almost apologetic, and they were targeting families with kids: families who, though sympathetic, didn't have much spare cash to hand over to two jumpy teenagers. Mei's desperation was becoming apparent, as was Allyson's reluctance to take other people's money. In an hour, they'd collected only $32.

It was Sam and Henry he found riveting, though. Sam had convinced Henry that their best move was to find a Disney cast member who was getting off his shift and see if he'd let them borrow his badge. If they could use his badge to get in and find the address, they could return the badge and be out before everyone else. It almost worked. What they weren't counting on was that all the cast members were wiped out and just wanted to get home. No one wanted to hang around while the kids traipsed around the park looking for some address.

Henry's frustration and anxiety was evident. "Come on, man," he said, after they'd been turned down by yet another apologetic employee. "We've got to go back and start finding money to buy our tickets. The other teams might be in by now."

Sam looked past him. The camera followed his gaze to a guard shack that sat about one hundred feet away, with a large wooden arm preventing vehicles from entering without credentials. A truck had just pulled up. The camera got a close-up of the side of the truck. O'Neil Construction. The guard was gesturing back from where the truck had come.

Sam smiled. "Dude. That's it."

Henry looked once at the guard shack and then back at Sam. "What? The guard? We've asked him. He said he couldn't help us."

"Not the guard. The truck. Construction. Which means that somewhere is a construction entrance. Which means that there are guys with hard hats going in and out. Guys who"—he looked meaningfully at Henry—"might have brought their son and his friend by to see the job site today."

Henry's eyes registered understanding and he put a finger to his lips, considering. "Okay, let's try it. But now, before we're the last team out here, okay?"

It worked. Within twenty minutes, they'd found a construction entrance, explained to an older guy in a hard hat what they were doing and why. He called over a tall man who looked like he might have a kid around Sam's age. And they were in. That easy.

Sam and Henry. Lucy and Cassidy. Tyrell and Hiroshi. With three teams now inside the park, the Benefactor knew it would now be a matter of figuring out the clue and finding the address to their new residence. From there it wouldn't be hard. A cab ride, really.

He drained his water bottle and sank back into the couch. He knew who he'd put money on if he was a betting man. And, if he was right, he was pretty sure future viewers would be surprised by the outcome.

July 9, 12:49 p.m.
Disneyland—Anaheim, California

God, it was hot. Sweat dribbled down Cassidy's neck and collected in her cleavage. She was stressed that her makeup might be smudging, her hair dull and lifeless. But Lucy—drill-sergeant, keep-it-moving Lucy—wouldn't let her pop into a bathroom and check.

Lucy was worried. She'd had a plan, or so she thought. Let Cassidy work her magic outside. Then get a map and start asking employees once they got inside. But she didn't know what to ask them. "I'm looking for some kind of address . . ." didn't seem to be working. They'd been in the park for an hour and had no idea what the hell they were looking for. They'd asked every Disney person they ran into if they'd seen anything. They'd run from Fantasyland to Adventureland to the hot, treeless, futuristic land with Space Mountain in it. Nothing. And dumb-as-dirt Cassidy was fretting about her lipstick smudging. It took everything Lucy had not to go off on her. But the camera was rolling, so she stayed calm. Or tried to.

Tyrell and Hiroshi kept coming back to the last thing the host woman had said. "I offer you the best of luck, and the hope for a peaceful and unified world."

Something about what she'd said seemed like it ought to offer a clue. Because who sends you off on a race with the hope for a peaceful and unified world? But they didn't know what that had to do with Disneyland or Walt Disney.

They'd asked a few less-than-helpful employees, then wandered around, hoping to come across a ride that had to do with peace and unity. Tyrell, who'd been to Disney World in Florida, was sure it was It's a Small World, this ride where all these little kids sing from different countries. But they'd stood in line, listened to the incessant song for the full fifteen-minute ride, and got nothing. They were now back at the park entrance, wondering where to go next.

Sam and Henry were working their way methodically through the park. Sam had grabbed a map from the first kiosk they'd seen and decided that their best move was to walk in one giant, looping circle, marking off places as they went. But he didn't know what they were looking for and that was frustrating him exponentially. And it wasn't the only thing.

Henry had a frenzied energy that Sam was finding hard to keep up with. But the guy was great with people. He knew how to work a crowd. In every line they stood in, Henry would strike up a conversation with somebody. They made a lot of friends. Just not a lot of progress.

Mei was ready to call it quits. Allyson was proving to be a far more difficult challenge than the actual challenge. When Mei tried to approach certain people, Allyson would freak out and say, "No, not them. We can't ask them for money. It's not right." It wasn't like Mei was totally comfortable asking *anyone* for money. But they'd been given this task; they had no other choice. Why couldn't Allyson see that?

Mei dropped heavily onto a bench in the outer plaza, wiping her moist forehead with her T-shirt sleeve. The camera moved in for a close-up. Mei's eyes drooped from exhaustion and defeat. She looked up at her partner, whose shoulders sagged and whose face registered a desire to be anywhere else.

"We have eighty-nine dollars and thirty-five cents," Mei said dully to Allyson. "What do you want to do?"

Allyson stared out at the plaza where families were gathering in clumps before entering the park. Her index finger and thumb rubbed mindlessly at the cross on her chain.

"I'm sorry," she said softly. "This isn't easy for me."

Mei swallowed. "It isn't easy for any of us. We didn't come here because we thought it would be easy."

Allyson blinked but didn't meet Mei's gaze. "You don't understand," she said tonelessly.

"Of course I don't," said Mei. Her posture was rigid as she stood in Allyson's line of sight. She kept her words even. "I don't know you. I don't know why you're here. But I know that there's a reason you came and that you need the scholarship as much as I do."

Allyson's face didn't change.

"We have just about half of what we need. I think we can get the rest. Can we please at least try?"

The camera alternated between Mei's steady look and Allyson's indecisive one. Then Allyson nodded weakly.

"Okay." Silently, she pleaded, *Dear God, please help us get this done quickly!*

Without saying another word, Mei turned and headed toward two women who'd just made their way through security, hoping they'd brought a little extra cash. Startled, she felt a hand grasp her arm. She turned, expecting to see Allyson either melting down or changing her mind.

Instead, the camera focused in on a small group of girls—likely college-aged—as diverse in their skin colors as their clothing. One, a short girl with shoulder-length black hair, large brown eyes, and skin the color of tree bark, moved forward.

"You're one of those kids trying to get in the park, right? For that show?"

Mei's look must have been skeptical or confused because the girl rushed to explain.

"We saw the cameras." She giggled self-consciously. "And so, of course, we had to find out what was going on."

Mei just nodded. She kept her face impassive. She felt Allyson press up behind her.

"Look, we know what it's like to want to get into college. And how hard it is. We're all"—she made a sweeping gesture—"students at UCLA. We thought that maybe we could help you."

She held out two tickets. Two ready-to-go tickets to Disneyland.

She looked sheepish. "We got these discount tickets through school, but two of our friends couldn't make it, and . . ."

Mei felt warmth surge up her throat, behind her eyes. She swallowed it down hard. And she kept her face blank. "Thank you. Thank you so much." She half bowed as she reached for the tickets, holding them close to her chest, and glanced back at Allyson, hoping the other girl would show gratitude as well. Without warning, Allyson stepped forward. One by one, she hugged the girls.

"Thank you," Allyson whispered when she was done. "And God bless you."

The first girl who had spoken met Mei's eyes again. "You know where you're going? Once you get in?"

Mei shrugged helplessly. "We have only the clue the woman gave us. Something about a hope for a peaceful and unified world."

A dark-skinned girl with a thick ponytail spoke up. "It's a plaque in Tomorrowland. A dedication plaque." She ducked her head sheepishly. "My dad used to do these scavenger hunts when we came here as kids, so . . ."

"You're such a dork, Nat!" said one of the girls. They all laughed.

"Listen," said the first girl. "Kick butt, okay? Really, when this thing airs, we want to see you two in the finals."

Mei nodded and let her eyes travel over to Allyson. Allyson was nodding, too. Like maybe she meant it.

Minutes later, they were in the park, heading for the Tomorrowland plaque, where they became the first team to find the box of sealed envelopes, the address of their new house, and the twenty-dollar cab fare to get them there.

"Thank you, Jesus," Allyson breathed, hugging the envelope to her.

Mei thought maybe their gratitude should be directed at the girls who gave them the tickets. But she was just glad to have the task done and not be the last team. Before hailing their cab, they found a large family and handed over the money they'd collected earlier—the entire $89.35, explaining how they'd gotten it and why they wanted them to have it. The family was all smiles and hugs. Allyson's eyes lost some of their dullness.

At about three p.m., their stomachs rumbling every time they passed a kiosk selling popcorn or those Mickey-eared pretzels, Hiroshi and Tyrell were starting to wonder what their next move should be, when they got lucky. In line to watch *Great Moments with Lincoln,* which Hiroshi was convinced might have something to do with a peaceful and unified world, they started talking with an older guy who'd been coming to Disneyland since he was six. He knew everything there was to know about the park. When they mentioned the phrase to him, he immediately told them about the plaque in Tomorrowland.

At 3:16 p.m., they were the second team to grab an address and the twenty dollars they needed to get a cab ride there. After some loud whoops, a leaping high five, and a shoulder-bumping guy-hug, they sprinted off to the main entrance.

Sam and Henry were nearing the end of their park-wide tour. They'd hit every land. Henry had talked to employee after employee, and most seemed baffled by whatever it was they were supposed to find. Sam felt like they were trying to find a needle in a haystack—but they didn't even know what the needle looked like. Even their cameraman was complaining, and he'd been able to refuel with a large turkey sandwich, a bag of chips, and a mouth-wateringly cold Coke.

It was 5:15 p.m. Time was ticking. Sam was pretty worried at this point that they were out of the race. Both his and Henry's stomachs were complaining, their legs were aching, and their skin had that raw, caked-on salty feeling from having been sweating in the sun all day. Henry's nose was dangerously pink, though he was still relentless in his determination to find the clue. Sam couldn't decide if he was grateful for Henry's focus or annoyed by it.

By six p.m. the sun was heading toward the horizon, and Lucy and Cassidy were starving. Any hope of winning this thing was gone. Lucy wasn't speaking to her teammate; she wasn't really speaking at all. Cassidy was nursing a blister on her heel and trying hard not to complain. Too much.

Henry and Sam were walking from Frontierland to Tomorrowland, passing in front of Sleeping Beauty's castle, wondering where in the world to go next, when Sam looked up at a gray stone monument of a smiling, proud Walt Disney and Mickey Mouse.

"You know," he said. "That last thing the woman said—*I offer you the best of luck, and the hope for a peaceful and unified world.* Does that sound funny to you?"

Henry gingerly touched his forehead to wipe some sweat. "Yeah, maybe. Now that you mention it."

"A peaceful and unified world. You think maybe that's a clue?"

"Aw, dude." Henry slapped his palm to his thigh. "What do you bet that's written somewhere? Like on a sign or something?"

Sam glanced up at the statue.

"Or a plaque," he said slowly.

Henry looked around. "We need to find any and every plaque in this place. Now."

And that's when they asked a passing Disney employee about plaques, who told them about the Tomorrowland one. And how, by 5:31 p.m., they ended up being the third team with the address in their hands, heading for the front gates and the waiting line of cabs, exhausted but anxious to get in the front door of that house before the last team.

At 6:15 p.m., Cassidy and Lucy were traipsing through Main Street for the four hundredth time, their cameraman trudging behind them, when a trio of guys, maybe college-aged, blocked their path. A tall, lanky one, his Jack Sparrow hat slightly cockeyed, grinned at Lucy.

"Looking for something?"

Lucy glared. Seethed and glared some more. Cassidy dragged behind her, trying vainly to tuck her damp, limp hair behind her ears and muster up a smile. She had vague thoughts of lipstick.

"We don't have time for this right now," Lucy said, her annoyance unfiltered.

Jack Sparrow raised his eyebrows at his two companions. "What if we could point you in the right direction? What might that be worth?"

Lucy shook her head. She started to turn away. "We don't need your jacka—"

Cassidy shouldered her. "Come on, Luce. Listen to him. It can't hurt. We're probably already last."

Lucy crossed her arms and sighed again. "Fine. What you got, Captain Sparrow?"

The guy grinned goofily. "You're on that show, right? The one where you're trying to win a scholarship?"

Lucy's eyes narrowed. "Where'd you hear that?"

"We asked one of the guys with the cameras. Anyway, I think I know where your clue or whatever is."

Cassidy smiled eagerly. "Awesome! Can you tell us? We've been walking around for, like, hours."

Lucy glared at her to shut up.

Jack Sparrow exchanged a look with his two companions. "We'll tell you, sure, but you gotta do something for us."

The look of distrust on Lucy's face deepened. She stayed silent. Waiting.

"You gotta ride the Teacups with us," he announced proudly, as if this was genius and everyone within earshot should probably applaud.

"You're kidding me," Lucy scoffed, already stepping backward.

Cassidy grabbed her arm and leaned in close. "Come on, Lucy," she said quickly. "What can it hurt? We've been looking all day. If they know where the clue is, what is one more ride?"

Lucy stared at all three guys. "Why? Why the Teacups? And why us?"

Jack Sparrow shrugged. "You're both cute and we might get on TV. Why not?"

And that's how Lucy and Cassidy found themselves squished into a purple teacup, spinning wildly with three rather nice guys from a town called Claremont, who, true to their word, led them right to the plaque in Tomorrowland as soon as the ride ended and, with friendly hugs, wished them a lot of luck in the competition.

Which they were absolutely going to need.

In that box was the last clue. The last envelope. Lucy's head dropped. She opened it and read the address. She handed it wordlessly to Cassidy and turned toward the main entrance.

They were last. One of them was going home. Tonight.

Oh God, Lucy thought. She hadn't counted on this. She never lost. At anything. It was how she coped with two moms who didn't understand that the world outside their door wasn't ready to embrace an all-girl family. And how she managed a dad who didn't seem to care one way or the other if she existed. She won. Debate team? Winner. Softball? Winner. Cafeteria social scene? She controlled that sucker.

How could she lose this? How had that wimpy Asian chick and that other girl who she didn't even really remember—how had they beaten her here?

Her only hope was that whoever would make the decision would think her more deserving than Cassidy. Surely, he'd see that she'd led today, right? He had to see that she was far better college material than this whining rag doll she'd been dragging around all day. Right?

Cassidy read the address printed neatly on the card. Newport Beach. Dread pulled at her throat and heart. Her chance to live at the beach, and she may never get to. She looked ahead to Lucy, striding off down the center of Main Street. Would the Benefactor, whoever he was, want to keep that bossy Texan with her know-it-all attitude? Cassidy would have to figure out a way to make him see. Show him how much she needed this.

She'd tell him the truth if she had to. No way could she let little Faith down. She had to make sure she got a college education. For sweet Faith. Her daughter.

One of them was going home tonight. It couldn't be her.

EPISODE 2
THE BEACH

"Education, therefore, is a process of living and not a preparation for future living."

—John Dewey, 1897

July 9, 10:13 p.m.
Malibu, California
The Benefactor

Brutal. That had been brutal. He should have expected it, and yet what he'd felt, watching those girls . . .

There had been tears, of course (not his). Some manufactured for both him and the camera. But some very real. And a gamut of emotions: anger, fear, anxiety, and finally relief. And frustration and regret, too.

And for him? Crushing doubt. Had he sent the right one home? He felt hollow. He wondered if this competition was justified—the right means to the right end.

He'd been naïve to think the Eliminations would be a cakewalk. Actually, he hadn't really given much consideration to the Eliminations other than buzzing, caffeine-fueled planning sessions with Yaz in which they'd excitedly come up with how they would work: only the bottom two kids would face off on couches in one of the common areas of their beach houses, cameras zooming in on every blink, every gulp, every heated exchange. The other contestants would be sequestered in their rooms, left to wonder who would be saved until the morning. The Benefactor would stay safely in his Malibu office, a dark shadow on a television screen: mysterious, removed, imposing, Godfather-like.

He'd loved the idea. It wasn't like he was a super-identifiable guy in public (people didn't stop to ask him for autographs in the supermarket), but he had name recognition. So the idea of keeping his identity a secret was appealing. Viewers (and contestants) would want to know—who was the Benefactor? Who was behind the show? Who was fronting the money for the scholarship and pulling the strings necessary to guarantee acceptance to the winner's school of choice?

The secrecy, the distance from the contestants, the air of them being his pawns—it all sounded fantastic. He could ax them from the comfort of his home and never soil his hands with any of that reality-show nonsense. But then he'd seen those two girls on those couches and gotten . . . twitchy. That irrepressible urge to crack his knuckles. Or ride until his quads ached. Or reach out and reassure them that it would be okay. *They* would be okay.

Lucy, with her stone-cold, fiery eyes, looked ready to claw Cassidy to shreds, but her hands had been quivering—a dead giveaway that her arrogance was all bravado. Cassidy tried valiantly to swallow her panic as she struggled to stay on top of the exhausting volley of slams that Lucy lobbed like a pro. They were fighters. He admired that.

"Why should I keep you?" he'd asked. The girls had been on the couches for over an hour, rehashing the mistakes of the day, firing blame at each other. The other contestants, wearing pity and relief like medals, had long been banished to their rooms.

Lucy was the first to answer. She crossed her arms and swung one leg over the other.

"I know we lost," she said, cutting a withering look at Cassidy. "But we wouldn't even have finished today if it hadn't been for me. I had a plan, and even though it took us longer than I expected, it was something. *She* had nothing."

Cassidy sat on the couch like she was a princess in etiquette training: her posture was ramrod straight; her chin was lifted; her tanned, perfect legs were pressed firmly together; her hands were folded tightly in her lap. She hadn't moved much in the last hour. She didn't move now.

"That's not true," she said quietly, but her bottom lip quaked. "Most of the money we needed to get into Disneyland, I got for us." Tears seemed imminent. "Once we were inside, neither of us had any clue where to go. We both had ideas, but they were just guesses, and obviously they didn't work. If it weren't for those three guys telling us, we would still be in there wandering around."

She dropped her chin to her chest. One hand came up and swiped at her cheek.

Lucy's eyes narrowed into deadly slits. She seemed enraged by Cassidy's emotion. It was probably good that there was a camera rolling and a coffee table separating them.

"I watched the tapes, so I know how the challenge played out," the Benefactor said, choosing his words carefully. "That doesn't tell me why I should keep you. Why are *you* more worthy of this scholarship than the others?"

Cassidy studied her hands in her lap.

Lucy, however, released her arms and gripped the edges of the couch. She leaned forward toward the TV that covered the entire mantel, where the Benefactor's image was projected. The camera zoomed in on her face—fierce, beautiful, passionate.

"Because I play to win. I don't quit. I don't let blisters," she spat, "or broken bones or how other people feel about me get in the way of what I want or need to do. I. Don't. Lose. If you keep me, I'll do whatever you ask, whenever you ask it. You want me to swim with sharks? Done. You want me to organize a cocktail party for fifty people? Fine. You want me to dance naked on the beach? Great. I understand that hard work is necessary and that the road to success is uncomfortable. So bring it on."

She sat back and crossed her arms again. Her mouth was firm. She didn't smile. She only glared—at Cassidy, at the cameras, at him. And the Benefactor had no doubt that every word she said was true.

Cassidy gulped, visibly shaken. Her eyes darted around, her discomfort palpable. He knew her background—single mom, two siblings, All-American girl. What could she be hiding?

"You should keep me because I will represent you well if I win the scholarship," she said, her voice soft but sure. "I mean, yes, I get that there will be hard work ahead, and I'm not afraid of that. Really, I'm not. I've watched my mom have to take care of three kids—two teenagers and a two-year-old—by herself. There's no shortage of work in my house. *Ever.* It may not look like it now, but I'm not afraid to get dirty or to sweat."

Lucy snorted.

Cassidy continued. "But I think there's more to this whole competition than that. Life is not just about winning. It's about getting to know other people and figuring out how to work *with* them. I can do that. I'm really good at that, I think. And if you keep me, I will not only commit myself to winning, but I will do it in a way that is, I don't know, not mean or underhanded. So that when I'm at college—a college you are paying for—you'll know that you can be, like, proud of who you chose."

Then Cassidy nodded once, as if to say, *That's all.*

Lucy muttered, "Good God," and let her eyes arc toward the ceiling.

That's when it got hard. Extremely hard.

Because Lucy's face lost her confidence and her steely-hardness when she started talking about going home after only one day. Because her eyes became desperate and pleading, even as her arms stayed crossed and her left leg continued to bounce. Because Cassidy's voice, when she mentioned her brother and sister, became tender and scratchy as she explained how she hoped to be a role model to them, to others. Because it became very apparent to everyone in that room, just as it would to everyone who would watch this in a week or so, and to the Benefactor himself, that these girls had more to lose than a scholarship if they were sent home.

And yet, he had to send one home.

There would be many who didn't agree with his decision. Who would argue on blogs and recap shows that he had been played for the sucker. Others would champion his choice and say that she may not have been the stronger competitor, but she was definitely the better person.

But seeing the devastated look on Lucy's chin-lifted, proud, and defiant face when he told her made him rethink this whole stupid idea. When from the safety of his darkened room, he cleared his throat and announced, as he and Yaz had practiced, "Lucy, you are not the top candidate for this scholarship, and I'm sorry but I must reject your application," he felt like someone had filled his abdomen with mud. Like he was crushing somebody's dreams because, oh yeah, he was.

And he had to do this six more times.

Lucy stood abruptly, without glancing at Cassidy, who had her head slightly bowed. She might have been praying. She might have simply been avoiding Lucy. But then, just before Lucy took the first step up to the room that she would never sleep in, she paused. Her fingers gripped the banister.

"You talk about playing your fair and square game," she said loudly, and it wasn't clear if she was speaking to Cassidy or to him. Cassidy's head snapped up and she blinked uncertainly in Lucy's direction. "But I saw you today. You're full of crap, Cassidy McGowan from Chicago. It took me all of five minutes to figure you out. The rest of the world will, too. So will the Benefactor. You'll scratch and claw and sleaze your way to the top if you have to. You'll just do it with your pretty little smile and your coy looks."

Lucy looked back up at the screen. "You fell for her . . ." she said, pausing. She shook her head ruefully. "You fell for her act. You're no different than the rest of the imbeciles in this world. No different." She swept up the stairs and out of sight.

Most of the cameras clicked off; lots of high fives were exchanged. Such drama! The viewers would be riveted! Ratings would soar! Wait until his sponsors got wind of this!

But the Benefactor sat motionless in his desk chair, feeling the sting of Lucy's words. On one of the remaining feeds, he saw Cassidy hesitate. Saw the corner of her mouth jerk. She blinked several times, her eyes glued to where Lucy had just been standing. Then she closed her eyes and brought a cupped hand to cover her mouth as if the horror of it was too much. For a moment, she bent forward on the couch and the Benefactor thought she might burst into tears—Lucy's accusations overwhelming, cutting, heinous, and untrue.

But she didn't cry. She kept her hand over her mouth, her other arm wrapped protectively around her stomach. Then he saw her eyes. They crinkled. Not in horror or humiliation.

In laughter.

He leaned back in his chair. Cassidy was giggling. Maybe it was nervousness or relief. Maybe it was a bubbling up of joy, knowing she'd been spared. But his stomach soured. What the hell had he just done?

On his screen, the camera closed in on Cassidy's face, catching the change in her expression as her eyes sobered. She looked around the room uncertainly and stood. Most of the show's staff seemed to have forgotten her now; they were packing up equipment, huddled over clipboards, or bent over a monitor in the back of the room, no doubt reliving the drama of the last few minutes.

Cassidy hesitated. She stared at the place where Lucy had just been sitting, had just been lashing out at her venomously. Again, Cassidy's expression changed—her eyebrows furrowed together as she reached forward for something left on the coffee table. Cassidy fingered it just long enough to let the camera get a close-up.

A ticket stub. Lucy's Disneyland ticket.

Cassidy stared at it before tucking it into her shorts pocket. Then, she looked right up into the camera, right at him. Her smile was sad and heavy. But underneath it, he could see what was already taking hold. Hope. That tomorrow would be better.

And for her sake and maybe his own, he prayed she was right.

July 10, 7:43 a.m.
Newport Beach, California
Cassidy McGowan

Brutal. God, what that girl wouldn't do or say to try to make herself look good. But it hadn't worked. The Benefactor had seen right through Lucy's Texas tough-girl act.

She flipped over on her back and stretched luxuriously, feeling the clean cotton sheets rub lightly against her bare legs. Her room was too awesome for words. It didn't overlook the ocean—Mei and Allyson had been able to grab those rooms since they weren't forced to battle it out downstairs. Still, through her open window, she could hear the crash of the waves, feel the damp sea air, and know that the Pacific Ocean was about fifty steps away.

"Ahhhh!" she squealed, throwing back the sheet and light blanket she'd slept under.

She wanted to climb up on this four-poster bed and dance and scream until her lungs were sore. Instead, she let the softest mattress she'd ever known envelop her as she savored her new room. It was painted a light sage with gleaming white wood paneling from the waist down. One whole wall was part built-in closet, part cupboards and shelves, one of which held a flat screen TV and several books with shiny covers. A white desk under her window offered a small lamp, a laptop, a spiral notebook, and a cup of freshly sharpened pencils and felt-tip pens. The floor was hardwood, but a creamy rug—the kind where your feet sink in at least an inch—covered a good portion of the room. Her own small bathroom jutted off to her left.

She'd almost missed this. Almost been sent packing last night. She wouldn't let that happen again.

Her stomach rumbled and she rolled off her bed. Knowing there would surely be cameras on her once she stepped out of this room, she'd have to dress carefully before she could find out what was for breakfast or even how that was done around here. But she didn't care. They could eat cookies for breakfast. Rice cakes. For all she cared, they could skip breakfast!

She was living on the beach. In an utterly gorgeous home where the dishwasher surely didn't flood and there was no Formica in sight. Not only that, but she hadn't had to spill her guts about Faith yet. A prickle of sadness lodged in her throat thinking of her little girl. She inhaled deeply and forced the guilt that tugged at her heart to release. She was doing this *for* Faith. She flung open her suitcase.

Now, what to wear to make sure she got noticed?

July 10, 9:13 a.m.
Malibu, California
The Benefactor

Sweat tickled its way from his temple to his jawline. His still-gloved hand swiped at it absently. One of the show's backers, a fifty-something guy whose net worth far exceeded his common sense, had roped him into riding a loop through Topanga Canyon: a forty-three-mile beast with over eight thousand feet of elevation change. His legs hadn't quite forgiven him yet.

He chugged his recovery drink—some lime-flavored thing that his trainer swore would help prevent muscle soreness but didn't seem to be doing jack—and let his eyes roam over the bank of screens. The kids were wandering out of their rooms for the day, getting their first real looks at the condos they would call home for the coming weeks. And he didn't want to miss a minute of it.

The guys were sprawled around their common area, looking like the day was already kicking their asses even though it was barely past nine. It appeared that nobody knew how to cook breakfast. The most anyone had done was open the door to the refrigerator, pour a glass of juice, and then look at their house custodian, Colin—a mid-twenties English guy who'd been hired to babysit the kids when they were at the condo—with hopeful eyes.

Colin poured a splash of milk into his tea and stirred before getting up from the counter that divided the small but first-rate kitchen from the main room. "So, mates," Colin announced to the room in general. "I know you're a bit knackered and all, but we've got some ground rules to cover before things get rolling today."

Colin chuckled good-naturedly. No one else did.

"Well, yes, then," Colin said, clearing his throat. "I'll just read this other bit of business, while we're all gathered . . ." He pulled a folded piece of paper from his front shirt pocket.

"Contestants competing on *The Benefactor* will live in houses based on gender—one house for female contestants and one for males. Contestants are *not* permitted inside the other house, unless escorted by their house custodian"—Colin looked up—"that's me, mates." He laughed uncomfortably. Again the room remained dismally silent.

"Contestants must be in their own rooms nightly from eleven p.m. until six a.m. Alcohol, cigarette smoking, or any illicit drugs are not permitted for use by any contestant and are cause for immediate removal."

There was a snort somewhere in the room. The Benefactor couldn't tell if it was because this was an obvious rule or because the person thought it was unreasonable.

The rest of the rules were pretty cut and dried: no sex; keep the place tidy; no physical attacks on other contestants; they were responsible for preparing their own meals—though the kitchen would be kept well-stocked—and they couldn't leave the immediate area around the beach house unless they were escorted by their house custodian.

"Any questions?" Colin said, tossing the paper on the coffee table.

Tyrell was sprawled on the couch. He pulled his arm from over his face and looked at Colin through heavy-lidded, bleary eyes. The Benefactor couldn't help but notice he had the hard-seasoned muscles of someone who worked out and did it often.

"You gonna read me a bedtime story, too?" Tyrell said.

The Benefactor mentally scrolled through Tyrell's bio, which he knew as well as his own: star receiver on his high school football team—until a torn ACL sidelined him last season. From Missouri. Little sister had sickle cell anemia. Chip the size of his state on his shoulders. (That last part wasn't in the bio.)

Colin lifted his eyebrows. "You gonna supply the book, mate?" he asked.

Tyrell's head swiveled. Colin leveled his eyes at the kid's glare. The sluggish mood of the room shifted. Tension now.

Hiroshi, in basketball shorts and a white V-neck T-shirt that pulled tightly across his muscled chest, sat rigidly on one of the straight-backed chairs, his eyes cast up toward the ceiling. From the uncomfortable way he kept tugging at his shorts, he was the clear introvert in the room.

Henry claimed the other chair. In a light-blue golf shirt and neatly pressed khakis, he looked ready for a day on the links. With his upbringing—his older, well-established parents were vets; he wanted to be a writer; no siblings—that wasn't surprising. His legs were jiggling so badly, the

Benefactor had to wonder if he'd already had a few espressos this morning. The guy looked amped.

It was Sam who was the most relaxed. His chest was stretched tightly under a threadbare T-shirt that the Benefactor was pretty sure he'd worn yesterday, plus some ragged boxer shorts. His face was slack, one knee pulled up, eyes hooded. Somehow, though, he gave off an air of being amused. The Benefactor mentally tagged him. From Seattle. Parents MIA. In and out of rehab. Had a killer voice and was good with a guitar.

Colin leaned forward and set down his teacup.

"Look here," he said. "I'm certainly not out to make your lives more difficult. I'm tryin' ta help you stay focused on what's important and that's winning this thing."

"You bein' from England and all, you able to whip us up some eggs Benedict?" Tyrell said from the couch.

"That's as American as apple pie, bud," Henry corrected, left leg jiggling. "You want food from across the pond, you get bangers and mash." His grin was friendly, not challenging.

Tyrell pivoted from Colin to Henry. "You know quite a bit about eggs and such. Sounds like you're our breakfast chef."

Henry crossed his arms and leaned back. His legs jiggled. "I cook, what's in it for me?"

Tyrell swung his legs around so he was sitting up. "Well, first off, we're going to get you a different shirt. 'Cause, man, you ain't never gonna meet a chick looking like you hang with the sixty-five and over crowd." He guffawed.

Henry's mouth tightened, a button of red appearing on each cheek.

Tyrell's eyes slid over to Hiroshi's. A look of understanding passed between them. "Then, we're gonna take our eggs Benedict, some toast, and maybe bacon, too, if my man, El Benefactoro, was kind enough to provide it, and you, me, and Yamamura are going to go up on that rooftop deck."

Henry didn't say anything. He jiggled away, glancing between the two guys. Once he looked over at Sam, whose expression remained amused and unconcerned. Henry seemed to be unsure about forming a bond with Tyrell and Hiroshi, when he'd clearly had some kind of alliance with Sam already. Everyone in the room appeared to understand that something was happening—something bigger than breakfast and bantering.

Finally, Henry nodded slowly. "Yeah. Okay. I got breakfast. Somebody else will get lunch, though. I'm not getting stuck playing mommy to you ass-wipes the whole time I'm here."

"Deal." Tyrell grinned and smacked his hands together loudly.

Sam stretched and yawned loudly. "Well, there's that." He casually locked eyes with Tyrell. "I'm happy to do cleanup, since Polo's cooking."

Sam unfolded his long limbs and stood up.

Tyrell glanced at Hiroshi and then lifted his chin toward Sam. "Nice of you to offer," he said guardedly.

"I'm a nice guy." Sam smiled.

For a second, Tyrell and Sam locked eyes: Sam half-smiling, Tyrell suspicious, his palms flat on the coffee table.

"See you up there, then," Tyrell said slowly.

Henry grinned. "Heard the view is . . . spectacular."

"Wouldn't miss the opportunity to see that . . . magnificent sea," Sam added.

Tyrell's grin spread slowly. "Nothing like the big, blue ocean to start a day off right."

Henry's eyebrows lifted in feigned innocence. "Ocean? Who said anything about an ocean? I'm talking about chicks, a lot of chicks."

Laughter. The tension melted away. Even Hiroshi cracked a smile.

The Benefactor took another swig and grimaced at the sour liquid coating his throat. He'd enjoyed watching their banter, but he hoped Polo cooked fast. The second challenge started at noon and the boys would want to be well nourished for this one.

July 10, 9:33 a.m.
Newport Beach, California
Mei Zhang

From Mei's window, she could see the ocean. All night, she'd laid in a bed that was far too large for her small body and listened to its steady pulsing, hoping it would lull her to sleep. But her mind was jumbled and her limbs felt as if someone had lit a fuse at the end of each one. She couldn't keep still. She couldn't focus on one thought for more than a few seconds. And even that rhythmic crashing outside would not calm her.

Today she felt only weary. It was time, she knew, to descend the stairs, face the cameras, and learn which of those two girls had not survived last night. She and the others had been banished to their rooms after a quick on-camera recap of the challenge. And though she'd thought she'd been savvy when she'd cracked open her door, her unabashed attempt to eavesdrop had been squelched immediately by a squat woman hunched over in a folding chair, whose sole job was to keep Mei sequestered. Mei had closed her door again without a word. Apparently, the Benefactor had anticipated curious teenagers.

Mei felt a familiar welling of pressure in her throat. It was the moment to figure out how her time in this house would work, who was in charge, what this next day would bring. Who might be her friend. If she would even have one here.

But instead she sat leaden on the edge of her bed and looked around her room. It was lovely—painted soft beige, with gleaming hardwood floors. A flat screen TV sat on a black dresser to her left. Her bed was covered in a thick red comforter and loaded with black and white pillows. It was the kind of room she had dreamed of living in. But being here made her heart ache.

A curtain of heaviness threatened to topple her, force her eyes closed, and cut off her air. But Mei rose steadily from the bed and walked evenly to the door. It was what her grandmother, her parents, and her sisters would expect her to do.

Downstairs, the other two girls were seated at a long wooden table that divided the kitchen from the great room. Another girl, unfamiliar and older with thick, black, glossy hair and skin the color of her father's ginger marinade, sat at the head of the table. She welcomed Mei with a wide, toothy smile.

"You must be Mei," she said. "I'm Nisha."

She was pretty, with large espresso-colored eyes and perfectly white teeth. She wore a tight yellow T-shirt and broccoli-green shorts and sat with one leg tucked underneath her. Her hand rested lightly on a half-empty cup of coffee.

Mei slipped into a chair across from Allyson, who fingered the cross at her neck while offering a smile that did not quite reach her eyes.

Cassidy was the only one at the table who looked anywhere close to ready for whatever the day might bring. Her makeup was flawless, setting off her wide blue eyes and rosy, full lips. She wore white shorts over tanned legs and a flowered baby-doll shirt with a scooped neckline. Her hair gleamed. Her smile shone. Her eyes sparkled. Mei glanced to a corner of the room where a trio of cameramen was setting up for the day. Cassidy was going to be the star.

Which meant Lucy hadn't made it. Something uneasy stirred inside her. Not because she'd liked Lucy all that much; her first impression was that Lucy was quick-tempered and scheming. But she was gone. Already. And Mei could be next.

"So, here's the deal, guys," Nisha said cheerfully. "We have a few rules to go over. And then we've got to figure out who's going to make breakfast. No maids here." She grinned.

Cassidy's shoulders seemed to dip in disappointment.

For the next few minutes, Nisha went over the house rules. No alcohol. No sex. No taking off. Curfew times. Mei listened with her hands clasped neatly on the table in front of her, her eyes lowered, her face intentionally expressionless.

"Any questions, ladies?" Nisha said, tossing her script onto the table and reaching for her coffee mug.

"Do we get to hang out on the beach when we're not, like, competing?" Cassidy asked hopefully.

Nisha smiled. "Sure. You just need to let me know where you are. And expect to be followed by cameras."

Cassidy looked longingly toward the spectacular view of sand and, beyond that, blue ocean and lighter blue sky out their bay window.

Nisha clapped her hands and leaned back. "Before we do breakfast, I want you guys to know that I'm on your side. Don't be afraid to ask questions or just, you know, stop me if you need to talk. This is pretty intense, what you're going through. So, let me know if you need to work through anything, okay? My room is right downstairs."

Nisha scanned the table with her sincere brown eyes. Mei appreciated her openness. But she knew she would never talk to her. Not the way Nisha was suggesting, anyway.

"So, anybody want to take the first breakfast shift?" Nisha asked, raising her eyebrows. "Throw together some scrambled eggs, maybe?"

No one responded. Somewhere a loud clock ticked. The waves crashed. A child screamed in delight. A seagull simply screamed. Cassidy stared out the windows, playing with a strand of her hair. Allyson toyed with her necklace. Mei focused on her hands.

"I think," Allyson said slowly, "that maybe we should all pitch in. It would help us to, you know, get to know each other a little."

If speaking could be painful, it seemed that it was for Allyson. Mei looked up at Allyson's face. It was clear she was trying. Whatever demons were pressing on that girl's soul, she was fighting them. Nisha nodded encouragingly.

Cassidy sighed. "Yeah, okay," she said. "And then we'll go to the beach, right, girls?"

Allyson shrugged without enthusiasm. Mei glanced out at the ocean. Something about all that water, those pulsing waves, felt imposing. She wasn't afraid of water. But looking at that expanse of blue, she felt overwhelmed.

"Sure," Mei said, her voice calm, even as the pounding behind her eyes grew louder and the dread in her belly made the thought of scrambled eggs nauseating. At any minute, she was sure, the next competition would start. How long could she really expect to keep her . . . problem hidden? How did she possibly think she could win this scholarship in the first place?

July 10, 10:21 a.m.
Newport Beach, California
Sam Michaels

It was an interesting alliance. Tyrell was intense. Sam wasn't sure he liked the guy, much less trusted him. But he'd been welcomed into this small Band of Brothers, and he hadn't felt it wise to show reluctance. That they all distrusted one another was understood; it was part of the setup, like any reality show. They were competing for hundreds of thousands of dollars. No one was gonna make nice when this thing went down at the end.

But right now, it wasn't a bad thing that these guys might have his back. If they really did. Sam wasn't so sure.

"So, look," Tyrell said, taking a huge swig of orange juice and shoving a whole piece of bacon in his mouth. "We don't really know what to expect next, right? But we know one chick went home last night. Either the hot blonde or her partner. The bitch from Texas."

Sam smiled at the descriptions. "Cassidy," he said evenly. "Or Lucy."

Tyrell narrowed his eyes. "How'd you even get their names, bro? We only saw them for what, like, ten minutes?"

Sam shrugged. "I remember names."

Tyrell's gaze tightened before he continued. "So, okay. One of 'em's gone. And those other two"—he looked pointedly at Sam, almost daring him to interject with their names—"can't possibly be much competition. I have no idea how they beat us here, but they had to have gotten lucky. Or got help somehow. They were struggling when Yamamura and I saw 'em outside the gates. The one dressed for prep school was probably two seconds from a meltdown."

Sam shrugged again. "They don't look tough, but sometimes those are the ones you gotta watch out for."

"Exactly, bro," Tyrell said, pointing at him appreciatively, while simultaneously scooping the last of his eggs into his open mouth. No small feat. "Which is why I think we should stick together, you know? Like, uh, form one of those alliances. Keep an eye out for each other until we only got guys left. Then it's every man for himself."

Henry finished his eggs and neatly folded his napkin under his plate. He leaned back in the deck chair, his expression hidden by black Ray-Bans.

"What if the next challenge is individual? What do we do then, man?" he asked.

"I'm not saying that we risk losing for another guy, but we can help each other in little ways. Pass on information. Offer assistance. Promise right now not to backstab another dude in this house, if we can help it. Try to take down the girls first."

Hiroshi had been eating and not really looking at anyone. He took his last bite and, without a sound, set his fork on his plate. Carefully, he raised his eyes but looked only at Tyrell.

Sam sloshed the juice around in his cup. "I'm not saying your plan is a bad one. But," he said, setting the cup down, "why would we want to keep each other—probably our toughest competition—and get rid of the girls, when we might be able to beat them in the end? Why wouldn't I want to try to get rid of, say, you and Hiroshi, who might be tough to beat in a physical challenge?"

Henry raised his eyebrows and looked at him over his Ray-Bans. "No offense taken."

Sam laughed good-naturedly. "Who knows, man? You might be the world's greatest jiu-jitsu artist ever and I'm gonna eat my words. Or maybe you kick ass in logic puzzles or something. Or run a four-minute mile."

Henry chuckled. "Nope. Hated PE. Played badminton in high school. But that was just to meet girls."

Tyrell curled his lip. "Badminton? For chicks? Really?"

Henry shook his head. "Nope. But didn't know that until it was too late. They're cool, though. The kind of chicks you can hang out with on a Friday night when you can't get the cheerleaders to go out with you."

Sam laughed. "I gotta remember that. Badminton. Who would've guessed?"

For a second, it felt like four guys hanging out. Not four guys who were gonna have to turn on one another.

Sam cleared his throat. "I guess my point is this: I don't know you guys or your strengths. But my guess is that you three are tough competition. I don't know those three girls either, but I'm willing to bet that at least physically, I could probably take them. So why wouldn't I align myself with one of them and try to take you guys out?"

Tyrell wadded up his napkin and began squeezing it in his fist.

"Fair point, I guess," he said. "But here's my offer. Stick with us right now and let's at least see what this game is all about." He glanced at the cameras, filming every word, and then down at the wadded-up napkin in his hand.

When Tyrell spoke next, his voice was lowered. "We don't know what we're up against. That Disneyland challenge? I have a feeling that was just the beginning. Let's use each other's strengths until we know how this game works." He looked up and locked eyes with Sam. "Then, you want to go after us? Go after us."

Sam sat back and fingered his chin. It wasn't a bad offer. At least through this next challenge.

"I'm in," he said, leaning forward to place his elbows on the smoked-glass table. "All for one and one for all, or whatever."

Henry and Tyrell laughed. Hiroshi kept his eyes down.

Sam wondered if he was the one to watch. Maybe he wasn't just an introvert, a non-conversationalist. Maybe he was a player.

July 10, 11:49 a.m.
Laguna Beach, California
Hiroshi Yamamura

The cameras made him intensely nervous. All he could think of when he saw them hovering, like bees in a field of honeysuckle, was that Maggie was watching. Maggie would see him on her television. And she would know. She would know instantly why he was doing this. And she'd probably be pissed.

He could picture her. She'd have her legs tucked underneath her, and she'd be on the floor. Maggie was a floor person. Offer her a couch or a chair and she'd flop right down and announce, "Naw, I'm good."

Her reddish-blond hair, pixie-short, and probably tipped in purple or pink, would be tucked behind her ears. She would have no makeup on. She didn't need it. Her complexion was flawless, her eyes a smoky green. Her lashes, pale and long. When she'd kissed him, she'd always tasted like cinnamon—the gum she chewed constantly.

Until Maggie, he hadn't dated much. An Asian guy in a white world has a hard time of it. Girls would flirt; they would drop hints. But when he asked? Excuses. Always.

Until Maggie. A drama student who slipped into the desk next to his in AP art history in September and slipped into his heart by Halloween. By December he was skipping practices to watch her rehearsals. By January his calculus grade had slipped to a B. By February his physics and history teachers were raising eyebrows when they handed back his tests, and his coach was all but threatening to cut him from the team. In March he asked her to prom in the corniest way possible, by pretending to be Romeo outside her window and offering her a single rose. And then in May his parents had given him their ultimatum, pulling the rug from under his feet, so that on the night of prom, while Maggie waited for him—in her purple-flowered dress with the wreath of lilacs he'd bought her circling her perfect head—he sat on his bed, his head in his hands, and cried.

He'd applied for this stupid competition the next week.

If he won, he could go back to her. Because his parents would have no hold over him.

If he won, he would ask her to senior prom and show her the best night of her life.

If he won.

The cameras closed in as he pushed himself out of the van and blinked in the blinding sunlight of wherever they were. Tyrell crawled out behind him.

"It was the Texas bitch," Tyrell muttered.

A few feet away, the three girls were climbing out of their own van. He saw the blonde who'd been in the Elimination last night. Behind her were the other two—the serious Chinese girl and the dour-faced brunette. No Lucy, with her fierce eyes. He wondered where she was, what she was doing. If she was mad or relieved.

They were on a car-packed, narrow street that ran along the coastline. Between them and the ocean was a strip of lusciously landscaped park, crisscrossed by paved jogging paths and dotted with stone benches and a few statues. Beyond that, it looked like there was a steep drop-off to a sandy beach and then ocean—as far as the eye could see.

The air here, even though it was July, was breezy and crisp. The kind of air that made you want to stand for a moment and just breathe. It was the kind of air Hiroshi was used to, having grown up in seaside La Jolla. It was the kind of air that made people flock to southern California beaches. Where there was this amazing feeling of life and vitality. This realization that you'd made it to the edge of the map and yet there was still more.

Without being told, the seven of them instinctively headed toward a roped-off area of newly cut, pristine grass where Molly, their host from yesterday, leaned casually against a metal railing. Her loose-fitting, sleeveless tunic billowed in the sea breeze, in contrast to the shapely white skirt that clung to her very curvy bottom half. Strappy white sandals showed off well-toned, tanned legs. She was striking, if not beautiful, though overdressed for the beach.

Laid out in a neat semicircle before her on the grass was an array of boxes—seven large ones paired with seven smaller ones. If Hiroshi had had to guess, he would have said the big ones contained furniture. They were about the length and width of a coffee table, maybe three or four inches thick. They were all set upright like some weird cardboard Stonehenge and as he walked closer, he could see that they were each labeled with one of the participants' names. Each of the larger boxes had a small box—probably just a couple of feet high and a foot or so wide—sitting next to it.

Henry blew out air. "Please tell me we don't have to assemble something," he whined. "Me and power tools do not get along well. Don't get me wrong, I enjoy a good screw as much as the next guy, but . . ."

Sam chuckled and stuck a fist out for Henry to tap.

Hiroshi kept his face expressionless but felt a surge of hope and relief in his belly. He had an engineer's brain. If they had to assemble something, he'd be in decent shape. What he was really hoping for, though, was that in that box was a boogie board or a kayak. Something that got him on the water. He was king on the water.

"Come on over, guys," Molly beckoned with a wide, camera-ready smile. "Today, we're going to see how you do in an activity the Benefactor loves. An activity that's going to test not only your endurance but your attention to detail."

Hiroshi felt a buzzing start in his head as he walked toward those boxes. Maggie was watching. He was sure of it. He had failed her so miserably already. Redemption was possible. Starting now.

July 10, 12:52 p.m.
Laguna Beach, California
Allyson Murphy

For the first time since she'd stepped foot in California, Allyson felt something loosen behind her eyes. The minute Molly explained the challenge, Allyson knew. She knew her prayers had been answered. God was watching out for her and He wanted her here. Those prickles of doubt, that He didn't exist, that He didn't care—because who let someone as beautiful and loved as her mom die?—those doubts subsided. And she realized that maybe she was supposed to be here. Because He wanted her to be.

The challenge had two parts. The first part required them to assemble the brand-new mountain bikes that were in each of these boxes. Once their bikes were assembled, and then adjusted and deemed safe to ride by the bike technician waiting nearby, he would give them a helmet and directions to a location they would ride to in order to complete the challenge.

Allyson didn't know how any of this fit into the Benefactor's overall plans. She didn't understand how this made them better college students or more worthy of a scholarship. But she did know this: she and her dad had been fixing up old bikes since she was big enough to hold an Allen wrench. And she'd been riding with him—sometimes just to their church, sometimes on long rides that lasted hours and took them all over Colorado and even into Nebraska—for as long as she had memories.

She found the box with her name and felt a bubble of excitement. But as her competitors tore into their boxes—Tyrell swearing, Mei anxious, Hiroshi already laser-beam focused on the task ahead—Allyson stopped. She rested her palms on the top of the box and closed her eyes.

She could feel a camera inch up next to her. But she wouldn't offer this prayer aloud for the world. This was between her and God.

Thank you, Jesus, she prayed silently, *for giving me a challenge that I am so fully capable of doing. For infusing me with confidence in a moment when I was feeling so lost. I will do my best in these next few hours to honor You in my actions and in my words. In Your most holy name, Amen.*

But then she did offer the camera a few words. Words she knew would let her family know that she was still in this. Each word felt heavy, but she forced them from her lips. "We got this, Dad," she said.

Allyson ripped open the top flap of her box and started to remove the very familiar contents inside.

July 10, 12:52 p.m.
Laguna Beach, California
Cassidy McGowan

Cassidy wanted to cry. The pieces of the blasted bike lay scattered in front of her on the grass. They all looked like stuff that should be on a bike: handlebars, seat, pedals, wheels. And then there were the things to help her set up the bike—some small metal tools, a tire pump, a sheet of instructions, and a three-foot-tall thing that she assumed was a stand—that had come in a separate box.

It should have been obvious where all this stuff went and how it should go on, right? So why did this feel like sitting in physics class when Mr. Leung talked about vector components and Cassidy's brain felt as if someone was running it through a meat grinder?

She glanced worriedly over at Allyson. Her bike looked like a . . . bike. The usually grim-faced girl was tightening her pedals, her top teeth biting her lower lip in total concentration. It was the first time that Cassidy could remember seeing the girl not fingering that stupid cross on her neck.

The four boys had dragged their boxes to form a tight circle as soon as Molly yelled, "Go!" It was clear they were working as a team. All four of their bikes, while not as far along as Allyson's, were at least starting to resemble bikes.

The only one who seemed to be struggling as much as her was Mei. The tiny girl kept picking up a part, peering closely at the one page of instructions they'd been given, and then setting the part back down, only to pick up another. So far, she'd attached her seat to the frame thingy and somehow managed to get her handlebars on—which was more than Cassidy had done.

For the eightieth time, Cassidy picked up the black seat that had a long, tube-like metal piece jutting out from the bottom of it.

"Think," she muttered, fighting back tears, knowing they would smear her mascara. She was panicked both by the task and the camera blinking dangerously close by.

She reached for the directions, but the words and diagrams all swam together, much like the algebra problems on her homework. And here there was no Luke or Jake to call. Helplessly, she looked around again. Realization was sinking in; she was on her own.

Allyson was wheeling her bike toward the guy who was going to adjust the gears and brakes, snap a small pod under their seat that contained a spare tube in case they got a flat tire (not that Cassidy'd have a clue how to change it anyway), and give them the final okay to ride. Cassidy gripped the seat post harder. Her directions were becoming a pulpy, sweaty mess in her other fist.

Laughter erupted from the circle of four guys. Henry was attempting to juggle the tools they used to tighten stuff on the bike, while Sam helped Tyrell wind on his last pedal. In a few more minutes, all four of them would be finished.

She was swimming in fear. Drowning in panic. She'd be in the bottom two. Again. The Benefactor wouldn't save her twice. She had to turn this around. Somehow. Now.

Quickly, she grabbed the blue frame that had been in her box, tucked the seat post under one arm, and made her way to Mei.

"Hey," she said softly, only too aware that every word of hers was being captured for the world to see and to judge.

Mei looked up, her face nearly expressionless, as Cassidy had come to expect. But hidden deep within those brown eyes, Cassidy was sure she could see some of the same panic, the same helplessness.

"I'm not doing so well," Cassidy said and forced a small laugh.

Mei sat with her legs neatly crossed on the ground, the parts lined up in rows. She sighed, surveyed her work, and then looked questioningly at Cassidy.

"We could team up, maybe?" Cassidy offered. "I mean, I don't know what I'm doing either, really, but at least we'd be able to talk through it together."

Cassidy nodded toward the guys who were gathered around Henry's bike now, waiting for him to tighten his last pedal. They would be off to the bike technician soon and riding away shortly after that.

Mei looked down at the instructions in her lap. A breeze lifted the ends of her straight dark hair. She tucked them behind her ears.

Then she looked up.

"Yes," she said to Cassidy. "Yes, I think we should."

July 10, 1:03 p.m.
Laguna Beach, California
Sam Michaels

This was a mistake. If he'd known what the challenge was going to be . . . how this would play out . . . he never would have agreed. He needed to unalign himself from these guys.

Put together a bike? Sam could do that in his sleep. When you're a hungry teenager on an island of rich kids, you learn quickly what you can do for cash. Fixing bikes was easy money and the local bike shop didn't care if he showed up in ripped jeans, slightly stoned, as long as he managed to adjust handlebars and true wheels and tune gears.

Tyrell, on the other hand, obviously didn't know an Allen wrench from his left nut. And Henry was so far out of his league, he could have been in Indonesia. Hiroshi was the only one who looked like he might have been able to slog his way through it alone. Regardless, Sam would have smashed all of them easily. Only Allyson would have given him any competition. The girl knew bikes.

Instead he was stuck playing "seat post connects to the top tube" when he should have been chasing down Allyson already. He regretted ever agreeing to an alliance. He'd just have to find a way out before the next challenge.

He watched the bike tech give each of their bikes the once-over and check their brakes and gears. When he got to Sam's bike, he inspected it appreciatively.

"Know your way around a bike," he stated.

Sam shrugged coolly. “Easy transportation where I’m from.”

The guy gave his brakes a tug. “You’re in good shape.” He appraised Sam. “You don’t make it in this competition, you let me know. I got a job for you.”

Sam smiled. “Thanks, but I’m not planning to go home any time soon.”

Might have been his imagination, but he thought he heard Tyrell snort.

“You got directions for us, boss?” Tyrell asked.

The bike tech tossed them each a silver helmet and an envelope.

“Good luck,” he said, shaking his head. “That girl has a good lead on you. Gonna be hard to close the gap.”

Sam pictured Allyson. She weighed maybe a hundred and ten and looked afraid of her shadow. They could catch her. They *would* catch her. Sam snapped the helmet on his head and ripped open his envelope.

“Thousand Steps Beach?” he heard Henry ask. “Any clue where that is?”

“Let’s get out on the street,” said Tyrell. “Get moving. We’ll figure it out.”

Sam would have preferred knowing where they were going first. He would have made a plan, then moved forward. He and Tyrell didn’t work the same way. Another great reason to break this bond.

Before it got him somewhere he didn’t want to be.

July 10, 1:13 p.m.
Laguna Beach, California
Mei Zhang

As much as she hated relying on someone else, Mei was grateful to have Cassidy working with her. When she'd been alone, she couldn't stop the letters on that instructions page from lurching around and jumbling together senselessly. Yes, there were diagrams she should have been able to follow. But the simple directions below them just taunted her. So a loud buzzing erupted in her brain. And kept her from focusing. On anything.

"Okay, so I think we put this front wheel in between these two little prong thingees," Cassidy said, glancing at her instruction page and up at her bright yellow bike frame. "Does that make sense to you?"

With Cassidy reading the instructions, a lot was making sense to Mei. And not just the bike assembly.

Now that the buzzing in her head had subsided, she knew she was going to have to fight for her life at the Elimination. Unless Allyson or the boys got lost, it was going to be her and Cassidy sitting on those couches, facing off. Maybe she'd get lucky and the Benefactor would choose to send Cassidy home since she'd been in the bottom twice. Somehow, Mei had to make sure that happened. Make sure that the Benefactor saw why she was worth keeping.

Which meant speaking up for herself. And actually believing what she said.

Slowly, she slipped her front wheel onto the frame and tightened the lever so that the wheel snapped into place.

"It says we need to pump up our tires now," Cassidy said. "I think this thing here is the tire pump."

"Does it say how much air to put in?" Mei asked.

"Umm . . . thirty-five to sixty-five is the number it gives here. PSI or something like that?"

While both girls attached the pumps to their tires, Mei considered what she might say to make conversation. She was hardworking. She'd had to be. She was creative—at least when it came to drawing and painting. She was a rule follower—a follower, period. But she didn't think that was a good thing.

And that's when the doubts flooded her. She wasn't athletic or outspoken. She wasn't really passionate about anything, except maybe her art. She did decently enough in school, but had to work so, so hard. She wasn't unfriendly but she wasn't outgoing, either. She was . . . forgettable. Why she'd been chosen to be here in the first place was baffling.

And she couldn't read.

Not true, she argued with herself. She could. If she went really slowly. If she used some tips given to her by her fourth-grade teacher—the teacher who came closest to figuring out that Mei might be dyslexic and didn't blame everything on her being a "second language learner," which she wasn't, because her parents had made sure she'd learned English and learned it well. Yes, she could read. She just couldn't do it fast. Especially when the pressure was on.

"I think that's all the air they need," Cassidy said, unclasping the hose from her tire valve. "We're almost ready to go," she finished cheerfully, smiling at Mei.

She watched Cassidy bend over the instructions again, her eyes scanning the final lines on the paper. Mei's stomach plummeted. She couldn't do this. She couldn't continue to fake her way through. She didn't deserve to be here.

July 10, 1:43 p.m.
Malibu, California
The Benefactor

Allyson was the dark horse, no doubt. He hadn't seen that coming. Not only had she assembled that bike like a pro, she'd then gone on to ride with ease the almost five miles from Heisler Park to Thousand Steps Beach. And that was along Pacific Coast Highway, a traffic-heavy, somewhat rolling route along the coast.

She'd then left her bike and run down the seemingly endless steps to the beach below where a marked board (set up earlier by a wheezing Yaz, who for all his efficiency was apparently in really lousy shape) showed only a large image of a red, British-style phone booth. Allyson had to figure out that this particular phone booth was a longtime landmark of downtown Laguna Beach, ride her bike there, find the clue tucked inside, and then finish at the nearby café where she would wait for the rest of her fellow contestants to arrive.

Allyson sailed through the entire challenge. She flew down the stairs so quickly the cameras lost track of her and didn't pick her up again until the bottom. After studying the image for about thirty seconds, Allyson hauled back up without breaking a sweat. At the top, she grabbed her bike, and with a look of determination that he hadn't seen from Allyson yet, reached for the arm of a woman passing by.

"Excuse me!" she said breathlessly. "I'm looking for a red phone booth. Like maybe an old-fashioned one. Is there something like that around here?"

The startled woman and her friend, both beachgoers, shrugged. Without missing a beat, Allyson flung a leg over her bike and headed down toward a crowded intersection just half a block away.

There she struck gold.

"Downtown Laguna Beach," said an older man, his skin leathery and brown from many summers in the southern California sun. "It's on Forest, I think. Just north of PCH. You can't miss it. It's been there for years." He pointed back in the direction she'd ridden from earlier and smiled, his teeth bleached brilliant white.

It was nearly four miles back up the Pacific Coast Highway to the street he'd named, but she found it easily, along with the note inside that told her to make her way to the café and find the marked table. The Benefactor watched her enter the restaurant and for the first time since he'd laid eyes on this small-town girl, a real smile spread across her face, lighting up her eyes. The camera caught it all. Within seconds, she was seated at a long, reserved table, being interviewed by one of his staff, Yaz nodding smugly—"Good girl!"—nearby.

The Benefactor then turned his attention to the boys, whose alliance was holding strong, despite a clear weakness in Henry's cycling skills. Crescents of sweat had appeared under Henry's armpits, staining his perfectly pressed polo.

"Jeez," he said as he caught the other three at a stoplight. His breathing was labored and sweat dribbled down his temples. "You guys want to slow down, maybe? We in the Tour de France and I don't know it?" His laugh was forced.

Sam made no attempt to hide his scowl. The light turned green. Henry groaned.

"Any idea how much farther?" Henry asked. His bike wobbled awkwardly as he tried to find his balance, pedal, and talk all at once.

Sam called over his shoulder. "The guy said it was maybe five miles. I'd say we've gone three."

Henry's face fell. Sam rode on, radiating mild contempt for his uncoordinated teammate. Frustration seemed to simmer just below the surface even for Tyrell and Hiroshi, who were not strong cyclists, but both fit, athletic guys who were ready to kick this challenge in the butt.

Which probably explains why they did what they did next.

What no one expected, though, was how much it would ultimately change the entire game.

July 10, 2:02 p.m.
Laguna Beach, California
Sam Michaels

Sam was sick of Polo's whining. If he pedaled any slower, he'd be going backward. If Sam had been alone, he could have been there by now. Frustration—with Henry and with himself—made his neck tight and his back teeth gnash together.

They were pedaling toward the Third Street intersection, a slight uphill climb. Sam glanced back. Predictably, Henry was lagging well behind. Hiroshi was just a few bike lengths back from Sam, with Tyrell third, working hard to stay on Hiroshi's wheel. Sam was nearly through the intersection, out of his saddle, and leaning hard on his pedals to push the last few yards when he heard Tyrell behind him.

"Dude! Light! We gotta wait for Polo."

Sam twisted back. The light was red. Sam, Tyrell, and Hiroshi had made it. Polo was still chugging along on the other side. Sam figured they had to be about a half mile from the beach they were looking for, based on the directions they'd been given from the guy in the Mercedes back at Heisler Park. They could (a) wait for Polo here and bumble along at his pace; or (b) go ahead and wait for him at the beach.

It was a no-brainer.

"I'm gonna keep going," Sam yelled over his shoulder. "Beach has gotta be close. I'll meet you guys there."

He didn't wait to see what Tyrell or Hiroshi would do. He lifted up off his seat and felt the release in his quads as he pushed hard on the pedals. With the cool sea breeze coming from his right and the solid feel of a brand-new bike under him, Sam relaxed. This was riding.

At the next light, he glanced over his left shoulder and noticed that Hiroshi and Tyrell weren't far back. Polo, on the other hand, was nowhere in sight. For some reason, this made Sam grin. Things had just gotten interesting.

At Thousand Steps Beach, he leaned his bike against the metal fence at street level and barreled downward, dodging beachgoers and couples with as many apologies as he could gasp out. The image at the bottom puzzled him for a fraction of a second before it clicked that they must have to find it somewhere and that it must be close. Game on.

Back up those stairs was harder, but adrenaline was on his side. Now that he'd made the decision to bust his pact with those guys wide open, he'd have to beat them—stay far ahead of them—because they weren't going to be happy.

Hiroshi and Tyrell were coming down as he was about halfway up.

"What's down there, dude?" Tyrell asked, stopping to lean against the stairs and wipe his shirt across his face.

"Just a picture," Sam said, already moving past them. "You'll see it easy."

Tyrell grabbed the tail of his T-shirt. Sam turned. Tyrell's eyes were challenging. Intense.

"Tell us, man," he said. "You save us a trip."

Sam glanced at Hiroshi. He wouldn't look up, but stared instead down the long flight of steps still awaiting them.

Sam's answer was slow and purposeful. "No can do, man. Pretty sure you got to complete every part of the challenge yourself."

Tyrell jutted out his chin and made a deliberate show of looking around. "No cameras here now, man."

Hiroshi shook his head slightly. He took a step down toward the beach. Tyrell's eyes narrowed.

Sam grinned. "Listen, bro." He pulled out of Tyrell's grasp. "You and Yamamura are my biggest competitors. I mean that as praise, man. You're tough and you're smart.

You're probably going to kick my ass. I can't stay teamed up with you two. I just can't. I gotta do this alone. And if it makes you guys my enemies, I have to risk that. I'm sorry."

Before Tyrell could react, Sam bounded up, up, up the rest of the stairs, never looking back.

At street level, he grabbed his bike and gave a quick glance down the street. No Polo yet. Which was odd since he hadn't been that far behind. Sam shrugged. He'd made his position clear with Tyrell. He needed to find that red phone booth. Polo was on his own.

July 10, 2:12 p.m.
Laguna Beach, California
Henry Stone IV

He was alone. Abandoned. And his dad would see it.

He wasn't the world's best bike rider or in the best shape either. But did they have to totally bail on him? They were dicks. He didn't need any of them. His IQ was probably at least thirty points higher than all of them. In fact, he didn't need this ridiculous competition. What was he doing here? Riding a bike along the beach to follow some inane clue left by whom? A guy who hadn't even revealed himself yet? What the hell did any of this have to do with higher education?

Which is exactly what he told his cameraman at the next stoplight. The guy was following along, hoping for something TV-worthy. So fine; why not give him something to film?

The anger usually started somewhere near his groin. Funny place, he knew, for anger to build from, but that's where he would feel it first. Then it fingered out into his belly, licking its way into his chest and up his throat. By the time it filled in behind his eyes, it was a full-blown rage, and he was helpless to do much but let it play out. Lash out at whatever—whoever—was nearby, and hope they could withstand his beating. He might not even remember it afterward.

Today, it was a circular lens and a blinking red light.

"This whole competition is . . . is a freak show," he said, his eyes wide and manic, his face flushed. Whether this was from the exertion of the bike or the passion of his words was hard to tell.

"What are we trying to prove? That we're better than the system? Or that we're unable to compete with the thousands of other high school kids out there who all want to get into college, too? And so what? I can't ride a damn bike, so I'm not worthy of Harvard? Yale? USC? How does any of this make sense? Do you know what my IQ is? It's 146. Yep, you heard that right. One forty-six. I think that's, like, genius or something, right?"

The light changed. Henry tried to maneuver his pedals around so he could get started, but his feet got tangled up and he toppled over. He caught himself at the last minute. Angrily, he got off the bike and started walking it through the intersection. The car with the camera stayed with him, moving slowly, its hazards blinking.

"So effing genius I can't even ride this effing bike. Good stuff, right? Good TV? And my three *pals*"—he drew out that word slowly and emphatically—"were so kind and willing to wait for me. That little alliance lasted all of about two hours. I've taken showers that lasted longer. God. What a remarkable joke this whole thing has turned out to be."

Once he'd crossed the street, he lifted his bike and flung it into a small grassy area at the corner of the intersection. Several passersby skittered out of the way, then turned to stare. Henry ignored them.

He plopped down next to his bike, bent his knees up, and dropped his head into his hands. And as much as he wanted to let the anger seep through him, he knew what came next. He'd cycled through this many times. And it worried him.

But that's not what scared him most. What scared him most was that his dad had been right. He was going to come home from this competition a loser. And end up at that damn vet school in Iowa.

July 10, 2:20 p.m.
Laguna Beach, California
Cassidy McGowan

There had to be a law against this much silence. She had to sing or hum or something. Anything but silence. This riding along without talking at all was making her feel edgy and anxious. Or maybe that was from knowing they were last. Or maybe it was both.

Cassidy dropped back so she was riding side by side with Mei in the wide bike lane. The passing cars made for a loud and constant backdrop.

"So, do you think we have a chance?" she shouted.

Mei kept her eyes forward. She didn't smile. "I guess there's always a chance," she said evenly, her voice barely carrying above the traffic.

"But, really, do you think maybe one of the guys got lost or something? Got a flat? Could we still beat somebody?" Cassidy's voice surged with hope.

Cassidy glanced at Mei. Was there a hint of irritation curtained behind Mei's guarded eyes?

"I think we should just focus on doing what we can," Mei said, her voice still even. "We can't really worry about what we can't control."

Cassidy sighed. Mei would have made a terrible team captain. Cassidy always made sure to tell the girls what they needed to hear when they were losing. Things like "We can still pull this out," and "We're the better team," even when it was clear they couldn't and they weren't. Cassidy pedaled to get in front of Mei and tried to tell herself they were still in this thing. Even when she knew they weren't.

Except that there was a guy up ahead on the grass who looked a lot like one of their competitors. She squinted. Yeah, it was him! It was the guy from Portland—the guy who'd flirted with her yesterday at Disneyland. Henry. What was he doing sitting there on the side of the road?

The light turned green just as the girls hit the intersection. Cassidy led Mei through it and then pulled up onto the sidewalk by Henry.

"Hey," she said.

His face popped up from between his knees. His eyes stared at her guardedly.

"You okay?" Cassidy asked.

She heard Mei brake behind her. Henry's glance volleyed between both girls. There was something unfocused about his eyes. Like he couldn't quite register who they were.

"Cassidy," she said gently, and then tipped her head behind her. "And Mei. We're pulling up the rear here, obviously." She laughed lightly.

Henry looked sideways toward the ocean and shook his head several times slowly. He didn't speak but his expression was hard, accusing. Maybe angry.

"You okay?" she asked again. "You got a flat or something?"

Recognition finally snapped in Henry's eyes. He blinked and glared up at her.

"You stop to think, just for a second, how completely and utterly stupid this whole thing is?" he said, casting his gaze down, each word more cutting, more razor-sharp, than the last.

Cassidy felt herself recoil. She glanced anxiously over at the car that had stopped near them. The one with the camera in it. That was surely filming all of this with interest. Relaying every word to the Benefactor.

"Um . . . stupid? What? The competition? Or the bikes?" she asked lightly. She was stalling. This was bad news. For him. For her, too, if she didn't distance herself. Quickly.

Henry lifted his arm and swept it in front of him, much like Molly, their host, had done earlier. "All of it. Jumping through these asinine hoops to get into college. For what? A degree? Do you even know what you want to be?"

His eyes were pleading. Kind of bleary. Was he on something?

Cassidy stole a look at Mei. No expression. Shocker.

Cassidy shrugged. "Sure, I've thought about it. A nurse, maybe. I think I'd like to help people. Or a physical therapist. I hear that's going to be a growing industry. Or I might just major in business, you know?"

Henry shook his head and scoffed. "See? That's exactly what I'm talking about. You don't really know. And yet, you're out here, busting your ass on a friggin' bicycle with all these other freaks so you don't have to bust your ass on the SATs and APs and scholarship apps and FAFSA, right? It's . . . insane, is what it is." His head swung left toward the ocean, which was still visible down a side street, through a line of houses.

"I ought to pull the plug. Go to the damn school my dad wants me to go to. It'd be so much easier," Henry said softly.

Cassidy was speechless. She wasn't the smartest person here. She was sure of that. And she definitely wasn't great at assembling a bike or even riding it. But giving up? That wasn't even in her vocabulary.

Mei inched her bike forward. "Maybe we should just go, Cassidy," she said quietly. Her expression was clear: if we leave him here, we are not last. We still have a chance.

But Cassidy glanced back at Henry, picking blades of grass from the ground. Henry would be last, sure. But that still left one of them to join him in the bottom two. She thought back to last night's Elimination. What she'd said to the Benefactor to get him to keep her. And suddenly it became very clear to her how to play this.

She nodded to Mei. "You go on ahead," she said. "We'll catch up in a sec."

Mei stared at her hard. But then the tiny girl spun her pedals and pushed off.

Cassidy slid a leg off her bike and laid it down by Henry's. She flopped onto the grass next to him.

"Tell me about your dad," she said.

July 10, 2:35 p.m.
Laguna Beach, California
Mei Zhang

Mei couldn't figure out Cassidy's game, and that worried her. She knew there was something she was missing. Because why would Cassidy volunteer to stay back with Henry when she knew she would be in the bottom two? Again. Facing almost certain elimination from the game.

Mei pedaled faster and faster, her mind spinning. She wasn't good at this. This gameplay stuff. She wasn't good at reading people or manipulating people. She was good at drawing people. When she drew, she could see things that she hadn't seen before.

That was it.

That's what she had to do. She had to imagine she was drawing Cassidy. While her legs steadily drove the bike forward, she let her mind picture a blank white page in her journal. And then, she started sketching. First, Cassidy's slender, egg-shaped face. Her wide, eager eyes. Her wide mouth and long, wavy hair.

Gradually, Cassidy took shape on her imaginary page, and Mei found herself relaxing. Her hands no longer held the handlebars in death grips. Her shoulders were no longer hunched up. Her chest loosened a little. And she began to see Cassidy more clearly. Why had she not done this before? Mei smiled.

For the first time, it felt as if she had a plan. A plan that could carry her forward in the game. No, she couldn't read well. But this . . . *this* she could do.

July 10, 2:41 p.m.
Malibu, California
The Benefactor

He watched, disbelieving, as Mei rode past the entrance to the Thousand Steps Beach. What the hell was she doing? Not only was she riding past it, but she was smiling broadly, as if she knew something everyone else didn't. She just kept pedaling, her eyes a million miles away, not even bothering to look over to see the sign that announced the stairwell down to the beach. How could she not have seen the entrance?

He watched the cameraman zero in on the entrance to the beach and then film Mei's retreating form. Another camera got a close-up of her face. She was smiling, leaning forward in a determined way he hadn't seen in her before. He couldn't help but notice that she was quite pretty when she finally smiled.

He flipped his attention back to Cassidy and Henry. She was something else, that one. He was pretty sure what she was up to, and it was a bold, potentially risky move. But the viewers would react to her. Her ratings would soar.

She was casually listening to Henry pour out his heart. He seemed to have forgotten that there were cameras nearby. He was blasting his mom and dad (dad mostly), for pushing him into the family business, for ignoring his love of literature, for insisting he enjoy animals when he clearly detested them. His powerlessness and hurt came through with every word, as did Cassidy's genuine empathy. It made for great TV.

But the kid was a whirlwind of emotion. One minute, he was riding high—flirting with Cassidy, cracking jokes. The next he was raging against the world. And now, he looked about ready to crawl into a hole and die. And he'd only been on camera for a total of about forty-eight hours. Something was up with this kid.

The Benefactor leaned forward on his couch. Watched Cassidy pull Henry up with one hand. For a moment, they both stood there.

"Come on, Henry," Cassidy said gently. "Finish this leg of the race with me. And then we figure out what's next. It's a bike ride and then we take it one step at a time. And if you want to quit tonight, quit tonight. But who knows? Maybe you won't."

Henry's face was a tangled mess of emotions. Part of him clearly wanted to believe her. Another part wanted to cling to his anger.

He blew out air. "Okay." His smile was forced, grimace-like. "You're a persuasive girl. Let's do this bike ride. I got nothing better to do."

Impulsively, she reached forward and hugged him. The camera caught his face. It was surprise and something more—a tender vulnerability that showed just how much Henry wanted, or maybe needed, someone to believe in him.

Within five minutes, they were at the entrance to Thousand Steps Beach, leaning their bikes against the fence and readying to bound down the steps.

Mei was nowhere in sight.

EPISODE 3
THE BREAKDOWN

"We need intellect, and there is no reason why we should not have it together with character; but if we must choose between the two we choose character without a moment's hesitation."

—Theodore Roosevelt, 1895

July 10, 11:45 p.m.
Newport Beach, California
Henry Stone IV

He'd failed. And he'd done it miserably and publicly. On a bike. Like a pathetic loser.

His father would watch this, sipping his nightly martini and puffing on that infernal pipe of his—though his doctor strongly advised against both. He would shake his head ruefully, self-righteous pity oozing out of every judgmental pore. He would inevitably conclude (in sidebar discussions with his tech assistants and longtime patients) that his son, though so bright and truly a gem of a kid, was nevertheless simply incapable of completing tasks involving athleticism and mechanics—hadn't he said exactly that before Henry left for this ridiculous game? Henry, therefore, must certainly come to his senses and return without delay to Portland, where he would bring honor and glory to the Stone family name by attending that damn veterinary school in Iowa.

Henry wadded up his pillow into a tight ball. The stupid room was abominably hot; his skin moist and damp. The sheets clung uncomfortably to his legs. He ripped them off and sat up so fast the room tilted. Where was the air conditioning? Could their esteemed Benefactor not afford air conditioning?

His rib cage felt like it was being squeezed by giant pliers. His head pounded. He couldn't stop reliving the challenge—the nightmare of being left by that laughable alliance, breaking down in front of the whole world, and then being saved—cue the violins, please—by the lovely Cassidy. Sitting through that humiliating Elimination with her and Mei. His father would . . . oh, God.

Damn him. Damn them all.

He didn't need to be here. There was money. Plenty of money. There'd always been money. He could have his pick of schools. Should have been able to have his pick of schools.

The anger was building, seeping, flowing; starting in that low spot and tendrilling its way into his belly. He rose to his feet, not sure what he intended to do, only that he needed to be moving. He staggered forward and caught the edge of the dresser. He leaned in to stare at his image, his glassy, manic eyes. From the moonlight streaming in his glass doors, he could see his flushed cheeks and taut mouth.

He was smarter than this game. He pounded his fist down onto the dresser's surface, relishing the pain that flooded his pinky finger and shot up his arm. He was being played a fool. In front of the world.

His gut raged, as much out of control as his thoughts. Did he not have what this game took to win? His throat ached to yell. His fists to pound. His legs to run.

He spun wildly, grabbing the first thing his fingers touched. A tablet. He lifted the thin computer, feeling primal, senseless, rampaging. Heedless of who might hear or what could result, Henry hurled it angrily. It smashed against the closet door with a satisfying, splintering sound, and he watched it fall to the faux hardwood floor below, where its screen shattered and pieces of the metal case broke off and scattered. Unusable, useless pieces.

For soundless seconds, then minutes, he stood staring at those pieces. His breathing was rapid, shallow, distressed. His vision was alternately blurry and crystal clear. The walls of the room seemed to inch closer somehow, until it felt like he would have no more air to breathe.

Scattered in those pieces on the floor, he saw his father's patronizing expression.

He saw Sam, Tyrell, and Hiroshi riding off when that light turned red.

And he saw Cassidy, leaning toward him, her look both sympathetic and horrified.

He collapsed to the floor, all of the rage sucked out of him, leaving him empty. And tired. So tired. On knees and palms, he inched forward toward the broken pieces of the tablet. How could he have let it go this far? How did he always let it go too far?

Slowly, with painstaking care, he picked up the pieces of the tablet, wrapped them in a pillowcase he pulled from his bed, and tucked the wad in a back corner of his closet. Maybe they would never know. Maybe he would never have to explain.

He eased himself back into bed, his body heavy, his eyes heavier.

He hadn't deserved her compassion. She should have left him there on the side of the road and ridden on. Instead, she'd reached out, urged him to finish, stayed by his side. Risked her own stake in this game.

That thought racked him with guilt. He was safe; safe here in this suffocating room, while she . . . she could be on a plane home.

He curled into a tight ball. What had he done?

July 10, 11:48 p.m.
Newport Beach, California
Sam Michaels

Had she been sent home? He flipped onto his side, feeling the twisted-up sheet braid with his legs. His mind raced as his eyes rhythmically watched his ceiling fan circle again and again and again.

Moonlight streamed in through the open window. Something . . . or someone . . . slammed around loudly in the room next to him. Henry. Packing angrily? Or just collapsing into bed after battling it out in the Elimination?

Sam flipped to his back, lacing his hands across his chest. He thought about earlier in the day, in the café. His heart did a funny little gallop. He'd been sitting across from her. She'd smiled, not her flashy, look-at-me smile, but a gentle smile. A real smile. And she'd said, "Well, I think I screwed that up big time."

He'd been wary. Like maybe this was gameplay for the cameras. He'd taken a bite of his crusty sandwich and swabbed at mustard on his chin. She was a pretty girl—would have been prettier probably, if she'd quit trying so hard.

"I suppose you won't know until the Elimination," he'd said evenly.

Her plate sat untouched—turkey sandwich, mound of potato salad, pickle spear, and the kind of homemade potato chips that he found irresistible. He almost reached forward and snagged a handful of hers. She didn't look like she was gonna eat them. And he hated to see food like that go to waste. He hated to see any food go to waste. Ever.

All seven of them were filed alongside the only long table in this small restaurant. Cameras and the show's staffers jockeyed for the little space remaining in what was clearly supposed to be a grab-and-go place. The contestants were eating but constantly being pulled out to a side patio where an artfully arranged backdrop was waiting for on-camera recaps and interviews. Two cameras circled the restaurant as well, capturing the intermittent banter going on between the teens. Everyone was either exhausted, anxious, or—in Tyrell's and Henry's cases—clearly pissed off.

Cassidy traced an imaginary line in the table with her pink fingernail. "I told myself to try to play this game, you know, honestly," she said. "I knew that I wasn't necessarily the smartest girl here or anything. But I figured I could be the one who stuck to her principles."

Her finger got to the end of the table and she let her hand fall away, watching it land heavily in her lap.

"What I didn't realize was how hard that would be," she said. "I guess these shows or maybe these contests have a way of twisting you into something you don't want to be. Or,

I don't know, revealing all the stuff about yourself you wish wasn't there."

She looked up at him, her blue eyes wide.

Sam quit chewing. He lost himself in her eyes, which, unless she was the greatest actress in the world, were completely guileless and sincere. And held more hope than anyone's eyes he'd ever seen.

She smiled then. Like she was only smiling at him, like she would only ever smile for him. Her smile . . . it made him think that a stoner from the northwest, one whose parents had long ago decided he wasn't worth getting their acts together for, maybe he was . . . deserving. Maybe he really could pull this thing off.

Then she went back to her sandwich. And he felt himself falling. As if he was running headlong down a steep hill at top speed, arms flailing, unable to stop. It was exhilarating.

He swallowed the gob of turkey and Swiss on wheat that had gummed up in his throat and washed it down with his lemonade.

"I think," he said, finding himself scrambling for words when words had always come easily, "that's the point. That's what the Benefactor wants to happen. He wants to see us all at our most vulnerable."

He could feel her eyes on him. Why did it feel like he was flying? With nowhere to land?

"So maybe," he continued, "you haven't screwed up at all. Maybe you're doing exactly what he hoped all along."

Cassidy's head tilted and an expression of gratitude washed over her. Her next words came out hoarse and deep and sexier than anything he'd ever heard.

"You have no idea how much I needed to hear that."

She was called away for some camera time and soon afterward, they were loaded back in the vans, banished to their rooms while their competitors battled it out during an Elimination, and he was left to shower and wonder about her fate. And wonder some more about why he cared. And lie in bed and curse himself for caring. Because all he could think about was seeing her again tomorrow. More than anything, he still wanted her to be in this competition.

And that scared the hell out of him.

July 11, 12:10 a.m.
Malibu, California
The Benefactor

He paced back and forth in front of the wall of windows that separated his bedroom from the Pacific Ocean. It was a spectacular view: the moon—nearly full—cast a brilliant yellow glow that shimmered lightly on the sea. But he saw none of it. His mind pinged restlessly while his hands reached for picture frames, books, cell phone, sunglasses—only to set everything back down almost immediately.

Twitchy.

He cursed, frustrated, trying to shove his hands into pockets that weren't there. Three days. Three days until he—until all of them, really—could hide no more.

Yaz had called him from the café, right after the last of the kids had arrived.

"We're good," he'd announced. It took several minutes of his translating Yaz-speak for the news to sink in: the network had an opening and was agreeing to bump up the series premiere. If the production team worked their asses off and got stuff cut and edited, they were good to air in three days. Wednesday night. Prime time. Marketing was going into overdrive to get the word out.

He didn't know whether to grab a drink to celebrate or grab a drink to calm his twitching hands. Three. Days. And then his whole little experiment went live.

He stood up, poured a finger of Scotch into a shot glass, tossed it back quickly, lay back on his massive bed.

Those kids. He pictured the seven of them as they'd sat in that café.

His legs, impatient and jittery, rolled him off the bed and marched him toward his enormous sliding back door.

It shouldn't matter this much.

So why did it feel like it did when he biked, flying down a steep and windy mountain road at full speed? Why did he have this sudden urge to call Yaz and tell him to cancel the flight, have her come back, figure out a way to let her stay? Why did he want to shut this whole thing down, write them all checks, and be done with this mess?

This *was* good for them. It certainly wasn't any worse than the real process they had to go through to get into college, right? And he was offering them a one-in-eight chance at a full ride. He should feel like a hero, a philanthropist. A *benefactor.* Instead, he felt like shit.

He moved out onto his secluded deck that overlooked a deserted beach. He felt like . . . a puppet master. Watching Henry self-destruct. Watching Cassidy try to save him. Watching Mei veer off course. Hearing them all try to explain. Listening to their rationales, some of which weren't rational at all.

It was hard to explain, really, why he'd done what he'd done. Saving Henry had been more of an altruistic thing than anything, he supposed. The kid had a lot of issues and it might have been easier to get rid of him. But Henry'd pulled it together for the Elimination. And frankly, he was more than a little curious to see what Henry would do, or who he'd *be*, next.

And the other two? Cassidy and Mei. Cassidy had been up for Elimination twice now, but still clung to this hopefulness, this eternal, almost laughable optimism that tomorrow would be better. That *she* would be better.

But Mei? Mei had just seemed lost. Which is why he'd sent her home.

July 11, 3:45 p.m.
Newport Beach, California
Cassidy McGowan

Her skin had that tight, sticky feeling of having been in the sun all day. Sand still clung to her ankles and feet. Her eyes felt heavy and her body tingly warm. Cassidy couldn't remember having felt this happy in a long, long time.

She lowered herself onto the soft leather couch while a few crew members scooted around adjusting lighting or tapping clipboards importantly. Gretta, her favorite makeup artist, lugging her trademark purple case of powders, liners, and creams, sprang forward to whisk a brush over Cassidy's cheeks and forehead.

"Oh, to have your skin, love," she purred, before she disappeared somewhere behind all the cameras and booms and grips and whatever else was crowding up their common room.

A producer, Mary-something-or-other, dropped into a chair across from Cassidy, smiling warmly. She tucked a pasty-white, freckled leg under her.

"Enjoy your day off today, Cassidy?" Mary asked pleasantly as a tiny black microphone was clipped to Cassidy's T-shirt. Mary had close-cropped gray hair, ice-blue eyes, and the most toned shoulders Cassidy had ever seen on a woman.

Cassidy lifted her arm so one of the crew could wind a cord under it to a small transmitter box strapped to her back. "Oh, my gosh!" she said. "It was *so* awesome. I mean, a whole day to just lie on the sand? Who wouldn't love that?"

It had truly been a gift: an entire day to themselves. No challenges. Time to do what they wanted. Or sleep. Or whatever. Just this one scheduled "confessional" with Mary.

As soon as Nisha told them about their unexpected vacay, Cassidy had grabbed one of the books in her room—not that she'd read a word of it—yanked her hair into a ponytail, slipped into her pale pink bikini, found a stack of beach towels in a hall closet, and claimed the most magical spot in the whole entire world—the sand right outside her doorstep.

Mary glanced down at her clipboard and then up at the camera. "We're rolling, then?"

Everyone cleared out of the way, so it was just Mary and Cassidy and a few well-positioned cameras.

"So, Cassidy," Mary said, folding her hands over her clipboard. "Two Eliminations for you now. How's that feel?"

She should have known Mary would waste no time going there. Cassidy breathed in deeply.

"Well, it sucks," she said, almost chuckling. "I'm lucky I'm still here. I know that. But until I get sent home, I'll keep trying to learn from my mistakes. I'll keep trying to win."

In truth? She probably shouldn't be here. She wasn't even sure how she'd made it through. Her only defense last night in the Elimination was that she'd thought it was more important to stay with Henry. That she wasn't even thinking about the game. That she was more concerned about him. Which wasn't really true, until she'd started listening to Henry. Then it kind of *became* true. She did care about him, enough to want to erase that pleading, hopeless look in his eyes.

As soon as they'd pulled into that café, though, she knew she'd screwed up. Again. Everyone but Henry and Mei had arrived before her. Looking at Sam and Tyrell and Hiroshi, who sat eating their sandwiches at the long table—a palpable wariness between them—it occurred to her that she didn't even know how to *be* wary, cautious, guarded. Not like that. And it was going to cost her everything if she didn't figure it out.

"Tell me about your strategy for this game," Mary said, her intense eyes meeting Cassidy's.

"My strategy?" Cassidy laughed lightly. "Does 'try not to look stupid' count as a strategy?"

Mary smiled. "I suppose it could."

Cassidy sighed. "My strategy, I guess, is to play honestly. I'm not super good at gameplay, so I'm just trying to focus on each task as it comes and not do anything I'll regret later. Not sure you'd call that a strategy, but it's all I got." She tried to smile brightly.

Mary had to know she was full of crap. Yesterday, riding that bike, she'd forgotten about the game. She hadn't been smart or cunning or fast. She'd been gullible and naïve. She'd played with her heart and not her head. And, for better or worse, that seemed to be the only way she knew how to play.

And last night, when the Benefactor—still only an imposing, featureless outline behind a desk—asked her, point-blank, why he should keep her around, *again*, she'd told him that. Picking uncomfortably at a thread on the couch, she'd said, "I told you last time I was here that I was going to play the only way I knew how. I could never knowingly try to get ahead if it meant deliberately taking someone else out." She shrugged. "I guess you saw that today. And, I don't know. If that was my mistake, I can't really say I regret it all that much."

She'd been honest. Maybe *too* honest.

"Were you surprised that the Benefactor decided to keep Henry?" Mary asked her now.

Cassidy dropped her gaze. "I'm glad that Henry is still here," she said softly.

"You didn't answer my question."

Cassidy looked up. "Yes. Yes, I am surprised. But I think maybe he just had a rough day is all." She shrugged.

Henry had been bleary-eyed at last night's Elimination. He'd slumped in a chair in their common room, saying little except that he'd wanted to give up, but eventually realized how much it meant to him to see this thing through. There had been something desperate about him. "I know I can do this," Henry had said, "but the challenge today was . . . physically demanding in ways that I wasn't prepared for. It got to me." And it must have been enough because the Benefactor dismissed him, and that was it: he was safe.

"How about Mei?" Mary asked. "Did she deserve to go home?"

Cassidy looked away and didn't answer.

Mei, typically, had said very little. She'd come into the café after everyone else, her face a mask. No one was really sure what had happened, since Mei had not spoken to any of them. She'd retreated to the end of the table, eaten her sandwich in silence, taken her turn with the cameras, and later, sat rigidly on the couch next to Cassidy in the Elimination.

Only then did Cassidy learn that Mei had missed the entrance to the beach, overshooting it by nearly two miles. And since Henry and Cassidy finished at exactly the same time, the Benefactor pulled all three into the Elimination.

"Mei," the Benefactor had said, "you were chosen for this competition because we saw in you the kind of qualities that we believe young people need today in order to succeed. And yet today you placed last in a challenge that required you to follow simple directions. Can you explain how such a bright, capable young woman managed to fail in such a simple task?"

Mei's posture remained stiff, her eyes blank. But she somehow appeared even smaller on the couch than she had a moment before. Cassidy resisted the urge to reach out a hand to her.

"I was . . ." Mei said, her words steady though quiet. "I was remiss today. I failed to pay attention and have only myself to blame for my loss. I am grateful for the opportunity to have competed alongside such deserving people."

Cassidy had felt dumbstruck. It was like Mei was surrendering. Admitting defeat when the Benefactor was still willing to give her a fighting chance. She couldn't imagine what was going on in that girl's head.

Unlike Lucy, when Mei was Eliminated she rose gracefully from the couch, nodded once to Cassidy, wished her the best of luck, and without another sound, disappeared up the stairs. It had been so fast. So unexpected.

Thinking of Mei, stoic and small, Cassidy looked up at Mary. "Do any of us deserve to go home? Probably no more than we deserve to be here."

Mary smiled, but it felt scolding. "You're sidestepping my question, Cassidy."

"No," Cassidy answered, feeling her chest tightening. "I'm not really. Mei didn't deserve to go home. But then, being here is a privilege. I mean, how did she and I get chosen out of thousands of teenagers to be on this show anyway, right? What I'm trying to say, I guess, is that it sucks that she went back to having to apply for college and everything, but that's what every other seventeen-year-old in America is doing right now. So I think your use of the word 'deserve' is wrong. That's all."

Mary's eyebrows came up, but she looked down at her clipboard and didn't respond.

"You spent the day on the beach, then?" Mary asked suddenly.

Cassidy nodded, feeling her shoulders relax at the change in topic.

"Yes," she said, "and it was probably one of the coolest days ever."

"So you didn't try to hang out with any of the other competitors?"

Cassidy paused. "It's not that I didn't want to be with any of them, I just really wanted to spend the day on the beach."

"So you weren't disappointed, then, when Sam joined you around, hmm, lunchtime, if I remember right? He set his towel right next to yours and, let's see here, offered you half of a turkey-and-cheese sandwich?"

Mary's look was slightly amused, maybe a little challenging. But Cassidy met her eyes squarely and grinned broadly. This was probably the easiest question she'd lobbed at her yet.

"Nope," she said, confidently, "I wasn't disappointed by that at all. Not at all."

July 11, 5:02 p.m.
Newport Beach, California
Henry Stone IV

It was showtime. Time to make good with everybody downstairs and convince the Benefactor that yesterday had been a lapse—nothing more than a bad day. That his absence all day was no big deal. A migraine. Nothing to worry about.

The headache had hit him first thing that morning, pounding away from the inside, hammering over his right eye until he couldn't see, couldn't think straight, didn't even care if he was standing, sitting, breathing. He'd puked up his guts twice, his whole body shuddering as he bent over the toilet, begging the world to end. But the pain raged on until mercifully, around noon, he'd passed out.

At some point, he'd felt a tug on his shoulder and forced one eye open long enough to see Sam hovering over him, his eyes downcast and concerned. "Dude, it's, like, the middle of the afternoon. You gonna wake up and join the party?"

That's when he remembered, in the muddle that was his brain, that he was competing. For something *big.*

He'd groaned and muttered a string of words: not feeling good, just needed sleep, he'd be down in a bit. Sam, good ol' Sam, brought him water and a wet cloth and pulled down all the shades in the room. He'd flipped on the overhead fan, which felt blissfully refreshing on his sweat-soaked body.

Henry had dipped in and out of consciousness for the next few hours, fighting nausea, raging against the pain, and sweating through his sheets.

But now he had to pull it together.

He cupped some water from the faucet in his bathroom and swooshed it around in his mouth. The sticky, stringy spiderwebs were still in there, clinging to his teeth and tongue, but his lips didn't feel so cracked and dry. He splashed water on his face, but his bloodshot eyes, the dark crescents underneath them, and the mats of hair that stuck to his forehead persisted.

Screw it. He'd say it was a migraine. Happened all the time. Really. No biggie.

He staggered downstairs, squinting against the shafts of sunlight that knifed into his eyes and sent shudders of pain through his brain. He was barely aware that the guys were gathered at the counter. He might have greeted them. Or simply ignored them.

Swallowing the nausea, he reached for a Coke and slopped up a hot dog that somebody had grilled, dropping it in the bun even as he was heading back toward the stairs.

"Thanks, guys. I'll get you back tomorrow, I promise," he thought he called over his shoulder.

Lumbering up the stairs was hard. His room was dank and stuffy, but blissfully dark and quiet. His unmade bed was pure relief. The hot dog sat heavily in his gut, along with the absolute certainty that he was homeward bound tomorrow, after the next challenge. The ceiling fan swished overhead, but its spinning propellers only made him dizzy, so he closed his eyes.

He was headed down the rabbit hole. And unless he could find his way back up to fresh air—and quickly—he was on his way home. To his dad's waiting agenda.

July 11, 7:02 p.m.
Newport Beach, California
Tyrell Young

He didn't want time off. He wasn't here to make friends or chill on a towel. He was here to win challenges, beat everyone else, and snag a scholarship. And then he could get home to his family and friends, his sister, and football.

He'd spent most of the day tossing a Frisbee around with Hiroshi, far from Sam and his new arm candy, who seemed to have about as much brainpower as a mushroom. He couldn't look at Sam without wanting to hit something. He should have trusted his gut, which had told him to stay away from that cocky son of a bitch. Apparently, his gut was genius. He wondered how long this new little alliance would last. Probably as long as she put out.

Didn't matter, really. He had his own alliance. With Hiroshi. And if things went according to plan, maybe that Christian chick from Colorado. The idea had hit him last night. And the more he'd thought about it, the more it made sense.

She was a clear underdog. She was making no attempt to score friends in the game. She was a loner and kind of weird. She'd spent the day curled up in a padded recliner in a shady corner of the girls' patio, reading. It wasn't until he'd passed by the fourth or fifth time that he'd figured out that the big book on her tiny lap was actually—get this—the Bible.

Here was the thing: he was a God-fearing guy. Went to church most every Sunday—'cept when his sister was feeling too lousy. He'd said prayers: for Shaina's pain to be gone, to make this time in the hospital be the last, to help his dad pay for the endless medical bills. He'd even cracked open the Good Book a time or two—but mostly in church.

He'd never sat down and, like, read the Bible, much less devoured it the way that girl was doing. Her eyes kinda roamed over the page like she was drinking in the words. Her lips moved, but soundlessly. And every so often, she'd stop and close her eyes, fingering her necklace—probably praying or something. It was weird.

But the girl rode her bike like Lance Effin' Armstrong. She'd cruised through that whole challenge, now that he thought about it. Which meant, despite having an intimidation factor roughly equivalent to his senile gram, this girl was tough. And he'd learned a long time ago, playing ball, that it was the small guys you had to watch out for. They were the ones who had something to prove.

July 11, 7:08 p.m.
Newport Beach, California
Allyson Murphy

"No, really," Allyson said, ducking her head, "I don't think that would work on me." Cassidy held up another top—bright purple, but a little less revealing.

"This one?" she asked hopefully.

Allyson eyed the shirt like it might have been sewn with poisonous threads. "I don't know," she backpedaled, wondering why she'd ever agreed to come up here.

She was sitting on the edge of Cassidy's bed, while the other girl eagerly pulled item after item from her suitcase (she hadn't even unpacked yet!), and begged Allyson to at least try something, anything on. To say Allyson was skeptical was an understatement. Though the girls were roughly the same height, that's where the similarities ended. Cassidy had curves that made Allyson's thin body look like a bookmark.

"It would really bring out the color of your eyes," Cassidy said, holding the shirt in front of Allyson. "Come on. Just try it on."

Tentatively, Allyson grabbed the shirt and swung her eyes around, looking for the bathroom. Cassidy laughed.

"It's okay," she said. "We're all girls here."

But it wasn't okay. Allyson's best friends back home were modest like her. They didn't parade around in bright pink bras and lacy underwear like Cassidy was doing. Allyson wished she had made an excuse and escaped to her room. This was *so* not her thing.

Taking a deep breath, she tore off her T-shirt and pulled on Cassidy's shirt in a single move, buttoning it as fast as her fingers would allow. It was a sleeveless, gauzy thing that clearly showed her plain white bra underneath. She crossed her arms over her chest, feeling exposed.

"Oh. My. God!" Cassidy squealed. "You look amazing!"

She grabbed Allyson and spun her toward the mirror over the dresser. Even with her arms in a large X over her chest, Allyson could see Cassidy was right: the color was a good match with her skin tone. But before she could say thanks and end it there, Cassidy was tugging her toward the bathroom.

"Come on," she said excitedly. "Let's do your hair and makeup!"

She wanted to protest. She hadn't slept well last night and there would definitely be a challenge tomorrow. But something in Cassidy—her overabundance of energy and enthusiasm—wouldn't let Allyson leave.

A half hour later, Allyson stared with disbelief into the mirror. Cassidy had transformed her. Her normally pale green eyes were awash with color: lined expertly in brown, her lids lightly shaded in greens and purples, her lashes just barely tipped in black. Cassidy knew just how much to apply—not so much that she looked overdone, but enough that her features became enhanced.

And her hair. Allyson could only run her fingers through it and stare. Blessed with light brown, wavy hair, Allyson kept it at shoulder length so she could tuck it out of her face. But that was all she did with it, unless she braided it or pulled it back in a simple ponytail. Cassidy had taken a straight iron to it, and now it framed her face perfectly and swung neatly when she turned her head. And somehow, with the straightening, her hair looked lighter; a golden tone was haloing her.

"Awesome, huh?" Cassidy said, unplugging the iron and standing back to check her out completely. "I think you might need a cami under that shirt." She dug in her suitcase, flinging a few garments carelessly. She tossed a tiny, white tank top with thin straps at Allyson.

"Put that on underneath and then let's go walk on the beach and show the world the new you!"

Allyson pulled on the littlest shirt she'd ever seen, surprised it fit anything other than a baby doll. But at least her bra was no longer showing. And as much as she'd been looking forward to a quiet evening in her room, something about a walk along the beach sounded kind of nice. She did look good. Maybe the others would notice.

Still, as she followed Cassidy down the stairs, smiling at their resident nanny, Nisha, who exclaimed over her new look, doubt flooded her. Allyson wondered if she should be making friends in this game. And whether Cassidy was a wise choice. Cassidy had been in the Eliminations twice. She didn't seem all that bright or even super driven. If Allyson had to guess why she was here, she would have said exposure, an opportunity to have some fun, and maybe, from the perspective of the Benefactor, to be a distraction for the guys.

But she was friendly. And she seemed sincere. So what was the harm in taking a walk with her on the beach?

Allyson saw a camera come up behind them. The red light started blinking. She ran a hand through her soft, silky hair, and felt herself smile. Tonight, the camera was going to get a New-and-Improved Allyson.

She caught up to Cassidy, who linked arms with her, just as some passing guys checked them both out. And Allyson felt a lightness run through her that she hadn't felt for a while. Maybe ever.

July 12, 10:15 a.m.
Newport Beach, California
Sam Michaels

"Get a move on, mates! Fifteen minutes!" Colin hollered up the stairs in his clipped accent.

Sam threw on denim shorts and a Bob Marley T-shirt and thumped down the stairs.

"Where is everyone?" Colin asked anxiously. "We should be headed toward Hollywood."

Sam's eyebrows shot up. "Hollywood?"

Colin shook his head. "That's all I know, so don't go asking me for details. But despite knocking on everyone's doors over an hour ago, I haven't seen hide nor hair of your three chums. Be a love and tell them to get down here in a tick."

Sam mouthed "a love?" and threw up his hands but bounded back up the stairs. He passed Tyrell and Hiroshi, already heading downstairs.

He poked his head in Henry's room, wincing at the overwhelming odor of sweat, feet, and maybe a hint of puke that accosted him. Henry was splayed out on the bed, facedown, a pillow covering his head. Sam shut the door and ran back downstairs.

"You probably ought to come up here," he said to Colin.

Colin set down his teacup. "Henry?"

Sam shrugged. "Still in bed."

Colin looked at the clock. He pointed at Tyrell and Hiroshi. "In the van, mates."

Colin took the stairs two at a time, with Sam close behind, and rapped on Henry's door before pushing it open.

"Henry?" Colin said softly. "Mate? Come on now. Whatever's on the blink we can fix in the van."

Henry didn't move. Didn't acknowledge he'd heard. Colin looked at Sam, who raised both palms helplessly.

"Polo, dude," Sam said. "You gotta rally."

For a second, though, he wondered why he cared. One less dude in the competition was . . . well, one less dude in the competition. And though Henry didn't bug him as much as Tyrell, he'd lagged behind painfully in the bike challenge. Maybe letting him wallow here until he was declared officially out or disqualified was what he deserved.

On the other hand, he and Sam had made a decent team for that first challenge at Disneyland. Plus, Cassidy seemed to like Henry for some reason. She'd mentioned his meltdown yesterday to Sam while they were chatting on the beach, and she seemed to have a soft spot for him. Helping Henry out might score him a point or two in Cassidy's book. Simply for the sake of gameplay, staying on Cassidy's good side was a smart idea.

Sam reached down and threw off the sheet, revealing a bare-chested Henry, clad only in sticky, damp boxer shorts. Sam nudged his leg. "Henry?"

There was groaning from the bed as Henry rolled to one side. He looked blearily from Sam to Colin.

"I'm out," he said dully. "Can't you see I'm out?"

Sam snorted. "You're not out. You had a bad day. Get over it." He took a step toward the door and flipped on the light. All three of them blinked, but Henry recoiled back into his pillows.

Sam marched purposefully to the bed. He grabbed at Henry's pillows one at a time until Henry was lying there flat on the bed, looking up at him.

"Get. Up." Sam took the cup of water on the bedside table and dumped it on Henry's face.

Henry sat up, sputtering and swearing.

"What the hell?" he said, wiping water from his eyes.

Sam laughed. "If you quit now, you'll never forgive yourself. Plus, you and I made a damn good team that first day. That's enough for me, bro," Sam said.

Sam looked over his shoulder. A camera was getting everything.

"Get your ass out of bed and in this competition. Cassidy and I will figure out how to help you make it through today. After that, it's all you," he said, tossing Henry a shirt from a pile on the floor.

Henry caught it. He blinked and pulled on the shirt, ran a hand through his damp hair, and rolled off the bed.

Colin looked at his watch. "Excellent. Now that's settled. Van leaves in one minute." He spun on his heel and bounded down the stairs.

July 12, 10:45 a.m.
On the 5 Freeway, traveling north
Tyrell Young

He had a pregame ritual that he'd been doing since Pop Warner ball. On the morning of a big game, he woke up and did fifty push-ups. Then he would take out the picture of him and Shaina and Mickey Mouse at Disney World, five summers ago, where her arm is slung around his shoulders and she is looking at the camera with happy, pain-free eyes. He would listen to Jay-Z or Kanye or Dr. Dre, and the beats and that picture would give him whatever fire he needed lit under him to get it done, to run hard and fast, because his sister never would.

He'd push-upped this morning. But then he'd gone to grab his picture, which he knew he'd stuck in the side pocket of his suitcase, only to find it wasn't there. And he'd checked frantically through his clothes and his carry-on and all around his room, his heart pounding. An almost frenzied feeling had come over him. He'd forgone breakfast, forgotten to shower, missed talking to Hiroshi about a game plan as he'd torn his room apart looking for that picture.

It wasn't there. It wasn't anywhere.

He leaned forward in the van now, his elbows on his knees. Whatever he had to do today, he wasn't ready. His stomach gnawed at him. His brain seemed fuzzy and unfocused.

Where was that picture?

He tried to think back to the day he'd packed. But that day had been a jumble of "do this" and "do that" from his mama while his dad kept moving in and out of his room—just looking, looking hard. Tyrell had remembered wishing he could just leave, leave and be on his way already, so he wouldn't have to feel his dad's penetrating gaze anymore.

He knew what was in that look. Disappointment. Disapproval. Remorse. Longing. It all felt like weights he was being made to carry along with him to Los Angeles. Like his dad's failed football career was somehow now on his shoulders. His burden to carry. And yet, Tyrell wasn't entirely sure that his dad thought this was the way to redemption.

He rubbed his forehead. Where was that picture?

His dad never said two words about what had happened on that field last September. Tyrell being carted off on a stretcher. The hours and hours of painful rehab, only to sit on the sidelines for the rest of the season. Just like his dad never said two words about LSU or why he never touched a football again after his junior year.

His dad never said a whole lot, actually.

Except that one time. Tyrell looked out the passenger window. Cars streamed by on the freeway, but he didn't see them. Instead he saw the field, that glorious green field lit by stadium lights. He was running behind the quarterback, faking right, then left. Then, the lateral from the quarterback and the ball was tucked safely under his arm. And more running, twisting by defenders, leaping, sailing, and diving into the end zone. Touchdown. Game over.

His dad had waited for him by the locker rooms. The team was headed out for burgers, but Tyrell saw his dad and jogged over, sure something had to be wrong with Shaina.

Instead his dad, hands shoved deep into the pockets of his faded jeans, had pulled his jacket collar up tight around him against the night's chill. And then, without looking Tyrell in the eye, he'd said, "Nice play tonight."

Tyrell had tripped backward a step. Nodded. Words gummed up in his throat.

"You ran that well," his dad had continued, finding Tyrell's eyes finally. "Like I would have."

And Tyrell's heart had exploded, but he could only nod, yes, yes, okay.

That one night. Before the torn ACL and the stretcher and the rehab and the uncertainty of any more seasons.

Where was that damn picture?

July 12, 11:38 a.m.
Near Hollywood, California
Allyson Murphy

Cassidy had barged into her room with a new shirt an hour before they were supposed to be downstairs—this one a soft green with a scooped neckline and empire waist. She'd had a makeup case and her straight iron and announced that she was there to make sure Allyson looked *a-MAZ-ing* on camera today.

Something had bubbled up inside Allyson as Cassidy stood behind her, tugging on her strands of hair to make them hang in that silky, soft way that they had the night before. Cassidy had this way of pulling you into her orbit and making you feel as if you were important. The girl looking at her in the mirror was someone she hadn't seen for a while. Someone she'd missed.

But now, on the way to the challenge, she felt guilty. Her mother was dying. What right did she have to look like that girl in that mirror? She needed to stay focused on what she was here to do. Because her mom was running out of time.

She reached up and rubbed her knuckles over each eyelid, trying to erase the work that Cassidy had done. Then, as the van pulled off the freeway and onto a congested street, filled with billboards and people, she reached back and began to twist her hair into a single braid down her back.

"Allyson?" Cassidy asked, gently touching her hair. "It looks so pretty down."

Allyson closed her eyes and kept braiding. "I know," she whispered.

July 12, 11:45 a.m.
Hollywood, California
Hiroshi Yamamura

They were ushered in the front doors, through the ornate and somber lobby, and led straight to the theater itself. Their padded footsteps echoed as they marched single-file down the center aisle to seats near the stage, where Molly stood waiting. The theater was grand, with rows of empty red-velvet seats, leading to a magnificent stage. Overhead an elaborate gold and blue ceiling arched to a massive light fixture in the center.

Hiroshi slid into a seat next to Tyrell.

"Whatever's coming," Tyrell whispered to him, "we're in this together, right?"

Hiroshi nodded, though skepticism was fast taking root. He admired Tyrell's competitiveness. He was, however, concerned about his integrity. Tyrell had been all too willing in the last challenge to coerce Sam into cutting a corner. Hiroshi was sure that if the Benefactor found out, they'd both be booted. He couldn't risk that kind of disgrace for his family.

"Maybe we're here to see a show," Tyrell said, sinking lower in his seat. "Hope it's not opera. I don't *do* opera. If it's opera, it's nap time."

Molly waited until they were all seated and the cameras were where they needed to be.

"Welcome!" she said, her voice echoing strangely. "This is the world-famous Pantages Theater, which first opened its doors in 1930 and has been home to many renowned, award-winning musicals. *Wicked, Disney's The Lion King, The Phantom of the Opera,* and *Cats* all had successful runs on this very stage."

Hiroshi found his stomach grumbling. He hadn't eaten this morning—he'd gotten up early, thinking an ocean swim would calm him, but afterward, there had only been time to shower, dress, and rush downstairs. When he didn't eat, his stomach did weird things, unpredictable things. He swallowed a bubble of air threatening to come up his throat.

"Today it will be the site of your next challenge," Molly said, with an ingratiating smile. "This one is rather uncomplicated."

Hiroshi's stomach gurgled again. Tyrell looked over. Hiroshi avoided his gaze but felt his cheeks grow warm. He hoped the cameras weren't picking this up. Maggie would be laughing her head off. His father would not.

"Your task is this," Molly said, surveying them dramatically. "Simply convince one hundred people to come inside these doors. That's all. One hundred people. Tell them whatever you'd like." She grinned. "But you must have one hundred people in this theater. All. At. The. Same. Time."

Hiroshi belched. He tried to squelch it with his fist, but he was too late. It escaped anyway. Tyrell guffawed. Sam chuckled. Even Allyson craned her neck around. Molly looked mildly annoyed.

All he could think of was Maggie. When she saw this, she would be rolling on the floor. They used to have belching contests. She always won.

"The Benefactor values many things, among them rhetoric. Just as he once had to convince investors to take a chance on a young kid from Quincy, Massachusetts, who had little more than an idea and big dreams, you will undoubtedly have to work hard to persuade and motivate others in order to complete this task. The last two competitors to collect their one hundred people will be up for an Elimination. And one of you will be sent home tonight."

Without a word, Tyrell stuck a fist toward him, quietly where no one else would see. Hiroshi tapped it.

"We got this, man," Tyrell whispered. "No problem."

Hiroshi hoped so. And that they could do it quickly. He was starving.

July 12, 12:00 noon
Hollywood, California
Sam Michaels

His mind was spinning. One hundred people. Three classrooms full, if he was thinking in terms of his high school back home. And even if he could get a group into the theater, he had to convince them to stay put while he went and gathered others. He had to think. And he had to think fast.

What was he good at? Not connecting with people. Not initially anyway. He took a while to warm up. But if he could get his hands on a guitar, he could entertain. While maybe someone else snagged them from outside. Entertaining he could do.

Cassidy was sitting just in front of him, her cascade of golden hair a distraction during Molly's spiel. *Cassidy.* She was his ticket in this challenge. She connected with people. Immediately. They could do this, if they worked as a team.

He glanced over at Henry, who was starting to look like he might make it through this thing. His eyes were open and he seemed to be focused on what Molly was saying. Which was a helluva lot better than he was half an hour ago. The guy had looked wasted. Or hungover. Completely not ready for a challenge. Sam questioned the wisdom of dragging this guy's butt out of bed earlier. He hoped he and Cassidy wouldn't regret teaming up with him.

Molly was running through the final rules—but Sam was only half listening. He had to get three hundred people in this theater. Because he'd promised Henry he'd help him—even if it was only for Cassidy's sake. And Cassidy was going to stay, too, if he had anything to say about it.

"So without further ado," Molly said, raising her arm as she always did before these stupid challenges, "the Benefactor leaves you with this quote as you begin this task: 'Truthful words are not beautiful; beautiful words are not truthful. Good words are not persuasive; persuasive words are not good.' Good luck!"

She swept her arm downward—their signal, he supposed—to leap ahead and start grabbing passersby. They'd been told to get a sheet of tear-off paper wristbands from one of the staffers at the door—his were blue; Cassidy's yellow—to give to each person they convinced to come inside the theater. That way each competitor's group could be easily tallied. And no one could cheat and claim someone else's catch.

But Sam didn't move. Neither did Henry. Cassidy spun around, her eyes puppy-dog hopeful in that way that made him want to forget this competition and take her to a movie. Or just grab her hand and take her somewhere. Alone.

"Listen, guys," Sam said, trying to ignore that Cassidy smelled like lavender and coconut oil. "I think this is going to be harder than it sounds. Getting people in might not be so bad. Getting them to *stay* is going to be killer."

Cassidy nodded. She looked like she couldn't wait to get out there and give this task a try. Even though she'd lost the last two. God, she was gorgeous.

"I think . . ." He cleared his throat and tried to focus. "We need to work together. Henry, you and Cassidy get them in the door. I'll take care of the rest." He punched his fist into the side of Henry's leg. Henry blinked. "I've seen you work a crowd. You guys should be able to get people's attention—your wit and her legs."

"Yeah." Henry nodded. Like he was waking up from a long nap. "Yeah. No problem."

"Seriously," Sam said smiling, "if I'm thinking this through right, we just each need to do what we're good at. And that," he nodded toward Molly, "ought to make us all safe from Elimination."

July 12, 12:15 p.m.
Hollywood, California
Allyson Murphy

She felt like she was outside Disneyland all over again. Only now Mei was gone. She was on her own. Approaching strangers and asking them to please go wait inside the Pantages so she could win a contest? It sounded lame. She was terrible at this. She'd talked to five or six groups of people, all of whom politely told her to get lost. She was wandering farther and farther from the theater with no game plan.

Plus, this place was a zoo. A freak show. It was crowded with people of all sizes, races, and religions. She'd passed a woman in a tiny tiger-print skirt (so short it barely covered her bottom), the highest heels she'd ever seen on a human being, and a black bra. And on closer inspection, Allyson wasn't even sure it was a woman!

There were homeless men pushing shopping carts full of blankets, rugs, and bags. There were street performers dressed like everyone from Batman to Marilyn Monroe, along with a sketchy, metallic-looking mime guy who started break dancing when you walked past him. There were tourists and same-sex couples who held hands unabashedly and a guy shouting out that the world was going to hell and Satan was taking over the earth. Two guys layered in gold chains wanted to sell her a T-shirt with a faded head shot of Michael Jackson on it.

This was Hollywood. Maybe it was supposed to feel glamorous or fun or colorful. But it just felt overwhelming. Maybe a little seedy. Definitely scary.

"Um, excuse me," she said to a mom herding two kids out of the Hard Rock Cafe. The guy she assumed was Dad was a few steps away, taking a picture of a gold star on the ground that said *Matthew Broderick.* "I'm on this TV show with some other teenagers who are all trying to win scholarships. For our challenge today, I have to try to get people to the Pantages Theater. Do you think you could, you know, help me out?"

"Would we be on TV?" asked the girl. She looked thirteen-ish, peering over Allyson's shoulder at the cameraman.

"You might be."

"Hey, that's cool," said her younger brother, who was maybe eight or nine. "Tell her we'll do it, Savannah. Right, Mom?"

The mom shrugged. "Go ask your dad. How many people do you need to get?"

Allyson took a deep breath. "One hundred."

Savannah's eyes widened. "Whoa. And, like, how many do you have?"

Allyson grinned sheepishly. "With you guys? Four."

Mom's eyes narrowed. "Where are you from, sweetie?" she asked. She eyed her husband, now handing over ten bucks to the gold-chained guys and happily holding up his new Michael Jackson T-shirt.

"A really small town northeast of Denver," Allyson said. "Look, it's okay." She took a small step backward. "You're probably on vacation and—"

Savannah grabbed her mom's arm. "No, come on, Mom. This is a TV show. Remember how cool we said it would be if we got to do something like this?"

Mom's eyes jockeyed between daughter and husband, who was now meandering into a gift shop, camera slung over his shoulder. She lifted one shoulder helplessly.

"One hundred people?" she asked Allyson. "You just have to get them inside a theater?"

Allyson quickly explained the challenge. The panic in her chest was loosening; and yet, something else was building there, too. Once again she was being helped by strangers. Once again, it seemed as if God had a plan to keep her in this competition. She glanced skyward. Why He kept choosing to save her was beyond comprehension.

"Isaac," the mom said to her son, "you need to turn on your Boy Scout charm, kid." She leaned toward Allyson and her tone was conspiratorial. "When he wants to, the kid can be the Pied Piper."

Isaac nodded eagerly. "This'll be cool! Will the camera follow us?"

Allyson looked over her shoulder. "It pretty much goes where I go, so yeah."

Savannah pointed across the street. "I say we start over there. See that line of people? They're all waiting to get tickets. I think to maybe *Jimmy Kimmel* or something. But, see, after they get their tickets, they're going to have to probably stall for a while until the taping."

Isaac hopped up and down on one leg. "Plus, if they are all waiting to see a taping of a TV show, then they'll probably want to be *on* a TV show."

Allyson laughed, feeling giddy suddenly. "I think I managed to run into the smartest family on Hollywood Boulevard. I can't thank you all enough."

Isaac's mom was herding them toward the crosswalk. "Let me tell your dad. He'll be thrilled to get some time to gift-shop hop. I'll meet you three over there." She turned and then paused. "By the way, what's your name, our new TV star friend?"

Allyson blushed. "Allyson," she said. "And I'm not really a TV star. I'm just trying to get to college. My mom's kind of sick, so . . ."

The mother's eyes softened, and she grabbed Allyson's hand to squeeze it gently. "I'll bet she'll be proud to see you doing this."

Allyson's throat constricted, and for several long moments she couldn't respond. "If she makes it long enough to see me at all," she said softly.

July 12, 12:50 p.m.
Hollywood, California
Tyrell Young

The problem wasn't *getting* the people; the problem was *keeping* the people.

They had a system. They were working together—him and Yamamura—starting from way down on Hollywood Boulevard, almost to the Wax Museum, and then slowly making their way back toward the Pantages Theater. He'd had to convince Yamamura that they weren't really lying. They were surviving. And it was a game, not real life anyway.

"Hey, the Pantages is where it's at! Just put this wristband here on and you will be one of a select group of people allowed inside for a special presentation."

But when they got to the theater to check their numbers, figuring they had to have herded about seventy to eighty people with green wristbands—Tyrell's color—they had twenty-five. And those twenty-five were looking restless.

"How long we gotta stay here?" one woman asked. She had a kid who was zipping up and down the aisles while she texted on her phone. "We got tickets to a show at the El Capitan in, like, twenty minutes."

Tyrell looked helplessly at his small crowd, all wanting an answer from him.

"We gotta do something, bro," he said to Hiroshi.

Hiroshi let his eyes travel slowly around the room. He inched closer to Tyrell.

"Give me your wristbands," he said. "I'll get people in here. You start working this crowd. Talk to them or something. Let the camera follow you around and maybe they'll feel like they're being interviewed."

Tyrell handed Hiroshi his sheet of wristbands and bumped his fist. "You're smarter than you look, Yamamura," he said.

Hiroshi allowed the edges of his mouth to curve up. "So I've been told."

Tyrell moved toward the texting mom. He couldn't help but notice that Sam had quite a crowd growing around him near the stage, but that Allyson, Cassidy, and Polo were nowhere to be seen. Confidence made him swagger just the littlest bit. They had this one in the bag. He and Hiroshi made an unbeatable team.

July 12, 12:59 p.m.
Hollywood, California
Sam Michaels

"Where you from?" he tossed out to a cute brunette in a tube top and short-shorts. She had inched her way forward in the growing crowd that circled him.

She lowered her eyes flirtatiously and stuck out a tanned leg for him to admire. He never would have given her type a second look. But it was all gameplay right now.

"Orange County," she answered, tossing a mass of highlighted hair over one shoulder. Somehow, he felt like she wanted him to be impressed by that. He tried to grin appreciatively.

If he hadn't been nervous about the numbers, this would have been a blast. As soon as Cassidy and Henry had jogged up the aisle and out the massive door of the theater, three large sheets of colored wristbands waving between them, he'd gone exploring. Turned out, the Pantages had been well equipped for a guy like Sam, who someday hoped to be on stage for real. In a dark, dusty room down a short flight of stairs, he'd found a set of wooden drumsticks.

His "Yes!" sounded cheesy and too loud in the deserted underbelly of the theater. But he didn't give a rat's ass. Even if a camera still documented his every move.

From there, it was a matter of collecting anything that could be banged, beaten, or crashed together. He snagged a huge plastic bucket and some pipe from a janitor's closet; a metal lid from a trash can out back; an abandoned wine bottle (empty) from what he envisioned was a rousing closing night celebration; a cardboard box like you might buy paper in; a tarnished silver tray with some fancy scalloped edges; and a Frisbee. He also happened upon a black fedora which, with his longer, shaggy hair, was going to give him a Kidd Rock look. He'd found a cape, too, but decided that would be too Harry Potter.

He had just assembled his "drum set" when his first groupies wandered in. They had blue, yellow, and orange wristbands on, which let him know they were his to round up and entertain. So, he did.

He sat on a stool he'd borrowed from the snack bar in the lobby. And as he beckoned people down toward him, he twirled the drumsticks expertly, planting his feet widely on the floor, feeling the muscles in his shoulders and back loosen up. This was something he could do. And do well.

Sam tossed a grin in the direction of the brunette who was now front row center. His sticks poised over the overturned plastic bucket, he said, "Help me out, then, Orange County."

With a rhythm that pulsed through him as naturally as his own heartbeat, he set up a beat. Orange County took the hint and started clapping; soon, the crowd joined in. Sam let the sticks fly over everything else he'd arranged, creating a melody somehow from the different timbres of the items he struck.

He closed his eyes and let the rhythm guide him. This was what he *did.* This was what he wanted to do forever. This was why he needed to win.

July 12, 1:09 p.m.
Hollywood, California
Allyson Murphy

She imagined it must look like a parade. A parade led by her, Savannah, Isaac, and her faithful cameraman. Together, they and their nearly one hundred new best friends wove their way down Hollywood Boulevard toward the theater. Isaac was awesome. He kept reminding everyone, in his squeaky, childlike voice, that they were "doing this for Allyson! And her sick mom!" She'd never had a little brother, never wanted one, but Isaac had her reconsidering.

Savannah was quieter, keeping pace next to her, enthralled by the camera and mesmerized by Allyson herself. The younger girl wouldn't stop asking her questions: Why'd you apply for this show? Where do you go when you're not doing a challenge? Are there cute guys in the house? Until finally her mom shushed her by reminding her that all of America would be seeing how nosey she was.

Allyson felt as if this were a dream. With this family by her side—the Lydles, who she learned were here on vacation from Wisconsin—she managed to work the line outside the *Jimmy Kimmel* theater, explaining what she had to do and why. Isaac jumped in frequently with his motivating quips. Savannah kept count. When they got into the high eighties, Mrs. Lydle suggested they start moving toward the theater and hopefully others would tag along.

For so many months, Allyson had felt like the rug had been pulled out from under her. Her mom's diagnosis. Watching her disintegrate before Allyson's eyes. The hair loss, the weight loss, the energy loss. In all regards, her mom was losing. Time had become so precious. And yet, she continued to make it clear to her daughter that she wanted Allyson's life to continue.

"Go to college, Al," she'd said one day as Allyson held her hand through another round of chemo. "Teach. Or something else. I know you love the outdoors." She'd smiled weakly—everything a battle, even a smile. "Just like your dad. Be a biologist or a naturalist or whatever will make you happy."

Mom didn't know how much her medical bills had drained the family. College wasn't an option unless they could get loans, but they had so many of those to pay off already.

That was why she was here. Spending precious minutes that could have been spent with her mom, with this legion of strangers traipsing past famous landmarks on a hot summer day. It had all seemed like such a long shot.

Allyson's group, when all the pink wristbands had been counted, totaled one hundred and three. She was the first of the six contestants to finish the task. Isaac and Savannah and Mrs. Lydle all hugged her and wished her the best of luck in the rest of the competition. She thanked them, thanked them all.

But mostly, she thanked God. Maybe He hadn't forgotten her after all.

July 12, 1:23 p.m.
Hollywood, California
Cassidy McGowan

Finally, a challenge she was good at. She just had to smile and flirt and talk to people. And, man, she was killer good at flirting.

Sam told her to hand out her wristbands first and then do his. But that felt wrong. She'd seen him in there, when she'd peeked inside after chatting up a group of college guys from USC. Sam was amazing. He'd had all the people she and Henry had rounded up gathered around him, clapping and cheering as he created the coolest sounds she'd ever heard—music made from garbage can lids and plastic buckets.

She'd felt a pull in her chest—like she wanted to go sit next to him, listen to him, claim him somehow. It was a strange feeling for her. She'd been so startled by it that she'd turned abruptly and headed back out on the street. She needed to be around people. Lots of people.

She'd gotten attached once. She'd been young. Young and dumb. He'd been older and convincing. Made her feel like she was special and mattered. But when he learned she was pregnant, he'd been gone fast. Without even saying good-bye. He'd never met Faith, never even learned the baby was a girl. The hate she'd felt for him had threatened to suck her under, until she'd held Faith and figured out that even assholes can leave behind something good. But her distrust of falling that deeply again was etched on her heart. Sharpie permanent.

She sidled up to a circle of guys waiting outside a pizza place. Within two minutes, she was handing them blue wristbands—Sam's color—and guiding them toward the theater.

They were in this challenge together. If Sam ended up in the bottom two, she wanted to be there with him.

July 12, 1:25 p.m.
Hollywood, California
Tyrell Young

Allyson was done. First again. Chilling in the back row. Something different about her today, too, but he couldn't put his finger on it. She looked prettier, maybe. Less uptight. Staring at her, though—all smiley-faced and relieved—he only wanted to grab her stupid necklace and yank it off her pasty white neck.

Sam had a huge circle of people all kicking it near the stage where he was banging on whatever it was he was banging on. Way more than a hundred peeps. Probably closer to two, maybe even three. Tyrell felt his mouth turn down in a scowl. It wasn't right what he was doing. The Benefactor said this was about rhetoric. Not lame-ass crap that was supposed to be music. Screw him and that loser girlfriend of his. Polo, too, since they'd obviously taken pity on the poor bastard after his crappy performance yesterday. Maybe they figured he was the weakest link, so the best choice to keep around.

Fine. Let 'em all gang up together. Let them die together.

"We're outta here, man."

Tyrell spun around. It was two guys who'd been around for a while, hanging quietly in one of the last rows of the orchestra section. They'd seemed legit, like they were in this for the long haul.

The guy stuck out a hand and Tyrell shook it. "Dude, we wish you lots of luck. But my friend and I got a movie to catch." He ripped off his wristband and handed it to Tyrell. His friend did the same. They both made their way up the aisle and out the door.

Two more casualties. Shit.

He looked around at his dwindling numbers. Forty. Maybe fifty. No way were they in this thing. Unless Ringo Starr broke a drumstick (or with any luck, an arm) and the crowd lost interest, they were way screwed on this challenge. He and Hiroshi were coming in last. Bottom two, baby.

And his ass would be on the line. Hiroshi was out there in the July heat, rounding up strangers, probably looking good to the Benefactor. He was in here, staying cool, doing a half-assed job of keeping these folks happy. He'd been trying, you know, to ask them stuff, seem friendly. But "friendly" wasn't his strength. If he could've started a pick-up game, tossed around the football with them, he'd have been in business.

Here, with moms and couples and teenage girls wanting to know about him and the show and crap he didn't want to share, he was nose-diving. Hard.

The crowd around Sam clapped and hooted. He watched Sam stand and grin, thanking them all for hanging around. Tyrell's gut felt like he'd taken a hard block from a three-hundred-pound lineman. He was gonna lose to that piece of trash. He wanted to punch something.

Two younger chicks in shorts and T-shirts were heading down the aisle toward him. Green wristbands. Excellent. He tried to smile at them.

"Welcome, ladies!" he said. "You don't know how much this helps us out. You guys from around here?"

He couldn't have cared less if they were from Los Angeles or Buffalo or Mars. But he pretended to listen and nod while his brain began doing some figuring.

He and Hiroshi were in the bottom two. He saw Sam, Cassidy, and Henry huddle up by the entrance, and knew by their hugs and high-fives that they were done.

"So what's this show called, anyway?" the brunette asked, snapping her gum obnoxiously and craning her neck around like she was waiting for some producer to discover her. He mumbled an answer and let her ramble some more.

How to get the Benefactor to dump Hiroshi and not him? What was Hiroshi's weakness? How could he play this?

The girl in front of him was babbling on and on, something about how she'd been in theater in high school and it was so cool to get to come inside the Pantages, which had been around *forever.*

Theater in high school. Those words nagged at him. *Theater in high school.*

And then, he knew. Maggie. As much as it would suck, he knew exactly what he would have to do. Because Tyrell wasn't here to make friends. He was here to win.

EPISODE 4
THE SECRET

"In 2010, about 74 percent of young adults with a bachelor's degree or higher were employed full time, compared with 65 percent of those with an associate's degree, . . . 55 percent of high school completers, and 41 percent of those without a high school diploma or its equivalent."

—National Center for Education Statistics

July 17, 6:29 p.m.
Malibu, California
The Benefactor

"You need to understand, Dick. I run the most prestigious university—"

"Chancellor Bingham," the Benefactor said, reaching for a paperweight on his desk and then setting it back down. He hated to be called Dick. Richard? Fine. Even Rich. But not Dick. "I appreciate your concerns. But surely you had to anticipate that I would be vetting these kids differently than the college application process. Otherwise, what would be the point of the show? Watching eight kids take SATs is hardly entertainment."

The chancellor's voice lost its friendly tone. "Don't patronize me, Richard. I've known you for many years"—the Benefactor stifled a laugh, unsure how a rejection a decade ago justified this statement—"and you and I both know what I'm referring to. We had an agreement: I'd allow my name to be attached to your show; you'd provide an endowment and make sure that whoever enrolled at my school was a worthy candidate. Having kids beg their way into Disneyland no more qualifies them to be a student here than if they could balance eggs on their foreheads!"

The Benefactor could have pointed out many things: first, that the Chancellor's name was not attached to the show, only his school's name and even then in a very remote way; second, some of the kids hadn't begged their way into Disneyland, and it was that ingenuity that made them strong candidates (in his mind, at least); and balancing an egg on one's forehead actually took quite a lot of practice, patience, and persistence, qualities that maybe he should place as much importance on as math aptitude or volunteer hours.

However, the Benefactor swallowed these comments. He needed this school on his roster.

"These kids are top-notch," said the Benefactor, feeling a surprising swell of protectiveness. "I promise you that the person who wins this competition will not only have earned their way into your school—if that's where he or she should choose to go—but will have proven their worth and their competitiveness with every other applicant you're considering. But you have to trust me to do this the way I've envisioned."

Silence. If the chancellor pulled out, others could follow, and the house of cards would fall.

"Tell me the kids aren't hitchhiking or working at McDonald's in the next episode, Richard."

The Benefactor forced a laugh. "McDonald's would not agree to our set of demands."

The chancellor did not laugh. "Seriously, Richard, these kids need to be proving they're not only bright and well-rounded, but we need to see the kinds of traits we look for in our admissions process: leadership, service to others, drive, and resourcefulness."

In other words, the Benefactor thought wryly, you want me to find exactly the same kid that your admissions officers would find.

"You act as if admission to college is akin to a kid's overall self-worth," the Benefactor said drily. He took a steadying breath. "I know the traits that are important for success. You're just going to have to trust that I can spot them in someone else."

He heard the chancellor sigh. "Obviously, we'll be watching, Richard. And if we have hesitations . . . well, I can't say that you can count on our support unconditionally."

The Benefactor closed his eyes. "And obviously, you understand that my endowment money hinges on your participation. However, I appreciate the heads-up. Thanks for the call."

He disconnected and dropped his phone on his desk.

Pompous ass.

He ran through his mental to-do list. Yaz was expecting a call from him about which shot of the kids to use in a full-page promo they'd bought in *People* magazine. His board members wanted an update. He had several reports to read from a possible investor and e-mails that were piling up. Not to mention at least one antsy chancellor.

But that wasn't what was weighing most heavily on him at that moment.

He had some news to deliver to one contestant. News he was dreading. And though he probably could've let one of the house custodians do it, his gut told him it should come from him.

He picked up the phone.

"Yaz," he said dully. "Patch me into the houses and call the kids together. I need to get this done."

July 17, 6:31 p.m.
Newport Beach, California
Sam Michaels

If the last four days with Cassidy had taught him anything, it was this: she had an unfailing sense of optimism and a laugh that made him forget he was competing for hundreds of thousands of dollars. And when he remembered, he wasn't sure he cared anymore.

The Benefactor had gone easy on them for the past few days. No challenges after the Pantages Theater. There'd been the Elimination, of course, which brought their number down to five. And then, nothing.

Well, not nothing, exactly. There had been regular interviews with producers, where he was asked everything from how he liked the food to who drove him the craziest to who he thought was going home next. There had been two field trips. The first was to *The Ellen DeGeneres Show,* where the contestants had ten minutes to vamp onstage with Ellen and then were presented with letterman-style jackets with Ellen's logo on the back. He'd hated being onstage, hated being primped and powdered. But when Cassidy'd grabbed his hand moments before the producer herded them onstage—grabbed him and leaned toward him, her excitement barely contained—he didn't want to be anywhere else.

The second outing was to Rodeo Drive in Beverly Hills, where they'd been given full makeovers by some of the top hair and makeup artists in the business. Then they were trekked to a nearby Macy's and introduced to some big-name fashion expert who preached about what clothes looked good with their skin tones and body types and who-frickin'-cared what else.

He'd hated that day and swore he would kill anyone who brought scissors within five inches of his scalp. They must have believed him because his hair was left alone, though they did force him into a crisp white V-neck T-shirt, a navy blue blazer, jeans that cost more than his last bike, and a pair of brown shoes that he was pretty sure he had last seen being rented at a bowling alley (but was assured were totally "hipster").

He'd felt like an imposter, more uncomfortable than he'd been since he'd arrived in L.A. for this crazy game. At least when he was in his worn secondhand shirts and the shorts he made by cutting off his frayed jeans, he could pretend he was still Sam and that he hadn't let go of that scrappy, soulful part of himself that allowed him to survive without parents, money, or guidance for seventeen years. In that snug blazer, he felt precariously close to being a suit.

Cassidy, however, seemed to like his new look, if the way she ran her hand up and down his arm and let her eyes roam over him was any indication. In fairness, though, she gushed over everyone's new look. Most of all, her own.

When she had stepped foot in the salon—some high-end place swathed in blacks and golds that had waif-like men with blond highlights who wielded scissors like they'd been born holding them—Cassidy's eyes had glazed over. A look of such bliss, such pure joy, came over her that Sam couldn't tear his eyes from her and he hadn't heard a word Molly said. He hoped that all the cameras that day had the good sense to stay trained on Cassidy. She was gorgeous when she'd walked into that salon, stunning when she walked out.

The following day was spent at a back-lot stage in Studio City. The five of them were schlepped in their separate vans (at an hour too early to actually be called morning) for some torture that Colin called "promotional shots." What it really meant was endless hours in front of cameras. Posing. Smiling. Taking directions from a woman with a tight smile whose hair was sloppily piled on her head but who managed to walk around in shoes that were at least five inches from the ground.

But, man, could she bark orders. *Hand on your hip. Chin lifted. Chin dropped. Look sexy, hon. Now, smile. That's right, and hold it.* He had no idea how incredibly exhausting it was to be a model. Cassidy, though, was on cloud nine—or cloud eighty-seven, if the clouds could go that high.

They were told that the pictures of them—staged group shots where they were supposed to look serious and determined—were being featured in magazines and on billboards, blasted out in e-mails, and made into thirty-second commercials.

It felt surreal. Like someone else's life. Three weeks ago, he'd been strumming his guitar on street corners and ferries with hands made greasy from bike chains. He'd had a joint rolled up in his pocket, Rachel mother-henning him to quit, his grandmother bitching at him to get the garbage out or find her missing bottle of Scotch, which he knew wasn't missing but drunk the night before as she'd lain half passed out in her housecoat on their stained and gritty couch.

Sam wasn't usually a doubting guy. He'd long ago quit trying to figure out if he was good enough for the world and just accepted that *this* was his world. He had talent—if the appraising looks he got from the passersby were any indication. And his music teacher at school said so. His music teacher being pretty much the only person who ever bothered, besides Rachel, to see past the frayed clothes and lazy smile to what was underneath.

But those four days in the spotlight flattened him. What would the people watching this from their homes see when they looked at him? The pot-smoking hippie loser that his grandma saw? A rising musician? The capable and calculating leader that Cassidy seemed to think he might be? Which then made him wonder . . . which of those Sams *was* he?

Right then, he wanted to be the Sam brave enough to reach across the glass table and lace Cassidy's fingers with his. But though her hands were there, resting inches from his for the taking, his own hands stayed folded in front of him.

"If it's your passion," Cassidy was saying, "then you've got to, you know, follow it."

Sam watched her tamp down a stray strand of hair and mindlessly pull it back to join the rest of her ponytail. She tilted her head and gazed at him with her saucer-like, candid eyes. They were sitting outside, across from each other on the second floor of his condo. The sun was well into its descent toward the ocean. The air was cool, salty, and a little scratchy against his raw, sunburned skin.

He leaned forward on his elbows. "So what's *your* passion, then, oh wise one?"

She laughed, low and sexy, and looked out at the ocean.

"My passion . . ." she repeated. He couldn't stop looking at her. Somewhere deep within him, shifts were taking place. He knew it. Things that had always been aligned were coming unaligned. Because of this . . . because of her.

"Well, Sam Michaels," she said, her tone light and teasing, "I love kittens and sunsets. The beach. Happy endings. Words that rhyme. My grandmother's spaghetti. The smell of nail polish. The sound of a train pulling into a station. And gumdrops."

He threw back his head and laughed. "Come on," he said, "the smell of nail polish? Really?"

She shrugged. "You asked. I answered."

"Be serious, Cass," Sam said. "What matters to you?"

Cassidy twirled a strand of hair and looked thoughtful.

"What matters to me," she said, her voice whispery soft, "is doing what's right. There are things, you know, that I've done . . ."

The French doors to the boys' condo flung open. Colin poked his head out.

"Sorry to interrupt, mate," he said, his gaze sliding from Cassidy to Sam. "But you've got to head down to the common room, and Cassidy needs to chivvy along to her own flat. The Benefactor has an announcement."

Sam's eyebrows shot up.

"About a challenge?"

Colin hesitated. He shook his head slightly.

"I don't think that's the gist of it, mate. I was told that he had to talk to you chaps. Something has happened, I think. Maybe at home. And it's gonna affect the game. For one of you."

Colin shrugged and ducked back inside. Sam started to stand up. Cassidy hadn't moved. He reached for her hand.

"You okay?" he asked gently.

She looked up. Her face was pale, even in the fading light. Her mouth was tight.

"Oh God," she said hoarsely. "Please don't let it be what I think it is."

Then, she'd gripped his hand, desperation bleeding from her like an open wound.

"Please," she whispered, "whatever he says, you have to let me explain, okay? And I have to know you won't hate me. Please, Sam? Say it, even though it will mean nothing in a few more minutes."

Sam had felt the warmth of her fingers and wanted nothing more than to pull her close and not let go. Whatever she was talking about they would figure out. Whatever secrets she had . . . well, he had secrets, too. They all did.

He'd squeezed her hand back. "It'll be all right, Cassidy. I promise."

July 17, 6:34 p.m.
Newport Beach, California
Cassidy McGowan

Faith. Something had happened to Faith. She was sick or had climbed up on Justin's top bunk and fallen off. Weren't she and Justin always reminding Mom to watch her more closely when they were gone? Faith was a climber—oh, how that girl loved to climb.

If something had happened to her . . . because Cassidy was here . . . not there . . . The fear threatened to pinch her throat closed, cut off her air. Crush her.

Even as she thought it, pictured it, she *knew.* Something terrible had happened to Faith. Because she was here, glamming it up for the camera, basking in the California sun, and laughing with Sam.

Sam.

Sam would find out. Now. Sam would know she was a *mother.*

A terrible mom who had left her daughter.

She wanted to tell him on her own terms. She'd even kind of scripted it in her head. She'd explain how she'd made one mistake two years ago, trusted when she should have steered clear, but that the result was sweet, pure Faith. Her baby. And though she regretted the mistake, she never regretted having Faith in her life.

And Sam would get it. He would commend her honesty and her commitment. He would see her heroic attempt to make a better life for them both. He would sympathize with the tough choices, the sacrifices a young mother like herself had to make, and see that this competition was her way of trying to make things right.

But somehow during these past four days, there had never been a good time to say all those things. And frankly, she'd been too busy, well, just soaking up this incredible life that was suddenly hers.

There really weren't words for her to describe how she'd felt. *Magical,* maybe. Though that conjured up images of

Disney princesses and seemed beyond corny. Words like *unbelievable* and *awesome* . . . they just didn't do it justice. Being in front of a camera for those promotional shots had felt like the most natural thing in the world to her—like she could finally exhale, after years of holding her breath.

And Sam? She'd known right away that he would make a good ally. He was smart—and just like all the other guys back home, he wanted to help her out, protect her. She was used to that.

What wasn't she used to? A guy who leaned forward on his elbows when she talked and, though his eyelids drooped slightly, making him so incredibly sexy, she knew he was listening. A guy who opened doors for her but also asked her opinion about things like whether or not they should stay aligned with Henry, or if she thought this competition would help them get into a college even if they didn't win. A guy who looked at her with, yeah, desire but also respect and curiosity, as if he couldn't quite figure her out, but he wanted to keep trying.

When Sam looked at her like that, it felt like a million bubbles were gathering in her chest and her throat. Little tiny bubbles, like the kind that fizzed up in the neck of a champagne bottle once it was uncorked. In fact, that was exactly what she felt like lately: a champagne bottle that had been uncorked.

But Sam hadn't even touched her really. A casual grazing of his hand across her back, which sent a buzzing up her spine and made her fight hard not to shiver. Once, he'd pushed a strand of hair from her eyes while she was eating, a gesture so familiar and thoughtful, she'd had to look down, afraid he'd see the longing she was sure was plain on her face.

But he hadn't made any effort to kiss her. Or to inch casually closer to her and let his hand rest on her thigh like countless others had done, as if they were entitled somehow to do such a thing.

As every hour passed, Cassidy found herself wondering when he *would* do this stuff. When he would show that he was just like every other guy. That he only saw the parts of her that, put together, were some universal definition of beautiful. And then, she would be able to shake her head, tell herself that she'd known it all along, and feel confident that she was a good judge of character. She'd learned her lesson—she wouldn't make the same mistake twice.

Because she *was* a good judge of character. It was just that one time. She'd learned her lesson.

So why did she feel this disappointment, this panging in her heart, every time he cocked his head and smiled at her, but kept his distance? Why did she feel the urge to reach for his hand, just to see how his long, bony fingers might feel wrapped together with hers? Why did she wonder, again and again, if his chest was as solid as it looked?

And why was she so worried, even as the panic about her daughter's safety pressed on her chest, that when he found out about Faith it would change everything?

July 17, 6:34 p.m.
Newport Beach, California
Tyrell Young

Tyrell leaned forward and placed his elbows on his knees as they waited to see what the Benefactor would say. He rested his forehead in his palms. What was this called again? When the universe figured out that you'd screwed someone and so it did its best to screw you back?

Damn.

His stomach felt heavy, though all he'd eaten for dinner was a grilled cheese sandwich and a couple of pickle spears. He'd been sure he was going home four nights ago. He and Hiroshi had lost the challenge. In fact, they'd never even gotten close to getting a hundred people in the Pantages Theater and had called it quits at about seven p.m. The Benefactor hadn't been kind in the Elimination, questioning their fortitude, their wisdom, and eventually, their alliance.

Hiroshi had been stoic. He'd refused to throw Tyrell under the bus. He'd defended himself, yes, but though the Benefactor prodded, Hiroshi stayed true to the friendship they'd formed on Day One. Tyrell, on the other hand, had played the one card he knew might save his ass and crush Hiroshi: Maggie.

After over an hour of rehashing and questioning, both of them coming under fire for everything from a lack of teamwork to too much teamwork, from lying to people outside to not lying to them enough, Tyrell sucked in a breath and faced the backlit outline of the Benefactor on the screen above.

"Look," he said, a cold resolve settling over him. It was the same resolve he got when it was fourth down and ten. "You know why I'm here? Because I got a little sister at home whose blood is wacked. Not a day goes by"—he swallowed, paused, swallowed again—"that my sister is not in pain. When it's cold? She can barely walk. She gets pneumonia two, maybe three times a year."

Hiroshi's face was closed, expressionless. Tyrell had to wonder what was running though his head.

"I'm here because my mom and dad can't afford to pay her medical bills and my college tuition. And though I had a football scholarship going for me at one point, I got an injury this last season that, well, erased it as an option."

Tyrell couldn't look at Hiroshi. They'd talked about this. Just like they'd talked about Maggie. When the camera was off. Which is why it wasn't right—what Tyrell did next.

"I love my bro over there. He's a fighter, like me, and he's got way more brainpower than I could ever hope to have. Which is why he don't need to be here."

Tyrell closed his eyes and clenched his back teeth. He had to do this.

"His parents have bucks," Tyrell said softly. "He's got the grades and the résumé to go to pretty much any school he wants. In fact, he's been recruited. Yep, recruited. By UNLV and UCSD. For swimming. And because he's a badass, in general."

He tried to smile at Hiroshi, but the look his friend returned was hardened.

"Hiroshi's doing all this for his girl," Tyrell added quietly. "Maggie."

Across the table, he heard Hiroshi's intake of breath.

"It's classic *Romeo and Juliet,*" Tyrell continued, ignoring the headache that was coming on like a freight train. "Which is ironic, since Maggie is in theater . . ."

"You son of a . . ." Hiroshi muttered.

"Something his parents were not fond of. So the choice was his: go to college on their dime or stay with Maggie. And my friend, Hiroshi, is very practical."

The room was dead silent. He could feel Hiroshi's rage, pulsing like it was another being in the room.

"You have to get rid of one of us tonight. Hiroshi and me—we've done all of our challenges together. We've finished them fairly equally. Performed roughly the same. You could argue, I guess, that there were moments I took some leadership. You could also argue that Hiroshi strategizes better than me. Is a better athlete. And you'd probably be right. But then I guess I'd ask you to consider our motives for being here. And the worth of this scholarship to us. If I go home today, I'm probably looking at community college. If Hiroshi goes home, his backup plan includes a top-rated West Coast school."

This is a game, Tyrell reminded himself. And every game had winners and losers. Casualties.

"I've also fought like hell to make you see that I want to stay, while Hiroshi has stayed mostly silent. I'm here because I'm probably the only one in my family who may ever go to college. He's here . . . well, because of a girl."

Tyrell knew how it sounded. It sounded like Hiroshi was privileged. Elite and pampered. And shallow enough to have chosen the security of his parents' money over love.

Which is exactly what Tyrell intended.

And it worked. Hiroshi was sent home a few minutes later, treading away silently without looking at Tyrell.

But there was no satisfaction in the win. No urge to gloat or slam a football between his legs and high-five someone. He'd wanted only to erase the memory of Hiroshi's face as Tyrell stabbed him in the back.

He was the biggest dick ever.

Which was why this was happening now. The Benefactor was going to tell him that Shaina was in the hospital again. Or that he'd found out about how Tyrell had tried to cheat on the biking challenge. Or how he knew Tyrell had done steroids, just that once, for a few months, right before his junior year.

Whatever it was, this had to be about him. Because he deserved it.

July 17, 6:35 p.m.
Newport Beach, California
Henry Stone IV

He was writing. Probably not his best work. But his room had a laptop (no Internet, of course), and since he hadn't hurled it against a closet door yet, he decided to spend some time jabbing his fingers at the keyboard. Sometimes, after one of his "bouts," he did his best work. Other times, what came out was more of a stream of consciousness, a kind of long-winded gibberish that was more journaling than writing.

Either way, it was cathartic. Either way, it got him away from the rest of the contestants. Either way, it helped him not think for a little while.

He'd gotten lucky. With Sam coaxing him from his "poor me" stupor. With Sam and Cassidy practically dragging him to safety in that inane Pantages challenge. The tragedy there had been that the challenge was made for him—tailor-made. Had he been less weighted down by his own uselessness, he would have kicked ass. Convincing others, networking—"rhetoric," the Benefactor had called it—man, he could nail that. Once again, though, he'd been sucked down by his own weaknesses. And it had been right there, broadcast for the world (and his father) to see

He'd been grateful for the past four days to pull himself together. Not that the makeovers or being paraded around like pageant queens had been his idea of a good time. But he had lots of practice at smiling and making like he was Prince Charming. And there were plenty of opportunities for him to steal away to his room to write.

He was wrapping up a short story when Colin stuck his head in the door.

"You're needed down in the common area, mate. The Benefactor has some kind of announcement."

Colin disappeared, leaving Henry to close up his laptop and wonder what the latest twist would be. He didn't like these unexpected turns. He would have much preferred a steady rhythm to the game—challenge, Elimination, downtime, repeat. He plodded down the stairs and slid onto the couch next to Sam.

"You know what's going on?" he asked quietly.

Sam shook his head just as the screen over the fireplace clicked on. The Benefactor's dark form appeared: an outline behind a desk, backlit by an orangish glow. Still unidentifiable.

"Good evening," he said in a low, even tone. "I won't waste anyone's time with pleasantries or carefully worded phrases meant to garner suspense and create tension. The reason I've gathered you is this: I have received news that concerns one of you. And it will, unfortunately, most likely affect your chances of staying in this competition."

Henry's throat pinched. A clamminess spread through his body. The Benefactor knew. Of course he did. He knew about his tirade five days ago. He knew about the broken tablet hidden in his closet.

And today, right now, would be judgment day.

July 17, 6:36 p.m.
Newport Beach, California
Allyson Murphy

Her mom. It was her mother. She sucked in a painful breath. She never should have come. She'd known in her heart that it would end like this. But her dad, he'd been so hopeful, so insistent. And her sister . . . Go, they said. It's what Mom wants.

Still, when she'd said good-bye that day, held her mom's hand, which was as feathery-light as a child's yet as bony as a woman's twice her age, she'd known, somehow, that it would be the last time she'd see her mom.

Waves of nausea hit her. She didn't want to hear like this. Not with these strangers. Panic blanketed her, and she felt suffocated.

She closed her eyes, pictured her mom—healthy, laughing, happy.

Yea, though I walk through the valley of the shadow of death, I will fear no evil: for thou art with me; thy rod and thy staff they comfort me.

It couldn't end like this. For her. For her mom.

I can do all things through Christ who strengthens me.

Dear God. Please . . .

July 17, 6:36 p.m.
Malibu, California
The Benefactor

He could see their faces through his screen, even though they couldn't see his. None of them deserved this. Especially the one who had to hear this news.

Say it, and be done with it, he told himself.

"We keep you sequestered from your families for a reason," he said, holding his voice as steady as he could. "We want to see how well you perform under pressure, without the support of the people you love and who love you. Harsh, I know. But sometimes, reality. Unfortunately, though, we've received word from one of your families that something has happened that requires you to return home. One of you will, I'm sorry to say, be leaving the game tonight."

He saw Allyson. She pitched forward and curled up. She was shaking, uncontrollably. Cassidy immediately enveloped her in a hug. He could see Cassidy's lips moving against Allyson's ear but could not make out what she said.

Tyrell's jaw clenched. He wouldn't look left or right. His eyes hardened into slits.

Sam's look was pensive. Curious. He glanced at both Henry and Tyrell and then back at the screen.

The Benefactor shook his head and blew out a breath. "I'm sorry, Henry," he said heavily. "Your father had a heart attack this morning. He didn't . . . he didn't make it."

For a moment, no one moved. Allyson's rocking stopped and she raised a tear-stained face. Cassidy continued to hold her tight, as they both gazed up at the screen, their eyes wide, dazed, confused.

Tyrell's head swiveled slowly toward Henry. Sam stood.

"Henry," Sam said, reaching for him with an extended hand. "Man, I am so . . ."

"What?" Henry jumped to his feet. "What did he say?"

"Your dad," Sam said, gently, "Listen, man, let's get you packed up. You need to . . ."

"My dad what?" Henry asked, his arms up, like he could physically ward off what was coming.

Sam glanced at Tyrell, who hadn't moved. Tyrell nodded, as if to say, *Do it, he needs to hear it.*

"He's gone, man," Sam said gently. "He didn't make it. Look. Come on. You need to get home. Your mom . . ."

Henry spun around wildly. He grabbed a vase of flowers sitting on the table and before anyone could react, he had it in his hands. Then he was throwing that vase. And it was smashing against the fireplace, shards of blue tile raining down, a stain of water growing where the flowers landed in a colorful array, almost as if someone had arranged them there.

Sam stepped forward cautiously.

Tyrell leaped up. "Come on, man," Tyrell said.

The Benefactor watched it all: Henry shoved Tyrell, who toppled toward the couch but caught himself. Henry stepped forward—just two steps—and his arm swept across the mantel filled with books and ceramic statues. Even before the last book hit the floor, Tyrell and Sam were on him, pinning his arms to his sides. Blindly, Henry kicked at them both, pulling and screaming—a deep, guttural, ugly sound.

"Henry!" Sam yelled, hugging Henry's arms from behind, while Tyrell was pushing and pinning him from the front. "Come on, man!"

For minutes, they wrestled—Henry raging, Tyrell and Sam struggling to contain him. Gradually, the fight seeped out of Henry. He sank against Sam, weeping. Exhausted.

"I'm sorry," he cried, burying his face in his hands and collapsing back on the couch.

Sam nodded, breathing heavily and swiping at a trickle of blood that wormed its way down the left side of his mouth.

Tyrell looked up at the Benefactor. "Can we turn the cameras off?" he pleaded. "Let the guy pull himself together or something, for God's sake."

Slowly, the Benefactor nodded and signaled to cut the cameras, watching as his screens went dark. And he stayed watching the bank of dark screens for a long while, until he had to press his thumbs onto both eyes to stop what he kept seeing. And his own tears.

July 18, 7:18 a.m.
Newport Beach, California
Allyson Murphy

"Dear Father God," she murmured into folded hands. "Please watch over Henry and his mom during this difficult time. Help them look to You for healing and to take comfort in knowing that their loved one is with You. I ask also that You be with Mom. Heal her body and make her whole again. In Your blessed name, Amen."

She pulled herself up from the side of her bed and sat on the edge of it. After the announcement last night, she and Cassidy had been given the chance to say goodbye to Henry. Seeing his empty expression and the mindless way he'd been led out to a waiting car had rattled her. That should have been her getting in that car. Wearing that expression.

Why had she been saved again?

Her heart ached, as if it had somehow grown too large for her chest in one short night. Sleep had not come easily last night. Her brain had pinged from Henry to her mom, and somewhere in all that muddling back and forth, when she'd fallen asleep, she'd had strange dreams of going to Henry's father's funeral only to look down and see her mother in the casket, alive and well and begging Allyson to let her out.

Allyson couldn't imagine how this day would unfold. They were down to four, just four. So quickly. So suddenly. Would they be expected to compete in a challenge? Maybe that would be preferable to sitting around the house all day, wondering and worrying about Henry.

During the makeovers two days ago, the stylist had used a more permanent straightener on her hair—some kind of keratin, he'd said—so it now hung in silky waves and shone like dark maple syrup. And she'd been given new clothes, too, in colors that Cassidy had said would bring out her eyes and make her skin look healthier, less pale. A makeup artist had shown her patiently how to apply eyeliner and how to layer different colors on her eyelids to make them bolder. She could now give herself defined cheekbones and full, rosy lips. She even had a pair of clip-on earrings that looked like small silver teardrops.

But today, she reached for one of her old navy button-downs, some knee-length khaki shorts. She pulled her hair back into a neat ponytail and scrubbed her face clean. Her only jewelry was the cross necklace that her grandmother had given her on her tenth birthday.

She didn't look like Cassidy. She wouldn't turn heads or melt hearts. In fact, she could already picture the disappointed expressions of the show's producers when they saw her. They would scowl and huddle together to cast pointed looks in her direction.

But this was who she was. Who she wanted to be. And if it didn't make her a good TV personality, they could send her home. Though, at this point, she was beginning to think she might just make it to the end. God willing.

July 18, 10:03 a.m.
Newport Beach, California
Sam Michaels

He'd lain awake all night, icing his swollen lip, reliving the night, watching again and again as Henry exploded. His rage was like something out of a movie. And finally, his grief and his collapse. It had happened too fast. And been so utterly exhausting.

But each time, Sam's brain found its way back to Cassidy. And like a detective drawn to an unsolvable crime, he desperately wanted to puzzle out the urgency in Cassidy's words. But he couldn't. Without Cassidy to provide the remaining clues, he was helpless.

Today, though, he didn't care if they had a challenge. Or if they were going on *Jimmy Kimmel* or modeling swimwear in front of a live audience. He had to talk to Cassidy.

And figure out what the hell she was hiding.

July 18, 10:35 a.m.
On the 5 Freeway, California
Cassidy McGowan

She wanted to talk to him. She had to explain. But there hadn't been time. They'd been loaded up so quickly. He'd have to understand. And wait.

Only she'd seen his face before he stepped into the dark confines of the guys' van. His normally sleepy eyes were suspicious and imploring. He deserved answers from her. But giving them meant . . . meant what? What *was* their relationship? Did they have one?

The van wasn't moving. Traffic was snarled and messy. Brake lights dotted the gray freeway ahead as the van lurched forward by what felt like inches at a time. She figured from Nisha's persistent checking of her watch that they were late. Still, what did it matter? What would happen if there were no challengers there to complete whatever task the Benefactor had dreamed up today? An image of Henry's slumped shoulders and deadened eyes popped into her head. What *did* it matter?

"Cassidy?"

Allyson's sad eyes met hers. She could be so pretty, if she only tried a little.

"I just want to say thanks," Allyson said softly. Her gaze slid downward, even as her hand found its way to the cross at her neck. "Yesterday. Last night, I mean. I thought it was my mom. I thought he was going to say my mom . . . and you . . . well, thanks."

"Your mom's sick or something?" Cassidy asked.

Allyson nodded, eyes still cast down. "Cancer. Stage four."

"Oh, jeez," Cassidy said and reached for Allyson. "I'm so sorry. That has to suck. Being here and . . ."

Allyson nodded again.

"You're pretty amazing, then," Cassidy said, feeling a swell of sympathy. "I mean, to be doing so well in these challenges while you have to be thinking about her and your family."

She watched Allyson's jaw tighten with emotion. Cassidy looked back out the window. Traffic was loosening up. The challenge was waiting. She leaned her head on the glass. So *many* challenges. For Allyson. For Henry.

For her. Sam. Faith.

How could the Benefactor throw anything at her that was harder than that?

July 18, 11:57 a.m.
Universal Studios, California
Tyrell Young

It was damn hot. The weather had been coolish, but today, walking out from the underground parking garage into the bright sun reflecting off the sizzling pavement, he felt like he was in a toaster oven.

He stood with Allyson, Sam, and Cassidy in front of a ten-foot-tall waterfall that proclaimed the entrance to Universal Studios Hollywood. Steps on both sides of it led to a long walkway lined with restaurants and stores, where gobs of people were already chillin'. The area around the fountain had been cleared of people—probably to film the intro to this challenge, but since they weren't actually doing that, he had to figure they were waiting on something or someone. Probably Molly.

He edged closer to Allyson.

"Yo," he said, hoping he sounded friendly-ish.

She sidestepped away from him and reached for her cross, as if she thought he might bite. So much for friendly.

"So, look," he said, keeping his voice low. "The two love-birds over there are no doubt going to team up on this. You and me, we could do this challenge. You know, work together, maybe."

He glanced around to see if anyone was eavesdropping. Of course, there was a cameraman. But Cassidy and Sam seemed to be deep in a heated conversation of their own. Scheming probably. Or picking the name of their first kid.

Allyson checked them out, too. Then, she zeroed back in on him.

"We don't even know what we have to do yet."

"Understood," Tyrell answered. "I'm just saying that if we can, you know, benefit each other, I think we should. We could make it into the final two, you and me, if we play our cards right."

Allyson gave him a once-over. He suddenly wished he'd worn his own necklace—the one with the heavy gold cross his dad had given him a few Christmases back.

"Just think about it, okay?" he said. "Pray about it. God works in mysterious ways, Shorty, and maybe He's got a plan for you and me, you know?"

Tyrell turned away in time to watch Molly trip down the steps in some flashy-ass yellow heels. He swiped at the sweat on his forehead. He was glad Molly had finally decided to show up and they could start this thing already. Allyson or not, he didn't plan to come in last place again.

July 18, 12:06 p.m.
Universal Studios, California
Allyson Murphy

She wouldn't align with him. His eyes . . . his eyes gave him away. Her dad had always told her that a person with nothing to hide will show you their soul. Tyrell blinked. A lot. And he slid his gaze sideways when he talked to her. He couldn't be trusted.

Still, the idea of doing another challenge alone terrified her. And he was right: Cassidy and Sam were clearly an unbreakable pair. They'd grown closer in the last few days, laughing in that intimate way people do when they're learning to trust each other, leaning closer when they talked.

Molly was being fitted quickly for her mike, and the cameras were circling anxiously. A crowd of people was gathering in a wide circle around them. But unlike before, they weren't quiet. Since the first episode had aired last week, people were calling out their names. As if they knew them. As if they already had this connection somehow.

"Sam! Sam! I hope you win!" yelled a tall girl in a tank top and miniskirt, waving from behind the taped barrier.

"Allyson! You don't deserve to be here! You and Mei were helped."

Allyson's head swung around. The woman was maybe forty or fifty with bleached-blond hair and cherry red lips. Her hands rested on a stroller. When her eyes met Allyson's, she glared and called her an ugly name. Allyson turned away and dropped her chin, fighting the tears.

The warmth of the hand on her shoulder made her jump.

"She's a loser," Tyrell whispered in her ear. "Don't let her get to you. She doesn't even know how to spell 'scholarship.'"

A weak laugh bubbled up her throat.

"Could be worse," he added. "Somebody just asked me where my hot Asian partner was. And"—he winked—"it was a guy."

She laughed harder now. All around them, the crowd was calling out to them. Some were asking for autographs. Others were shouting their support, while one or two were deliberately mean and antagonistic. Tyrell was right; she couldn't let them get to her.

Molly rushed toward them, smoothing her hair, even as a makeup artist ran alongside, brushing powder on her flushed cheeks. Then he scuttled off, and the cameras all clicked on.

"Welcome, competitors!" Molly said, flashing her too-broad smile. "My condolences on the loss of your teammate, Henry. Rest assured that the Benefactor has reunited him with his family and is making certain that they are all being allowed to grieve in private."

Allyson could feel the discomfort at the mention of Henry's name. Was he really being left alone? She hoped so.

"But, of course, our game must continue. And your next challenge starts now."

Molly paused and let her eyes sweep over the four of them and the gathered crowd.

"We've brought you to the famed Universal Studios Hollywood, one of the oldest studios still in use. It's often been billed as 'The Entertainment Capital of L.A.' In the summer, some call it 'The Coolest Place in L.A.,' though on a scorching day like today, I think we could argue with that."

Polite laughter rippled through the crowd.

"Tours first started here in 1915, allowing the public to see all the action of a working Hollywood studio for just a nickel. Even today, visitors can travel through the back lots and get a glimpse of dressing rooms and actual production. Sometimes visitors get lucky and spot a real-live star."

Molly dramatically tossed her perfectly styled head of blond hair.

"The Benefactor suspects you'll need far more than *luck* to succeed in today's challenge. You'll need resourcefulness, persistence, and audacity."

Allyson's pulse quickened.

"The actual task, like most tasks have been so far, is quite simple. Take a picture with a cast member of *Saturday Night Live,* many of whom live or work right here in L.A. That's all.

Track down an *SNL* cast member—past *or* present, though it must be a true cast member and not just a host or guest star—and convince them to snap a photo with you. You'll be given a phone and an envelope with a credit card and some cash. When you find your celebrity, you'll text that picture—with both of you in it—to a number provided by the Benefactor, and then your challenge is complete. The two of you who take the longest to complete this task will be up for Elimination."

Panic began cascading in waves throughout Allyson's body. This was everything she wasn't good at. Networking. Convincing other people to do something. Pretending to be socially confident and poised.

Maybe having Tyrell as a teammate wasn't such a bad idea. He'd been kind to her. How big of a jerk could he be? And even if he was a jerk, at least she wouldn't be alone.

"Oh," Molly said, tilting her head and putting one finger to her lips. "One last thing. You must do this task by yourself. No helping each other out on this one."

Allyson's skin prickled cold, even though the temperature outside was roasting.

"And the Benefactor would like to leave you with this advice, advice he was quoted as saying in a recent article in *Wired* magazine: *Don't assume a closed door is a locked door; even a locked door has a key to it somewhere.*" She lifted her arm and swept it outward. "And with that . . . good luck!"

The surrounding crowd erupted in cheers, but Allyson felt rooted to the ground, paralyzed. Cassidy grabbed her phone from the producer and began climbing the stairs purposefully, like she knew exactly where to find a television star. Sam had his new phone out and was scrolling through it, his thumbs frantic on the keyboard. And Tyrell jogged off, his phone already tucked in his back pocket, his credit card out and waving at a nearby taxi.

They all had plans. They all had resourcefulness, persistence, and audacity.

She looked over at the blond woman with the stroller. There was something smug in her expression. Allyson reached for the phone and envelope that was being handed to her.

Dear God, she began, *I might need a little more help . . .*

July 18, 12:34 p.m.
Near Universal Studios, California
Sam Michaels

He had to think. Or make a list. This challenge was everything he kicked ass at, if he could only get his head in the game. *Saturday Night Live* . . . who the hell was even on that show? Why could he not come up with a single name? Not one.

He knew why. He had a name branded in his brain already.

Cassidy. She'd sidestepped him at the challenge. Evaded his eyes and his questions and made light of what she'd said last night. Mumbled something about skeletons in her closet, but they all had skeletons, right? And then she'd giggled. Her annoying, insincere, squeaky high giggle.

She was lying. And though he'd only known her for a week, it pierced his heart as if they'd been best friends or . . . maybe more than that. He'd thought that she trusted him, that he was different from all the guys she flirted with. That giggle, that smile, those bronzed legs and suggestive, sultry poses were her defense. But he'd broken through them to the real Cassidy. Hadn't he?

Saturday Night Live . . . Come on, Sam. Will Farrell? Wasn't he on SNL *at one point?* Sam stopped walking, realizing that he'd been wandering aimlessly away from Universal Studios. He shaded his eyes and looked around. Near the bend of the road he was on, he could see a tall Sheraton Hotel. Perfect. He could get out of the heat and use the lobby to collect his thoughts and formulate a plan.

He needed to stay focused. No way could he lose today. And no way could he let his feelings for Cassidy McGowan become a factor.

Even as he suspected they were becoming just that.

July 18, 12:45 p.m.
Universal Studios, California
Cassidy McGowan

She loved *Saturday Night Live.* When she'd had to get up on those late nights to feed Faith, or take care of her when she was sick, it was a perfect way to pass the time.

She had to tell Sam about Faith. And she planned to. But it seemed like right before a challenge, when they both needed to focus, was bad timing. So she'd bailed out. But she hadn't missed the hurt look in his eyes. She wanted to get it off her chest, wanted to have him tell her it was all going to be okay. But she also knew that he could hear this news and run.

Which pierced her heart like a dagger.

There was just something about Sam that made her feel like trying harder, doing better, *being* better.

A yellow cab waited in the driveway ahead. She'd called for it as soon as Molly had set them loose. She read *People* magazine. She knew where the stars hung out. It was just a matter of being there when one of them showed up.

Quickly, she jogged over and slid into the backseat. Her cameraman slid in next to her.

"The Ivy, please," she said to the driver, "in Beverly Hills."

His eyes met hers in the rearview mirror as he put the car in gear and then eased into traffic.

"You're meeting an agent or casting director, no?" he asked pleasantly.

Her laughter filled the small car. "No, but thank you for thinking so. I'm hoping I have a date with a well-known actor. And"—she winked at him—"if all goes well, I'll be back on the beach in just a few hours."

July 18, 1:03 p.m.
On the 101 Freeway South, California
Tyrell Young

This was a risky move, but he didn't have a whole lot of other options. He'd made some calls almost immediately. Yes, there was a show tonight. Yes, he could score a ticket for him and his faithful cameraman buddy. Yes, Kevin Nealon was the leading stand-up act.

The show didn't start till eight p.m., which meant he had a lot of time to kill. But he was headed to The Laugh Factory now. Since he was putting all of his eggs in one basket, he better make sure that basket was as freakin' sturdy as they come. He planned to find the back entrance to this place and bribe a guard to let him hang there until Nealon showed up. Then he was gonna have to talk his ass off and get himself a picture.

Maybe the others were working something faster. Maybe he was gonna be screwed. Maybe he was gonna have to rush the stage during Nealon's monologue and snap one of them selfies, those reverse photos that Shaina did with her friends and then posted on Instagram all the time.

He was praying that Nealon wasn't sick. He was praying that the guard on the premises saw his cameraman BFF and gave him a free pass to hang out by the stage access door. He was praying that this Nealon guy had a big heart when it came to high school kids wanting to go to college.

And he was praying that Cassidy, Sam, and Allyson had ideas just as lousy as his. If not, he was going home. Tonight.

July 18, 1:45 p.m.
Universal Studios, California
Allyson Murphy

She was wandering around the outdoor mall outside Universal Studios. The walkway was crowded with tourists and shoppers, all basking in the southern California sun. Some part of her brain registered the second glances that she and her cameraman were getting. But mostly she was just trying hard, so hard, to think of how to complete this task.

She didn't have Mei to help stem the tide of panic that enveloped her at the thought of approaching strangers for help. She didn't have the Lydles gathering people outside the Pantages Theater, little Isaac rallying the masses. She didn't have her dad's voice guiding her through the bike challenge.

This was . . . and had to be . . . all her. It was time to step up to the plate.

She'd never watched *Saturday Night Live.* She knew what it was—kind of—and had heard kids at school quote from it or reenact what they'd thought was a funny skit from the weekend's episode. But it wasn't something her conservative family watched. So it wasn't on Allyson's radar screen.

So how was she supposed to find a cast member from a show she'd never seen? In a city of something like three million people? With a phone and a credit card?

She sank into an empty metal chair outside of a Coffee Bean, noting that people at tables nearby stopped their conversations to turn and stare at her. Cassidy would have winked and waved or said hello. But she wasn't Cassidy, so she pulled out her newly acquired phone and pretended to be texting.

Pretended to have a clue how she was going to do this.

Prayed that the answers might come to her.

Prayed that she would somehow magically find a famous actor.

Prayed that someone would come up and ask if she needed help.

But no one did.

She took a deep breath. She had to find an actor. How would you contact an actor? She was pretty sure that you couldn't just look up their address on the Internet, but it was worth a try. Quickly, she opened a browser, and typed in "Saturday Night Live cast." Wikipedia listed nearly a hundred names. She scrolled through until she spotted one that she at least recognized. Amy Poehler. She and her sister had once watched *Parks and Recreation* in a hotel room in Denver when their mom was going through chemo.

Swallowing, she searched Amy Poehler and found that, sure enough, her address did not pop up. But apparently, she had an agent. And her agent's address and phone number *did* come up.

In her heart, she knew that she was going to lose this challenge. Deep down, something told her that she had gone as far as she could. But she also knew that God had led her this far. And letting Him down was not an option. She would get to this address. She would explain, as honestly as she knew how, what she was doing, why it was important. And if someone listened to her, then she would know God still had plans for her in this contest. And if not . . . well, she wouldn't think about that yet.

She rose slowly from her chair.

"Allyson?"

She closed her eyes. Her back tensed. It was another woman who would tell her that she was undeserving. Another person who would explode the doubts that seemed to hover around her like a neon sign.

"Hey, Allyson," the woman said to Allyson's back, "keep the faith, girl. My daughter and I are rooting for you."

Allyson let those words echo in her ears as she hailed a cab and gave him an address to a talent agency in Beverly Hills.

July 18, 4:50 p.m.
Beverly Hills, California
Cassidy McGowan

She'd had a lovely lunch. The maître d' had graciously seated her at a darling outside table on a large patio encircled by a white picket fence. Under the shade of a white umbrella, she'd dined on a wild Maine lobster risotto in a pinkish sauce that had been buttery and too delish for words. Sure, the other diners kept throwing her skeptical looks—a young teen dining alone yet being constantly filmed. But she'd smiled her you-just-wish-you-were-me smile, and kept her eyes peeled for a familiar face. Any familiar face.

But three hours, four glasses of iced tea, and two desserts later, the lunch crowd was gone, her server was losing patience with her, and she was beginning to think that maybe celebrities didn't hang out at The Ivy except on weekends or something.

She flipped her credit card into the padded folder that contained the bill and took another sip of tea.

"Excuse me, miss?"

She looked up at a tall, well-dressed man towering over her.

"I couldn't help but notice . . ." He gestured at the camera and then the empty seat at her table. "You were waiting for someone who didn't show?"

Cassidy set down her glass and smiled warmly. "No, nothing like that. I'm actually on a reality show. " She laughed lightly as the man's expression changed to surprise and then intrigue. "I'm a high school senior trying to win a scholarship to college."

He stuck his hands in his pants pockets. Cassidy noticed that his suit was perfectly tailored and that he wore a very expensive watch, a Rolex, maybe. Whoever he was, he had money.

"Interesting." He nodded appreciatively. "I would assume then that you have to do challenges or something like that?"

She glanced toward her cameraman. "That's what I'm doing right now." She laughed lightly again. "I have to locate a cast member from *Saturday Night Live.* I guess I rather stupidly thought I'd stake out a place like this and manage to run into one." She shrugged. "Not the first time I've made a wrong turn in this game." Her laughter this time had a bitter twinge to it.

The man contemplated her for a moment. Then he slowly pulled out the chair across from her and lowered himself into it. Cassidy swallowed and glanced around. The patio was nearly empty now.

"I know who you are, Cassidy McGowan from Chicago," he said, his tone low but not threatening. Still, her heartbeat quickened. "I watched Wednesday's episode and frankly, I was surprised to learn you were still in this competition." She winced. "Then I did my homework."

He leaned forward and laced his hands together on the small table.

"Across the street, right now, is a legion of paparazzi," he said. "As soon as we conclude our discussion and you pay your bill, go ask any one of them where to find Jay Mohr or Julia Louis-Dreyfus. And for the right price and one of your gorgeous smiles, they'll steer you in the direction you need to go."

Cassidy let her eyes trail to where he was indicating. Sure enough, there were at least three guys lounging near parked cars with huge black cameras dangling from their necks. One smoked a cigarette. The other two pecked away at their cell phones.

"But," the man said, tapping a perfectly manicured finger on the table in front of her, "listen to me, first. Your desire to get a college education is admirable. I'm sure your parents are proud."

Cassidy had to hold back her snort.

"But you have something that we don't see often, Ms. McGowan," he said, his eyes zeroing in on hers so that she dared not look away. "Some call what you possess the 'it' factor. Some call it 'presence.' Others would simply say the camera loves you. Because, my dear, it very much does."

He reached into the front pocket of his suit coat and pulled out a small card. Deliberately, he placed it square in front of her so she could read it without moving.

Alex Ginsberg. Casting. 310-555-7832

Cassidy's palms were damp as she reached for the card.

"I don't know what to . . ." she whispered, trying to think, trying to stay calm.

Alex Ginsberg smiled, a big and broad and knowing smile. "There's a movie. Several, in fact. Obviously, we need to know if you can act, but I have this suspicion that's what you've been doing your whole life. Give it some thought, Cassidy McGowan. From Chicago."

He stood gracefully, his chair gliding backward as if it knew it should. He tipped his head toward the photographers.

"They'll help you out. But Robert Downey Jr. lives in Malibu. And I'd be surprised if he wasn't out on the beach on a hot day like this."

He winked at her and walked off.

Cassidy felt the sharp edges of that tiny little card in her hand. *There's a movie . . .*

Fireworks were exploding in her chest. She couldn't wait to tell Sam.

July 18, 7:01 p.m.
Beverly Hills, California
Allyson Murphy

She'd never seen so much white. The marble on the stairs was white. The leather couches were white. The ceiling was white. The floor was a glossy white. Perched on the edge of the couch, she felt glaringly out of place—sweat-crusted and plain and contaminating somehow.

The fact that she'd made it this far was nothing short of a miracle.

She'd called the agency nearly three hours ago. After telling her story to no less than a dozen different people, she'd finally been put through to an agent. The woman had been exceedingly kind, but could not guarantee that Ms. Poehler would be available since she was currently filming her TV series and therefore quite busy.

Allyson had listened politely and volunteered to go to wherever Ms. Poehler was.

"It'll take just a second," she pleaded. "I understand that she is extremely busy and this is an imposition, but . . ."—Allyson gulped—"this is for a college scholarship and my. . ."

She paused. She couldn't do it. She couldn't play the sick mom card.

"It's just really important to me. And my future," she finished lamely.

The agent had sighed. A deep and resigned sigh. But somehow she'd agreed to let Allyson meet her at the agency at seven that evening, where she would then escort her to CBS Studios in Studio City and get her into the back lot just long enough to let Allyson snap a picture.

At two minutes past seven, a woman with a mass of straight black hair and piercing blue eyes click-clacked her way across the white-tiled floor toward Allyson. Nervously, Allyson popped to her feet.

"You're Allyson Murphy?" asked the agent, extending her hand and smiling pleasantly.

"Yes," Allyson answered. "I can't thank you enough for meeting with me."

The agent tipped her head and gave her a once-over. "Well, kiddo," she said, "I've had folks call and pretend to be reporters. I've had people try to sneak in to see my clients. I've had paparazzi stake themselves outside just about every place imaginable. It's rare you get someone who comes along and simply tells you the truth."

Allyson instinctively reached for her cross.

"I can't guarantee that Ms. Poehler hasn't left for the day," the agent said. "But let's see what we can do." She winked. "I'm sure we can find *somebody* who's been on *SNL* who's willing to take a picture with you."

As she followed the agent out of the office, she fervently prayed that the woman was right.

July 18, 7:03 p.m.
Beverly Hills, California
Sam Michaels

Maybe she had a boyfriend? But then why wouldn't she just tell him that? Maybe she'd been in rehab or something? Jeez, if that was it, she could relax. Beer and weed were to him what pizza and soda were to a lot of other kids. They were his Friday-night friends. His reward for a test well done. Hell, they helped him relax enough to study for the damn test!

She didn't seem like a drugs-and-alcohol kind of girl, though.

So what the hell was she hiding?

He stepped off the golf cart as it rolled to a stop. He turned back to the security guard and held out a hand.

"Thanks, man," he said. "I'll make this quick."

The young Hispanic security guard hunched over the steering wheel. "Take your time, bro. Get a good one."

Sam smiled and sauntered toward the steel door he'd been told to use, his cameraman trailing behind.

The Internet was a vast and wonderful tool. A little over three hours ago, he'd found a plush chair in the Sheraton, ordered some sodas for himself and his camera guy, and started searching. *SNL* cast members. *SNL* cast members that lived in L.A. Agents of those cast members. Publicity agents. He'd started cold calling. Tweeting. Pulling up websites and typing out random e-mails. Concocting a story. He was the producer of a small radio show for teens and he was doing a piece on favorite comedians of the past year. Would so-and-so be available for a quick interview and photo?

He hit roadblocks. Closed doors. But then about an hour ago, he'd called the agent who represented Adam Sandler. And instead of his usual story, he'd gone for the truth. He was a kid on a quest for a scholarship. And he just needed a picture to make it one more round.

Sandler's publicist bit.

"Let me make some calls," she said. "You got something to verify what you're telling me?"

He had his cameraman plus the number that the Benefactor had given them to text the photo to. He gave her the number. It must have checked out because she called back twenty minutes later.

"Mr. Sandler is filming at Fox right now, but said he'd do a quick picture with you," she said.

He got an address and instructions, and he and his cameraman loaded into a taxi and headed toward Pico Boulevard in Century City.

Within minutes, if all went well, he'd be shoulder to shoulder with Adam Sandler while someone else snapped a photo from his phone. And then, Sam would be hitting send a minute later.

What the hell was she hiding?

July 18, 7:06 p.m.
Malibu, California
Cassidy McGowan

The beach here was stunning. The sand was pristine and soft, the waves gentle and caressing. She almost didn't care that she'd just met a famous movie star. Who'd taken not only one picture with her, but a whole slew, vamping it up as if they were long-lost friends. He'd had his little boy with him, a pudgy kid who waddled along on the sand like a penguin. Cassidy couldn't help but drop to her knees when she'd seen that sweet boy. Seeing him made her think of Faith, with her sausage-like toes and rosebud lips. Within minutes, Cassidy had his small hand in hers and they were chasing waves, running back and forth as the froth of the sea nipped at their bare heels.

And sometime, in between the sea chasing and sandcastle building, she got her pictures. She selected one to send to the Benefactor. And thanked Mr. Downey for a wonderful afternoon.

But as she loaded herself back into a taxi, brushing the sand from her legs and feet, relishing the cool air inside the cab, she knew the game had changed for her. Maybe more than the game.

From her back pocket, she pulled the business card.

Alex Ginsberg.

On the cab ride over, she'd checked the number on her phone. Checked out his name. He was legit.

There's a movie . . .

She smiled and leaned her head back against the black leather seat.

July 18, 7:09 p.m.
Hollywood, California
Tyrell Young

Damn. He was a genius. A freakin' genius! No way had he thought this would work. Bribe a security guard and then basically play stalker until Nealon showed up—it was genius in its simplicity.

And it had freakin' worked.

The Laugh Factory sat on the corner of Sunset and Laurel in Hollywood. It was a pale brown, stone building plastered with advertisements for upcoming acts. Tyrell had worked his way around to the back, which had been surprisingly small and easy to access. Two unmarked doors. A minuscule parking lot. One bored security guard patrolling. Tyrell had offered him fifty bucks, and the guy had jumped, spilling his guts about when Nealon usually got there, what kind of car he drove, and how best to make his move. Plus, he'd seemed kind of giddy to be on camera, which Tyrell played up as much as possible.

An hour before showtime, just like his security guard pal had said, Nealon pulled up. In jeans and a T-shirt, he stepped from his car and walked toward the back entrance, lifting a friendly hand to the guard. That's when Tyrell had sauntered over, pled his case, and gotten his picture.

Almost too easy.

He was a genius.

Now he was top three, baby. He folded himself into the backseat of the taxi and gave his Newport Beach address. Up until this point, he hadn't allowed himself to think of colleges. Hadn't wanted to get his hopes up. But suddenly, he realized that he could win this thing. He could actually win this thing.

He'd look good in an LSU sweatshirt. Really damn good.

July 18, 8:02 p.m.
Newport Beach, California
Sam Michaels

He'd been watching, his left leg jiggling like crazy. Not to see who came home first, who might have won or lost. There was no way to tell, really. Pictures might have been sent hours ago. Or not at all.

The taxi's headlights pulled up to the condo next door, and his chest felt full, even as his stomach dropped low. He couldn't shake the uneasiness. He stood up from the porch where he'd been sitting in the waning light. He wanted her to see him. And he wanted to see her.

He took a deep breath.

"Cassidy!"

She turned, her eyes brightening. She handed the cab driver some money and made a beeline for him. His pulse took off.

She unlatched the gate to the small patio on this side of the house, the non-beach side. Sandwiched between garages, it was tiny—barely room for two Adirondack chairs. She fell back into the one next to him.

"You finished?" he asked, drinking her in. There was a change in her face; something different. He couldn't put his finger on it. Like she was calmer, maybe.

She nodded, letting her head fall back onto the chair and closing her eyes. "Yep. You?"

He leaned forward and rested his elbows on his knees. Now he was sure of it. Something was off. She should have been eagerly rehashing the details with him, wanting his affirmation that she'd done well. She would have been hopeful and encouraging as she'd asked him about his own challenge.

"Yes," he said, guarded. "Got it done."

A smile played around her lips and she sighed contentedly. *What the hell?* They didn't even know where they stacked up against Allyson and Tyrell. One of them could be going home. And yet, she seemed . . . unconcerned.

"Cassidy?"

She opened her eyes and turned slowly to face him.

"What's going on?"

He knew they weren't a couple, really. A lot of flirting. Hours of talking and laughing. But he felt something when he was with her. And he had to believe she felt it, too.

So he reached out and took her hand in his. Molded her fingers so they were just the right fit. Then he slid forward in his chair and pulled her toward him. He saw her surprised look. And he didn't care. He'd wanted to do this for days. And, dammit, if he was going home, he was going to know how it felt to kiss her.

Her lips were salty and dry but soft. The minute they touched his, it was like he was weightless. The world slid away and he didn't give a damn if it ever came back.

Until he felt her hand on his chest. Lightly pushing him away.

"Sam."

No. Whatever she had to say, it could wait. He grabbed her hand. And squeezed it.

"Not now," he said, his voice scratchy and rough. "Just let this be, Cass."

She dropped her chin and shook her head.

"I can't." Her voice caught.

Her tear-stained face was enough to bring him to his knees. He stood and pulled her up with him. She fit so well under his chin, in that place where his chest and shoulder met. Her body shook gently.

"Hey," he said. "It's gonna be all right."

With a shaky breath, she pulled herself from his grasp and stepped back.

"Sam," she said. "That thing I've needed to tell you?" She glanced around. There was, of course, a cameraman a discreet distance away filming everything.

Cassidy stuck her hand in her back pocket and removed a small card, a business card. She fingered it for a few minutes. Then she raised her eyes to his, and in that single heartbeat, he saw her indecision, her hope, but most of all, her apology.

Without a word, she turned away from him and was gone.

EPISODE 5
THE CONFRONTATION

"[I]t is a characteristic of wisdom not to do desperate things."

—Henry David Thoreau, Walden, *1906*

July 18, 8:12 p.m.
Newport Beach, California
Sam Michaels

He watched Cassidy leave. With something that felt like a bike chain wrapped around his heart, he watched her unlatch the gate leading out of the side patio and disappear around the corner to her condo. She never looked back at him.

He let his forehead fall into his hands.

How could he have been so stupid? Impulsive. He'd gotten nervous. Afraid that he would lose that last challenge. Worried that his picture was texted through last.

He'd only wanted to kiss her, to know if . . . if she felt it, too. And now he'd screwed up everything.

He heard the light *clink* of the gate unlatching again. He allowed himself to look, allowed hope to bubble up. It was the camera guy, still filming.

"You okay, Sam?" he asked as he moved into the chair next to him, the chair Cassidy had just been sitting in.

Sam dropped his head again. "Fine," he mumbled.

"Tough break, kid," the guy said.

Sam snorted.

"She get a better offer?"

Sam let those words register before he raised his head again. "What are you talking about?" He looked past the camera at the guy behind it. It was one of his favorite camera operators. An older guy the contestants had nicknamed Bandana because he always wore one tied around his head. While some of the people assigned to film them seemed to think it was okay to get right up in their business—screw personal space or common courtesy—Bandana kept a respectful distance. And he talked to the kids the way maybe a coach or a hard-edged uncle would.

"The card she was holding," Bandana said. "Come on, you saw it, right?"

He had. Of course he had. She'd pulled a tiny business card from her back pocket, and then she'd bolted. For some reason, though, he hadn't given much thought to the card, just to the bolting.

Sam sat up. "You think she met another guy?"

Bandana shrugged, kept his camera running. "It's possible. She's a good-looking kid. But she's done nothing but smile and make eyes at you for the past week. You think a meet-and-greet during a challenge is going to erase all that?"

Sam rubbed his eyes. "What if it was the actor she met? The *SNL* star? I can't compete with that," he said.

"Nope, son, you can't." Bandana shrugged again.

"Gee," Sam said, throwing Bandana what he hoped was a scathing look, "not cut out for pep talks, are you?"

Bandana laughed. "Look, maybe she met someone today and he swept her off her Converse. But I saw her reaction when she kissed you, kid. She was into it. Until she wasn't.

Something's going on. Something to do with that little card. And I don't think it's another guy."

Sam fell back into the Adirondack chair, his brain jumbled and his body feeling like a beach ball with all the air sucked out. His instincts told him to move on, leave Cassidy alone. She was hiding stuff—lots of stuff—and getting involved with her would not only screw up his chance of winning this thing (if he was still even in it), but potentially leave him with a broken heart.

So why did he want to run after her? Demand that she tell him what the hell was going on? And figure out some way to prove to her that she could trust him? That they could do this thing . . . together.

"You want my advice?" Bandana said, switching off the camera and laying it in his lap.

Sam was surprised. In almost ten days of this competition, he'd never seen a cameraman do that unless the day was over and he was packing to go home.

"I know she's got a lot going on, Sam," Bandana said. "But she's a sweet kid. And you guys make a good team. Go—go track her down and grab those lovely shoulders of hers and don't let her walk away again until you get the full story." He picked up his camera and stood.

"I been doing this job a long time. And I've filmed a shitload of people who wouldn't know something good if it grabbed 'em by the ass. They walk around like they're entitled to happy, happy, joy, joy—but they don't want to do the work to get there. Do the work, Sam. Talk to the girl. And don't tell anybody we had this conversation without my little friend here documenting it, okay?" He gestured at the camera in his hand, dark and unblinking, and then padded out quietly.

Sam stood. Bandana was right. It was time to lay everything out there.

In his pocket, the cell phone—the one given to him by the Benefactor to complete the last challenge—buzzed. He pulled it out and read the incoming text: *Pls report to your condo common room. The next Elimination starts ASAP.*

Elimination. If he had to report, he must be in the bottom two.

Dammit. He looked up at the girls' condo next door. Wild desperation tore through him. He had to talk to her before he was sent home.

And that's when he made his decision.

July 18, 8:24 p.m.
Newport Beach, California
Cassidy McGowan

Her chest felt hollow. The tears were relentless.

She'd left him sitting there. She'd held her body nail-file straight and bit down hard on the pain in her throat long enough to make it around the corner of her condo, out of Sam's sight, before she lost it. Then she'd collapsed, bending forward, managing somehow to half-run, half-stagger past Nisha, with her noticeably raised eyebrow, up the stairs to the sanctity of her room where she'd flung herself on her bed and wondered what the hell she was doing.

There's a movie . . .

Was there really? Alex Ginsberg *was* a casting director. But could she believe him? Was she being gullible, naïve Cassidy from the Midwest who had great legs but no sense of how the world really worked?

Just let this be, Cass.

Sam had kissed her—such a sweet and pure and right thing—and said those words, and she'd known, she'd *known,* that she couldn't do it. She couldn't let him think she was who he wanted her to be. She had to tell him about Faith. But she couldn't. Not with the cameras rolling. Not with Alex Ginsberg watching.

So she'd pushed him away and bolted. But not before she saw his confusion and helplessness.

She curled up tighter on her bed as another wave of guilt and remorse crashed through her. There was no way to tell him without a camera around. And there was no way to tell him *with* a camera around. She had no choice but to break it off—whatever *it* was. Maybe they could figure something out after the competition. Or after she found out if this thing with Alex Ginsberg was legit. She could tell Sam the truth then—tell them *all* the truth—and see if he still cared.

Until then, she had to keep her options open. Fight to stay alive in this game. Put her best smile on for the camera so that Alex Ginsberg liked what he saw. She couldn't let her feelings for Sam screw this up. She had a little girl back home who was counting on her. And frankly, she had a future herself—a future that might not be as bleak as it once looked.

The cell phone in her pocket vibrated. She pulled it out and swiped at her bleary eyes to read the text.

An Elimination. Tonight. Which meant she was in the bottom two. Again.

She closed her eyes. She'd thought she'd done so well on this one. Tired and resigned, she pulled herself from the bed and did her best to clean up her appearance so she'd look good on camera. That, suddenly, was as important as ever.

With one last look around her room, she got ready to plaster on a smile. Then she opened the door of her bedroom.

And gasped to see Sam standing there.

"Sam?" she breathed, stepping backward. "What are you doing?" Her eyes darted behind him to the empty hallway. No cameras in sight.

Gently, he took her hand and steered her into her room, closing the door behind him.

"No!" Cassidy said, pulling her hand from his, even as she noted the warmth of his fingers. "You can't be in here . . . the Benefactor . . . Sam . . ."

Calmly, he leaned against her door and let his eyes take her in.

With a deep breath, he said simply, "Cassidy, we have to talk. Now."

July 18, 8:30 p.m.
Newport Beach, California
Allyson Murphy

She'd done it. For the first time, she'd conquered a challenge by herself. Sure, meeting the cast members of *Parks and Recreation* had been crazy and fun. But, mostly, she'd just felt satisfaction that she'd finished the thing without having to rely on anyone else. Not a single other person.

But the text. An Elimination. When she was just starting to believe that she was meant to be here, that she might have a shot at winning.

Who would she have to go up against? Sam? No way could she beat him. He was too confident, too eloquent, too sure of everything he said and did. She'd crumble. Tyrell? He would claw at her, unafraid to draw blood if it meant staying in the game. Cassidy? She'd been in Eliminations before. She knew how they worked. And how to talk her way out of them.

Allyson fingered her cross.

Dear God . . .

She stopped. What? What should she pray for? Guidance? Wisdom? Words? He'd gotten her this far. He'd opened doors, sent angels to help her when she needed them, provided direction when she was lost. No, it was time for *her* to step up to the plate.

Dear God . . . thanks for getting me this far.

She flipped off the light in her room and made her way down the stairs.

July 18, 8:31 p.m.
Newport Beach, California
Tyrell Young

He was sitting *alone* in this damn common room in his condo. Unless Sam showed up soon, this had to mean that ass-wipe made it through again.

His legs bounced and he glanced around the room uncomfortably. The TV screen remained blank, but there were cameras—three of them, waiting for the fireworks to begin. Eliminations were good stuff; he could just see all them producers gathered around editing machines and small screens, pointing to him and whoever else was gonna be in this Elimination. Hoping for yelling. Or tears. Or pleading.

Not this time. He wasn't gonna do any of that shit. He was gonna tell 'em what he did and why he did it. He'd say he had a plan, he executed it, and if it put him in the bottom, well, then, so be it. He'd tried. He'd keep trying. He'd go down trying. But he wasn't gonna sell anyone out like last time. Like Hiroshi.

Colin came down the stairs, his eyes taking in the room. "No Sam, huh?" he asked.

Tyrell shrugged. It was obvious he wasn't there.

“He’s not in his room, either,” Colin said.

“He s’posed to be here?” Tyrell asked. Maybe there was hope.

“Message I got said all you mates were,” Colin said.

Tyrell tilted his chin sideways. “Girls, too?”

Colin shrugged. “Dunno. Think so.”

The night ahead just got more interesting.

Colin headed toward the door that led to the front patio and the ocean.

Where the hell was Sam?

July 18, 8:33 p.m.
Newport Beach, California
Sam Michaels

“Cassidy,” he said. “We have to talk. Now.”

Panic exploded on her face. “But the Elimination,” she whispered. “And you can’t be here.”

“They’ll wait a second,” he said, taking a step toward her. He took both her hands again and gripped them tightly.

“Hear me on this, Cassidy McGowan,” Sam said, his eyes seeking hers. There was an urgency in his words. An intensity.

“I came here to escape from a life where I was invisible. Where I slid between the cracks of a society that wasn’t sure what to make of me or what to do with me. From a family who’d abandoned me years ago. I came to win a scholarship so I could play music for the rest of my life and maybe get paid doing it."

He chuckled, looking at her beautiful hands in his.

"I've spent my whole life drifting. Yeah, corny, right? Like a country song or something. But that's what I've been doing. Drifting. Without ever really latching onto anything because, what if that thing I got close to suddenly left?"

He felt those last words catch in his throat, but he forced himself to push on. He didn't have much time.

"And you know what? It sucks. When you drift through life, you miss getting to know what it's like to savor someone's smile. To learn the texture of someone's skin on yours. To feel lighter, or maybe happier, just because another person has walked into the room."

He saw the corner of Cassidy's mouth tip upward, and it encouraged him.

"I'd like to win this thing. I'd like to learn how to be a better musician and not have to strum my way through life on street corners anymore. But mostly? I'd like to quit drifting. I'd like to find someone who is passionate and hopeful and determined. I think, actually, that I may have found her already."

He searched her face. For something. A sign that she knew and cared and felt the exact same way.

For the longest moment of Sam's life, Cassidy looked back at him without speaking, without blinking. Her eyes never left him; but in them, he could see the emotion tearing at her. She hadn't pulled away, though.

Oh, man, please . . .

"I don't deserve you," she whispered.

A laugh escaped him, and he fought the urge to crush her against him.

Instead he softly said, “I know my charm and good looks can be intimidating, but give me a chance.”

She grinned and dropped her eyes. Then she did pull away.

“Sam,” she said, and now the urgency was hers. “Something happened today.”

A dark stain of dread. Spreading in his abdomen. *Bandana was right . . .*

“I can’t give you all the details now, but . . .” She reached into her back pocket and handed him the same small card from earlier. It was black with simple white lettering.

“Alex Ginsberg?” he asked, reading the card. “A casting director?”

“He said he has a movie for me. He’s seen me on the show, I guess.” She shrugged. “I checked him out. He’s legit, Sam. I mean, I don’t know if *what* he says is, you know, true . . . but he is *who* he says he is.”

It took him a second, and then the pieces fell into place. “He wants you to audition. For a part.”

Again Cassidy shrugged. “I think so.”

There was hopefulness in her eyes. She seemed as if she was trying to squelch it, act matter-of-fact. But he saw it. She wanted this.

“Cassidy!” Sam said, grabbing her hand. “This is terrific. It could be the break you need!”

She half-grinned, kind of rolled her eyes. “It’s not a sure thing.”

He grabbed her shoulders. “Cassidy! He found you. *You!* And gave you his card. Girl! Do this! We’ve talked about how much you love being in front of people. The cameras. Why wouldn't you do this?"

She looked at the door.

"I might," she said. "I mean, I probably will. But I think I should finish out the game first, you know? What if I win? What if I could get a scholarship?"

He scrutinized her face. She'd loved that day, posing for the cameras. Sure, she could go to acting school, but this Alex Ginsberg could probably make that happen, too.

"What if he won't wait, Cassidy?" Sam said. "Do you want to risk that for a competition that's not a sure thing for you?"

Cassidy leveled her gaze at him. "What do you mean 'for you'?"

Sam shook his head. "I didn't mean anything by that. Come on, don't read into it. It's not a sure thing for any of us."

Cassidy stepped backward. Away from him. Toward the door.

"When you described me earlier—at least I think it was me—you said 'passionate' and 'hopeful' and 'determined.' You never said 'bright' or 'intelligent.' Or even 'capable' . . ."

"Cassidy . . ." Sam stepped forward.

She held up her hand. "You don't think I can win this. Do you?"

Sam sighed. "I think you can do what you want. But you *could* have a better shot if you . . . I don't know . . ."

And that's when she reached toward the doorknob.

"You almost had me, Sam," she said softly. "I was almost there. But though I'm a pretty face and 'hopeful,'"—her voice was barely above a whisper—"I *can* win this thing."

And for the second time that night, he watched her leave.

July 18, 8:45 p.m.
Newport Beach, California
Tyrell Young

"You're late, bro," Tyrell muttered when Sam slid onto the couch next to him.

"Bathroom," Sam answered, his eyes going immediately to the screen, where the Benefactor was waiting.

Tyrell didn't buy it. Colin had checked upstairs. If he was using the bathroom, it was in somebody else's condo. He watched Sam's face for a second, but the kid didn't flinch. Tyrell turned his attention to the Benefactor.

"Each of you performed admirably on this challenge. We received pictures from all four of you. And you're all quite photogenic, by the way."

Maybe the girls found that flattering and smiled. He did not.

"But I'm sure you are quite interested to know why all of you have been called down for this Elimination when our previous Eliminations have involved only two contestants, or in one case, three contestants because of a tie."

The Benefactor paused.

"It's actually because we don't need an Elimination tonight."

Tyrell's nerves started buzzing. No Elimination. Was this a good thing?

The Benefactor continued. "The rules of this challenge, specified by Molly, stated that each of you was to pose in a picture with a cast member from *Saturday Night Live.* And that you were not to receive help from another contestant."

His nerves kept buzzing. Something was wrong. Whenever somebody repeated the rules, it was bad news.

"Unfortunately, one of you failed to complete this task as specified. And, because of that, I am forced to disqualify you from this challenge and send you home. Tonight."

Tyrell racked his brain. He was positive Kevin Nealon had been on *SNL.* He'd double-checked, and then the dude had said something about it when they were snapping pics. And Tyrell hadn't worked with anybody on this. Unless the security guard counted. Man, was that it? Was it the security guard?

He glanced over at Sam, whose face was still expressionless. His eyes had their typical hooded look. If he thought he was about to go home, he was hiding it well.

"Tyrell," the Benefactor said. Tyrell gripped the arm of the couch. "We received the picture of you and Kevin Nealon, a cast member on the show from 1986 until 1995, this evening at 7:13 p.m. Congratulations, Tyrell, you will be moving on to the next round of competition."

He released a breath he didn't even know he was holding.

"Sam," the Benefactor went on, his voice deep and steady, his dark figure as still as stone, "we received a photo of you and Adam Sandler, a cast member from 1990 until

1995, at 7:15 p.m. That means that you, too, will be competing in the next round."

Tyrell watched Sam's face for a reaction. Nothing. The guy was as cool as a Popsicle on a summer day.

"Cassidy," the Benefactor said, "the picture of you and Robert Downey Jr., a cast member for only one year, 1985, was our producers' favorite. Congratulations, Cassidy, you will be competing in the next round."

He felt Sam exhale next to him. *Interesting,* Tyrell thought. *Did he care more about her safety than his own?* Something to tuck away for these final rounds.

"That leaves you, Allyson," the Benefactor said, and Tyrell was almost sure he heard their mighty mentor sigh. "You sent us a picture of you and Rob Lowe. Originally, it appeared you intended to get a picture of Amy Poehler, a cast member of *SNL* from 2001 to 2009. However, when you arrived on the set of *Parks and Recreation,* Ms. Poehler had left for the day and her agent convinced you to take a picture with Mr. Lowe instead, telling you that he had been on *Saturday Night Live* many times. She was correct; Rob Lowe has hosted *Saturday Night Live* a number of different times, most recently in 2000. However, he has never been a cast member."

Tyrell shook his head. Tough break.

"Allyson," the Benefactor said, "due to your failure to follow the rules of this task, I must inform you that you are not the top candidate for this scholarship, and I'm sorry but I must reject your application."

The boys' common room had no screen showing them what was going on in the girls' condo, so there was no way to know how Allyson reacted. But Tyrell pictured her fingering her cross, thanking the Benefactor, and then quickly heading for her room, leaving with as little fuss and fanfare as she'd displayed the entire game.

One more down. Allyson was a good kid; he'd even grown to respect her a little. But with her leaving, he was top three. Two more challenges, he figured, and he'd have that scholarship in his hand.

He could already picture his dad saying, *You ran that well. Just like I would have.*

Damn right.

July 19, 8:21 a.m.
Newport Beach, California
Cassidy McGowan

She was hoping makeup would cover all the remnants of yesterday. Too much sun. Too many tears. Too little sleep. But though makeup had saved her before, she wasn't sure it was up to the task this time. Unless there was a concealer out there that could hide her disappointment and mask the slithering uncertainty that kept winding its way into her thoughts. Otherwise, she was sunk.

Her shoulders, rigid from tension and fear, had gone slack with relief when she'd heard her name called last night. But Sam's name had brought an onslaught of conflicting emotions. Of course, she wanted him to do well. She couldn't deny what she felt around him. But if he'd gone home? Life would have gotten easier. Exponentially.

And yet, as she'd dragged herself up the stairs, tossing a mumbled good night to Nisha over her shoulder, she'd felt a small measure of satisfaction. She was the only girl still in the game. She'd outlasted them all—her, a teen mom from the Midwest. Maybe it had been her charm or—what had Sam called it?—her passion or hopefulness, but still . . . she'd done it.

So why, this morning, did she feel so empty? She needed to be on her best game now, the final days of this crazy competition. She needed to pull it together and show Sam and everyone else that she could win. Show Alex Ginsberg that she was sexy *and* smart.

Instead it felt like the first week of volleyball when Coach took no mercy on her team. When her sore muscles protested every movement and regretted an entire summer's laziness. Today, she felt beat. Wrecked. Tired.

She glanced over at the only item she'd placed in the room when she'd moved into it nearly two weeks ago: a framed picture of her and Faith taken earlier this summer. Faith was on her lap at a Cubs game, her pudgy face foamy white from an ice cream cone. Cassidy's heart was heavy from missing that little girl.

She pulled on a tank top, aware on some level that it could use an iron, and grabbed some shorts she'd already worn which had a tiny pinprick of mustard near the cuff. She knew these things, and yet something in her didn't care. She bent toward the mirror, seeing her puffy, pinkish eyes. She should wash her hair, dry it, and curl it. But her arms ached at the thought of blowing it out. She grabbed a band and pulled it back into a ponytail.

Quickly, she applied makeup and glanced once more at the girl in the mirror. *You're a warrior,* she told herself. *Regardless of what Sam thinks or says. You're going to win this competition and then use the scholarship money to learn how to act or model and show the Alex Ginsbergs out there how much you deserve their attention.*

She dropped her eyes from the mirror. What did she deserve anyway? She was lying. Lying to Sam. Lying to the Benefactor and Alex Ginsberg.

Mostly, lying to herself.

July 19, 9:03 a.m.
Malibu, California
The Benefactor

"What the hell are you doing?" he said, trying to keep his voice measured. Trying not to lose it. "You can't crash my reality show and not think I'm going to have something to say about it. You need to back off, Ginsberg."

Alex Ginsberg laughed lightly on the other end of the line. "Nervous that she's going to jump ship, Richard?"

The Benefactor ran a hand through his hair and reached for his pen. Clicked it open. Clicked it closed. Stood up. Paced his way toward the windows showing a blanket of clouds hugging the coastline.

"Well, you certainly gave her a good reason to, didn't you?" He scowled. "Is there even a movie? What kind of bullshit are you feeding her?"

He pressed a palm against the cool window. He wished he could slug the guy. He wanted to slug the guy. He'd never slugged a guy—but it might feel really good.

"Of course there's a movie," Ginsberg answered in that hedging tone the Benefactor had heard oh-so-many times. Maybe there was a movie; maybe there wasn't. But it wouldn't be whatever Cassidy was dreaming it up in her head to be. This guy was a sleaze.

The Benefactor wouldn't let the bastard do this to one of his kids.

One of his kids . . .

God. He let his forehead fall forward to rest on the window. When did it change? When did it become this for him?

He ground his back teeth together. "Look, Ginsberg," he said, fighting for control, "until this show wraps, she's mine, okay? You want to track her down after? Then track her down. But until she's either eliminated or the show wraps, she's mine."

Ginsberg chuckled. "Something going on between you and the blond one, eh? I get it, man. She's hot."

The Benefactor mashed his thumb onto the button that disconnected the call and turned around so he could slam his phone onto his bed.

Damn him. Damn that bastard.

He slid into the recliner that was usually only a spot to throw his bike clothes once he'd pulled them off after a long, tiring ride.

What the hell was going on? This game was getting to him. The kids. Watching Allyson last night—seeing her face crumple when he'd told her she'd failed. But then, watching her struggle to pull it together, to leave that room with dignity, hugging Cassidy, thanking him, fingering her necklace—he'd felt a tugging in his chest. He had to wonder if, after all these years of stomping on people to get where he was, he did, indeed, have a heart.

She'd needed this. Of all of them, Allyson probably needed this the most. He'd relished watching her find her way throughout the competition. And she had. She'd dug deep and discovered some reserve of strength and courage that she probably didn't know existed until this competition had forced her to find it. He'd wanted her to win. Just like he wanted Cassidy and Sam to win. And even Tyrell.

He could do it for them. He could write each of them a check. He had the money. Maybe he couldn't guarantee they'd all get into the schools they wanted. But this game, this exposure would open doors. The money would let them walk through. He could finish the game with a big post-show recap and write them all a check. Let them go to whatever damn school they wanted. Send them off into their futures with something. More than he'd had.

That's when the bullet found his chest. The bullet of resentment and remorse. Of wishing he could go back in time and give his dad the one gift he'd never given him. Of hating his dad for asking for that gift in the first place.

He had to stand up and move. The twitchiness was debilitating when it got like this. He reached for the bike clothes he'd been sitting on. He'd pound through some miles, hard miles, to make his legs stop aching. He ripped his T-shirt over his head and reached for his jersey, barely conscious that it was dirty and sweat-stained from yesterday's ride. He'd ride until his body was numb and his mind was clear.

Maybe then he wouldn't see Allyson's desperate eyes as she realized what she faced when she left that condo. Or Henry's blank, haunting stare before he got into the car to take him home. Or Sam's anguished look when Cassidy left him last night.

Or his dad's disappointment that morning—in Quincy, Massachusetts, so many summers ago. When his dad had backed angrily out their narrow driveway. But didn't come home.

July 19, 10:15 a.m.
Newport Beach, California
Sam Michaels

Sam sat across from Tyrell, trying to force down bites of burnt toast with grape jelly in between swigs of orange juice. He'd never been a breakfast person. There'd never been much breakfast around for him to be that person. And given the way his stomach felt at the moment, it didn't seem like a great time to start the habit.

But he knew a challenge was imminent. Colin had roused them a half hour ago with his annoyingly energetic "Shipshape, mates!" It took all of Sam's restraint not to hurl an alarm clock at him.

Tyrell had met him at the breakfast table, a dark scowl tightening his features. They'd eaten in silence, hadn't even exchanged a "Hey, how's it going?" Which was fine with Sam. He hoped by the end of the day that Tyrell would be on a plane back to Missouri.

It was Cassidy he was worried about. Not getting her *out* of the competition, but keeping her *in*. Which his brain kept telling him was insane. She'd made it clear how she felt.

He tried not to gag on the last bite of dry, scratchy bread in his mouth, chewing quickly and washing it down with the remnants of his juice. He stood so fast that the legs of his chair scraped loudly on the floor. Tyrell winced.

Good, he thought. Inflicting pain on that guy was exactly what he intended to do. For the rest of the day.

July 19, 2:02 p.m.
Union Station, Los Angeles, California
Tyrell Young

Something was wrong with the lovebirds. For the first time, they were riding in the same van to the challenge—him, Sam, Cassidy, Nisha, and Colin, all buckled in like they were on some special camp outing. And, of course, the mandatory camera guy, a young squirrelly dude who took up most of the front seat and kept leaning forward into Tyrell's space.

The guy was lucky he still had his camera. And both arms.

He figured he'd let the hippie-prince and his skanky princess have the back bench to themselves. So they could make out or whatever. Only when it was Cassidy's turn to climb in, she averted her eyes from Sam and slid in next to Tyrell. Trouble in paradise with a capital *T*. Maybe he could drive that wedge in a little more firmly.

He leaned toward Cassidy, making sure that his arm rested on the seat behind her—you know, to make old Sammy squirm.

In a low voice, he said, "Robert Downey Jr.? Nicely done, Miss Cassidy. That's high-end star power you managed to track down."

She offered him a thin smile, not her usual high-wattage variety. "I got lucky."

He shrugged, let his hand graze her bare shoulder as he brought it back to his side. "Maybe. But it landed you in the final three. Seems to me like that took some scheming on your part. You see another girl here? 'Cause I don't."

She looked at him sideways, like she was skeptical but wanted to believe him.

"Nice of you to say," she said.

"Not saying it to be nice," he said, looking straight ahead and avoiding her eyes. "I'm saying it because I always size up my biggest competition. And right now, that's you, girl."

He could see her, from the corner of his eye, staring at him. He wanted to smile but held back. Whatever was going on between her and Rasta-mahn, he wanted to build her up. Let her think she could win this, that she was totally capable. Which was crap. She had about as much a chance of winning this thing as Kim Kardashian had of winning the Pulitzer.

The van stopped and they unloaded in front of a huge 1940s mission-style train station. Unexpectedly, he felt his skin prickle. Sure, it was hot outside—nineties at least with no breeze, especially here in the heart of the city. But that wasn't it. He looked up at the building, with its high arch and adobe walls. Let Sam and Cassidy battle it out for second.

Those prickles on his skin? That rush of heat he was feeling? It was confidence.

Whatever this next challenge was about, he was gonna nail it.

July 19, 2:06 p.m.
Union Station, Los Angeles, California
Cassidy McGowan

Cassidy had grown up riding trains. She'd been inside Union Station in Chicago at least a dozen times with her grandpa and grandma. Her grandparents hated to fly; airplanes didn't make sense to them and especially after 9/11, there was no way they were going to get in one. But they lived in Florida. So seeing the grandkids, or having the grandkids come see them, meant riding the rails.

Some of Cassidy's best memories had taken place in a cavernous, bustling train station much like this one. Chicago's Union Station had the same old-timey feel: the high, elaborate ceiling; the worn wooden benches, though these were cushioned; the signs pointing to the train platforms; and the slightly musty, greasy smell, mixed in with the warm, bready scent of fresh-baked pretzels that instinctively made Cassidy look around for Grams and Gramps.

Molly, along with her posse of cameras, waited next to a square, wood-paneled kiosk with its clearly labeled sign: INFORMATION. Beyond the kiosk, shiny terra-cotta tiles and travertine marble created intricate floor designs that meandered under a high archway into a tunnel marked overhead with TO TICKETING AND TRAINS.

Today Molly was wearing a loose blue jersey with the word *Dodgers* scrawled across the front in white. Under that she had on tight jeans and new white Nikes. No tight skirt or heels. Definitely odd.

Cassidy fought the urge to keep walking past that information booth, where the rest of the group had stopped. Instead, she wanted to duck into the train tunnel. She loved trains. Loved everything about them, from their high-pitched whistles to the steady rocking that could lull you to sleep. She loved the way they were predictable and steady. Loved that they weren't rushed. That you could play a game of gin rummy, having just visited the dining car where your Gramps might have splurged on some red pop and chips, and know you'd have time for a whole round of games while America jostled by.

She hoped Faith loved trains someday. She needed to remember to take Faith on a train ride as soon as she got home. Maybe down to see her great-grandparents.

She blinked away those thoughts. She turned dutifully toward Molly, whose fake welcoming smile only made her want to bolt toward the trains that much more.

"Our illustrious final three contenders!" Molly exclaimed. Cassidy pasted on a return smile. Cameras were watching. Which meant Alex Ginsberg was, too.

"Welcome to Union Station in Los Angeles. This station, 'The Last of the Great Railway Stations,' opened its doors in 1939. Visitors walking through today see the buildings pretty much as they were in the 1940s, since little remodeling has been done, besides some sprucing up, of course." Molly smiled and nodded around her.

As before, a crowd was gathering. Cassidy was used to the attention by now, and she barely acknowledged the onlookers. She was also trying very hard not to notice Sam's presence just inches from her. Yet every time he shifted his weight or scratched his ear or stuck a hand in his pocket, she found her body reacting. Like her skin hoped he wasn't scratching his neck but trying to reach for her.

He didn't. He stayed those few maddening inches away.

What did I expect? she chided herself. She'd pushed him away. She had no right to hope for these things.

She took a small step away from him. She had to get herself under control.

"Today's challenge has two parts," Molly said, glancing at the contestants one by one. "Each part will show the Benefactor a different ability of yours. Or the lack of it."

Molly raised one eyebrow. Almost daringly.

Cassidy bit her bottom lip. She would not fail today.

"Thousands of people come through Union Station every month. Some are traveling on Amtrak to destinations all over the country. Some are commuters who simply don't want to fight L.A. traffic."

Sam tucked a strand of hair behind his ear. Cassidy felt her eyes stray toward his fingers. She forced her attention back on Molly.

"Among the crowd today are a number of people wearing bright orange ribbons, just like this." Molly gestured to a small ribbon she had pinned to her jersey below her shoulder. It was looped around once into an oval.

"These passengers are all headed toward cities throughout the U.S. to attend Major League Baseball games. Some are traveling alone, others with family members. But they all have a few things in common. First, they'll be seeing a Major League game in the next day or so. Second, they'll be traveling by train at some point to get there. And third, a few of them are missing their game tickets."

Molly revealed what Cassidy assumed were three tickets, though it was too far away to read them. Molly fanned them out in front of her and held them up for the cameras and the gathered crowd.

"Each of you will be given one of these tickets. You must match this missing ticket with its correct owner."

She lowered the tickets and tilted her head sideways.

"Be forewarned: there are lots of travelers wandering around this station with orange ribbons. Not all of them are going to the game for which you are holding a ticket."

Cassidy narrowed her eyes. This didn't sound super hard. Some trial and error, maybe, but eventually, she'd find the person who wanted to go to her game. Then Molly looked around and sighed. Loudly.

"Oh, and one more thing: the people with the orange ribbons? They will answer all sorts of questions that you ask them. A few questions they won't answer?" Molly ticked them off on her fingers. "What city are you traveling to? What game are you going to see? Who's your favorite baseball team?"

She winked and the crowd laughed.

Cassidy's brain started its predictable and dangerous shutdown. Without those questions, how could she figure out whose ticket was whose, then? What was she missing?

"Once you've found your correct baseball fan, they will be handing you a ticket of your own," Molly went on. "To Dodger Stadium. Using the new Dodger Stadium Express, a free service for Dodgers fans that starts right here at Union Station, you'll make your way to the stadium. Inside the stadium, you'll need to find famed peanut vendor Roger Owens. Mr. Owens has been throwing out bags of peanuts to baseball fans for over fifty years, at more than four thousand games by his own count. He'll be waiting for you with instructions and a tray full of peanuts. When the game starts later tonight, you'll have the opportunity to try your own hand at tossing out peanuts to hungry Dodgers fans. And once your tray is empty, you'll find an envelope taped to the bottom which will tell you how to claim victory—or defeat—in this challenge."

She held up all three baseball tickets. Apprehension started swirling in Cassidy's chest, and she realized it might quickly become a tornado if she didn't figure this out. *Think,* she told herself desperately. *What would Sam do?*

"The last competitor to completely sell their tray of bagged peanuts and retrieve that envelope will be eliminated." Molly looked at her watch. "So, sports fans, the Dodgers will throw out the first pitch at 7:10 this evening. Which leaves you just a few hours to determine whose ticket you're holding and get your own ticket to tonight's game. No time to waste!"

She let her gaze linger for a second on each of them. "The Benefactor knows what it's like to try to find a needle in a haystack. To have to use reasoning, logic, and common sense. It's how he was able to turn a small technology start-up into a billion-dollar empire."

She smiled. "Best of luck to each of you."

And then she waved her arm to start the battle.

But Cassidy was frozen. Her mind was a blank. Here was a venue in which she felt completely comfortable. Trains. My God, she *knew* trains. But how did this challenge relate to trains? It seemed to be all about baseball.

She felt a hand on her arm. Sam. Warmth cascaded up her body and made her cheeks flush.

She allowed herself to look at him. His eyes were kind. Concerned.

"You okay?" he asked gently.

She nodded.

"I'm sorry, Cass," he said, his voice so low she might not have heard it over the rumble of the background noise in the station. But he was standing close. And she was listening. Listening hard.

"My words last night didn't match my heart," he continued, lifting her chin to make sure that she was looking him straight in the eye. She was. "You are a wonderfully capable person. Capable in every regard." His gaze circled upward and around the room before settling on her again. "You mentioned once how much you love trains. Traveling on trains."

His eyes were so beautiful. So intense.

A slow, lazy smile spread from his mouth to his eyes. "I'll be hot on your tail, Cassidy McGowan. You know how to read these train schedules better than anyone else. But no one can throw a bag of peanuts like me."

He left his eyes on hers a moment longer. Then he winked and was gone. Gone to grab his ticket from Molly and find the passengers with orange ribbons.

Cassidy was left to breathe again. With measured steps, she grabbed her ticket from Molly and spun toward the tunnel that led to the trains.

The trains.

Oh, Sam. She closed her eyes and choked back the emotion in her throat.

You know these train schedules better than anyone. He'd seen the panic on her face and he'd reminded her that she could do this challenge. She felt the tears building just behind her eyelids.

She blinked hard and ducked her head for a minute, trying to read what was on her ticket.

The Chicago Cubs against the Colorado Rockies. In Denver.

Thanks to Sam she knew exactly what she had to do now. With a deep breath, she lifted her head and walked confidently toward the tunnel that led to all the train platforms. She had some orange ribbons to find.

July 19, 3:15 p.m.
Union Station, Los Angeles, California
Sam Michaels

It had been a little under an hour. He'd managed to find three people wearing orange ribbons. And he'd figured out immediately that the key was to ask them about what train they were traveling on or something like that. From there, he'd have to read the train schedule and put two and two together.

His ticket was for a Giants game taking place on Sunday. So he needed somebody traveling to San Francisco. He'd gone right to the giant electronic board of departures and tried to find a train heading north. There were none.

Without any trains going to SF, this wasn't going to be as easy as he'd hoped. He had to find some orange ribbons and start asking questions, and maybe piece together how somebody would get to the City by the Bay from their answers.

Except it wasn't working out so well.

The first orange ribbon he found was on an older gentleman carrying a beat-up, patched-together suitcase like you might expect to find in an old train station like this.

"Excuse me, sir," Sam had said, sliding onto the bench next to the man. "Can I ask you what train you plan to board?"

The old guy had lifted his chin to peer back at Sam with runny eyes under bifocals. "I believe I'm scheduled for the 422 train later this evening."

"Is that the number of the train or the time it leaves?" Sam asked.

The old guy looked at him over his wire rims. "That's the train number, boy."

"Where's that train headed?" Sam asked hopefully.

The old man shook his head and waved a wrinkled hand at Sam. "That's all you'll get from me, young man. The 422."

Sam thanked the guy and headed directly for the train schedule board. The 422 was bound for Phoenix. No help there.

And so it went. Sometimes the people with the orange ribbons gave him a train number. Sometimes they gave him a departure time. Or an arrival time. Or a city where they had to switch trains. Or they might give him a platform number, and he had to figure out what train left there. Or ask more questions.

Those orange ribbons didn't stay put, either. One orange ribbon—an abnormally tall woman traveling with her equally tall husband—gave him a number that didn't show up on any of the train departure boards. When he went back to ask her if she was sure that was the number, she was gone.

That stumped him for a bit. Until he thought to ask the bearded old guy at the information kiosk if maybe some busses left from this station as well. Indeed, they did. And when he found the tall woman's number listed among the busses—to his disappointment she was headed to Bakersfield and then to Portland—something clicked for him. Maybe there wasn't a train directly to San Francisco. Maybe you had to take a bus first?

That's when he found what he was looking for: busses that left for Bakersfield, where riders would board a train to San Francisco. With these numbers, he could ask the right questions. And hopefully get rid of this ticket pretty quickly.

He saw a flash of orange up ahead and made a beeline for it. It was a young couple, holding hands as they passed a salted pretzel back and forth.

Seeing them made him think of Cassidy. Without even knowing he was doing it, his eyes started roaming around the terminal he was in, looking for her neon-green tank top and blond ponytail. He'd given her the only clue he could. He hoped she wasn't pissed at him for it, as if he was somehow underestimating her.

But he knew if he could just steer her in the right direction, she'd have a chance. She knew train stations, if her stories of traveling with her grandparents were any indication. And she was great at getting people to talk.

The girl with the orange ribbon bent forward and grabbed the last piece of pretzel with her teeth. Her partner bumped her with his hip and scowled playfully.

Sam paused for a second, watching them. His heart snagged. He'd never looked at other couples and wanted what they had. In fact, he and Rachel had often ridiculed people like them. Did they even think for themselves? Did they value their independence? Did they know how stupid they looked?

Sam knew that couple didn't care if they looked stupid. And they would have given up anything to be together. Because that's how he felt about Cassidy, too.

Suddenly, it occurred to him what he was feeling in his chest. Jealousy. For the first time in seventeen years, he knew what jealousy felt like—and how much it sucked.

July 19, 3:30 p.m.
Union Station, Los Angeles, California
Tyrell Young

He freaking hated baseball. Baseball was a sissy sport. He'd never played Little League, never really even learned how to catch and throw or hit a stupid ball. Why would he? His dad had preached from the time Tyrell could listen that real guys played football.

His ticket said that the New York Mets were playing the Arizona Diamondbacks some time on Sunday. He had no clue where in Arizona the Diamondbacks played and had to ask some ancient janitor limping along behind his wide, dusty mop. Turned out it was Phoenix. Though why anyone would go see a baseball game in the triple-digit heat of Phoenix was truly mind-blowing.

His next step was to figure out which of these orange-ribbon-wearing peeps was just such an idiot. Most of his conversations went something like this:

Tyrell: You going to see a Diamondbacks game?

Orange Ribbon Idiot (some variation on a smirk): Going to see a baseball game.

Tyrell (testier now): What city you going to see that baseball game in?

Orange Ribbon Idiot (less friendly): Well, now, I think my train leaves at 4:02 this afternoon, OR whatever city number 213 is going to, OR I believe I'll be arriving there at 11:27 tomorrow mornin'.

Tyrell wanted to rip that stupid baseball ticket into forty thousand little pieces and throw it at any one of those idiots. Tell 'em all they were wasting their time; they oughta wait until football season, especially if they were going to spend freakin' fourteen hours on a train for a game. But he just pushed on, asking idiot after idiot, hoping somebody would finally tell him they were going to Phoenix, Arizona, and he could hand over the stupid thing, good riddance.

He'd just had one of those pointless exchanges with a ribbon-wearing dad and his teenage son—"we'll be leaving from Track 15 at 6:22"—when he saw Cassidy. She was talking with two older women, both of whom wore visors on top of blue-gray fuzz-heads, oversized T-shirts, knee-length pants, and white Keds. They reminded him of his gram. He watched as Cassidy nodded once and then laughed. Then she spun around and grabbed the arm of a tall guy in a gray suit who was striding by. With an easy smile, she handed him a camera and said a few words. Tyrell watched, reluctantly amused, as Cassidy slid between the two old ladies, her arms resting on their shoulders, all three of them smiling for a picture.

She then held up one finger to the two women and jogged back toward the main entrance. Curious, he blended in with the crowd and followed her. She went straight for the large board announcing all the departures. She strained her neck upward, her eyes scanning the long list of trains scheduled to leave. Then she stopped, drew a line across the board with her finger, and pursed her lips, shaking her head slightly. Her shoulders slumping a little, she headed back to where she'd left the women.

Cautiously, Tyrell made his way over to the board. And realized two things: he had completely underestimated Cassidy, *and* he was probably the biggest idiot on the planet. Bigger than those losers going to watch baseball games while sweating all over their beer and peanuts.

All of these people had been giving him information. Train numbers and departure times. One of them could have been going to Phoenix and he wouldn't have known it because he was too stupid to figure out that he had to use what they were telling him to piece it all together.

He'd figured this was simply a trial-and-error task. That if he kept at it, eventually he'd come across the right person who would say, "Yep, that's my ticket. I love me some Arizona Diamondbacks."

Damn. He was smarter than this. His dad was no doubt gonna shake his head in disgust and leave the room when he watched this play out on his TV.

He looked down at his ticket. He had some catching up to do. Starting with those two old chicks. He'd even pose for a damn picture.

July 19, 5:00 p.m.
Malibu, California
The Benefactor

He swigged his Sam Adams Summer Ale and leaned back in his favorite Italian leather armchair. This chair had been an extravagance. When it came to "stuff," he was a pretty simple guy: Levis, T-shirts. He drove a Prius. But this chair . . .

His dad had had a chair. A worn-out recliner that tipped dangerously to one side. His mother hated that thing. Always threatened to find the nearest yard sale when Dad went on one of his fishing weekends. Empty threats—she knew it, and so did everyone else. That chair was Dad's kingdom. Nobody sat in it. Even the cat figured out not to curl up there.

After his dad died, his mom had let Dad's chair sit untouched in the den for years. It was an eyesore, collecting dust—unusable and too molded to Dad's butt to give away. But when he'd suggested taking it down to the dump, she and his brother had gone ape-shit on him. Like he was suggesting they desecrate Dad's grave or something. He'd never mentioned it again.

He'd never understood how a guy could get so attached to a piece of furniture. It was a chair. Not a person or even a pet. How could it possibly mean that much?

But now he got it. There was something about this chair that relaxed him. That let him know in a way nothing else could that he was home—away from the crap. That also reminded him how far he'd come in this world. A working-class kid from Quincy, Mass. who now owned a friggin' empire. Who used to sweep floors at Nick's Pizza and now paid people to sweep up after him.

The Benefactor looked at his bank of TVs and took another swig of beer. He watched Cassidy approach two twenty-something guys draped casually on some chairs near the main entrance. One was short with cinnamon-colored skin, a mustache, and dark, weasel-like eyes. The other was heavier, with kind of a baby face. Their eyes roamed over Cassidy appreciatively. The short guy nudged his buddy and made an obscene gesture when Cassidy wasn't looking.

The Benefactor's eyes narrowed. They'd have to edit out the gesture. But it still made him feel like he wanted to reach through his screen and grab the guy by his scrawny neck.

"You guys short a baseball ticket?" Cassidy asked pleasantly. She kept some distance. Wise girl.

The weasel-eyed one lifted his chin and grinned smugly. "What you got, *chica*?" he drawled.

Cassidy kept her smile in place but it lost a bit of its luster.

"You probably need to tell me where you're headed," she said evenly, glancing toward the camera.

"What you think, *cuate*?" Weasel Eyes said, spreading his jean-clad legs wide on the chair and laying an arm across the back of the seat. "Where are we headed?"

Cassidy sighed. She looked toward his pudgier companion. "You know what train you leave on? Maybe what time?"

The Benefactor took another drink but kept his eyes trained on the screen. They'd done a cold casting call for these people, who were mostly wannabes just happy for a little camera time. They were being paid a nominal fee to walk around the station for a few hours and deliver a handful of scripted lines. They hadn't really vetted them, though. This kid could be anyone, with anyone's problems and baggage.

But Cassidy had a camera with her. That gave her some measure of security. Plus, it was a crowded place. And there were producers staked out at key spots throughout the train station.

The larger kid also looked at the camera. He seemed nervous, if his sweaty upper lip was any sign. "We leave at 6:15 tonight," he said. "On train number four."

Something clicked in Cassidy's eyes.

"Train number four?" she asked, her voice rising excitedly. "Hold on, okay?"

She started to spin around, but Weasel Eyes was fast as lightning. Like a rattlesnake striking, his hand was out and wrapped around Cassidy's wrist. She was yanked back, hard enough that she stumbled and cried out.

"Hey! Knock it off!" she yelled.

The guy tightened his grip and leaned in close to her face. She bent backward. The Benefactor imagined the smell of alcohol on the guy's breath. He gripped the neck of his beer bottle harder. *Knee him,* he urged Cassidy silently.

Her eyes were wide with fear and repulsion.

"We gave you what you wanted," he said. "What you got for us, *chula*?"

The camera view was suddenly blocked by a hulking dark shape. For a second, the Benefactor held his breath, unable to tell what was going on. Once the view was unobstructed, Weasel Eyes was backpedaling. Cassidy was rubbing her wrist and biting her lower lip, sucking back tears.

And Tyrell was standing between both of them, looking menacingly pissed off.

"I don't know what they teach you where you come from, but in my neighborhood, when you grab a chick like you just did, you better watch your back, 'cause usually that chick got brothers or cousins that gonna come after you. Cassidy ain't my sister or my cousin, but I'll be damned if I'm gonna let any scum like you lay a hand on her. You read me, homie?"

The guy was holding up two hands in surrender and stepping backward. He was outsized by Tyrell by at least six inches.

"Come on, dude," Weasel Eyes said. "I was messin'. That's all."

"Well, you *messin'* with the wrong girl today, bro. And, before you go cryin' home to mommy, you tell this girl here exactly what she asked you," Tyrell said, waving Cassidy forward.

Cassidy was shivering like a leaf in a cold wind. "He said he was on train 4," she said quietly, swallowing. "I was just going to go check it on the board."

Tyrell kept his eyes trained on Weasel Eyes, who was glancing sideways toward his buddy and the exit.

"Why don't you go check real quick, while I watch Dickwad here?"

Cassidy jogged off as Tyrell and the other guy stared each other down. The pudgier buddy was looking scared shitless.

When Cassidy came back, she had her ticket out. "He's the one," she said to Tyrell, holding out her ticket, a note of disbelief in her voice. "He's going to Denver, and I have a ticket for the Colorado Rockies."

Tyrell took the ticket from her and glanced at it. Then he offered it to Weasel Eyes.

"This yours?" he asked, taking a step toward him.

The guy snagged the ticket quickly from Tyrell and pulled another ticket from his back pocket.

"Here," he said. He tossed it toward Cassidy, and it landed near her feet. He looked at Tyrell. "Who's *estupido* now? You gonna let some blond chick beat you?"

Tyrell bent down and picked up the ticket. He handed it to Cassidy.

"She's tough, bro," Tyrell said, shaking his head. "If you'd seen her over the last two weeks, you'd have known not to mess with her."

The guy shrugged. "Whatever," he said, slinking off. His buddy trailed behind him, looking over his shoulder twice.

Cassidy stood there a minute, staring at the ticket in her hand and taking a deep breath.

"Thanks for that," she said, finally looking up at Tyrell. "He was being a dick."

Tyrell shrugged. "I know the type." He nodded at her ticket. "I'll see you in a little bit, okay? Don't sell all the peanuts until I get there."

She grinned, some of the sparkle in her eyes coming back. "I'll save you a bag or two."

Tyrell started to walk off. Cassidy watched him go, appearing uncertain. Her head swiveled toward the exit and then back at Tyrell. Then she bit her bottom lip.

"Hey, Ty," she called out.

Tyrell turned back. His eyebrows went up.

"You're looking for a really old guy, glasses, dragging around a patched-up suitcase. Pretty sure he said he was getting on the 422 train. Also pretty sure that's headed to Phoenix." She smiled. "Good luck, okay?"

And then she strode toward the main entrance, her ponytail swinging, the camera and several pairs of male eyes following her.

Tyrell, too, watched her go. Without looking at the camera, he said quietly, "So long, Sammy-boy. You just got screwed."

Then he shrugged and sauntered off in the direction of the trains.

EPISODE 6
THE FINALS

"The great enemy of the truth is very often not the lie—deliberate, contrived, and dishonest—but the myth—persistent, persuasive, and realistic."

—John F. Kennedy, Yale commencement address, 1962

"Fewer than four in ten mothers who have a child before they turn eighteen have a high school diploma. Less than two percent of young teen mothers (those who have a baby before age eighteen) attain a college degree by age thirty."

—National Campaign to Prevent Teen Pregnancy, 2010

July 19, 10:34 p.m.
Malibu, California
The Benefactor

He'd foolishly thought he could do this show without becoming invested. Two weeks ago, he'd combed through their bios and submission tapes, eager, and even haughty, over the fact that he would get to ax them one by one. Then they were eight identities, eight characters. Names and faces only.

Tonight had been hard. Harder than it should have been. He hadn't expected the Union Station challenge to turn out the way that it did. And he hadn't been prepared for the Elimination. There was no need for questioning, hemming, or hawing—since one contestant had clearly arrived to the Dodgers suite last and therefore was out of the game. But the Benefactor had still felt off-kilter.

Cassidy got there first. Waving the piece of paper that told her to come to his corporate-owned suite on the club level, she'd burst through the door, breathless and flushed.

"I'm . . . done," she'd gasped, leaning onto a leather chair for support. Her neon-green tank top clung to her back, where sweat stains were visible.

A producer moved forward with a cold bottle of water. "Nice job, Cassidy," she said smoothly, taking the paper from her and guiding her to the couch. "You've beaten both boys. We'll be seeing *you* in the finals."

Cassidy uncapped the water and swigged it gratefully. The relief in her eyes was clear. She'd made it.

When Tyrell arrived an hour later, smashing the door open with such force that everyone in the room looked up, a camera closed in on Cassidy. But her expression stayed closed and guarded. She didn't show the surprise that might be expected. Or the disappointment. If the Benefactor had to describe her expression, he would have said she looked resolved.

It was Sam's arrival shortly afterward that caused all eyes to volley from him to Cassidy and back again. That caused breaths to be sucked in but not released. Even the Benefactor, safe in his viewing room nearly thirty miles away, felt the heightened tension.

Sam glanced at Cassidy. At Tyrell. Understanding registered on his face, and though he quickly let his eyelids drop into the hooded look the world was used to, the Benefactor caught the brief emotion there. The disappointment. Maybe a quick stab of jealousy.

But then Sam became the class act that viewers had come to expect. And love.

"Good job, you two," Sam said easily, walking toward Cassidy and squeezing her shoulder. Cameras rolling, he leaned forward and whispered something in her ear. She nodded without smiling.

Sam reached a hand toward Tyrell. "Congrats, man," he said, clearing his throat.

Then it was time. The Benefactor moved quickly into the small room he'd mentally nicknamed "the dungeon," because of its lack of windows. He flipped the switches, turning on the back lights, slid behind his desk, and tapped the button under the desktop that would start the cameras and project his silhouetted image to the kids—and the world.

There were screens set up so he could watch the kids' reactions as he pummeled them with questions, berated their performances, or sent them packing. Tonight he had little to say. He wanted to be done with this. Quickly.

"Good evening," he said.

Sam's head swiveled toward the screen in the suite, and as it occurred to him what was going to happen, he dropped into a seat by Cassidy, looking a bit dazed. Cassidy bit her bottom lip and closed her eyes. Tyrell nodded smugly.

"Excellent job today. By all of you. The task required a variety of skills, including logic and persistence. The three of you proved to have both of these in abundance."

Sam glanced at Cassidy, the yearning so clear in his eyes. She didn't look at him.

The Benefactor took a deep breath.

"Unfortunately, one of you must be eliminated tonight, based solely on your inability to complete this task as quickly as the other two."

He wanted so badly to grab something. Tap something. Throw something. But this desk was purposefully clean.

"Sam, you are not the top candidate for this scholarship, and I'm sorry but I must reject your application."

Sam closed his eyes. Nodded once. Opened them and stood quickly.

"Thank you," he said, staring up at the screen. "This has not only been a tremendous opportunity but probably the coolest few weeks of my life. Worth every minute."

He turned to Cassidy and Tyrell. "Good luck, guys," he said softly. Then he looked around uncertainly, but seeing no other option, he walked to the door and let himself out.

The cameras clicked off a minute later, but not before they caught Cassidy's face. She'd kept her head down until the door clicked closed. Then she looked up to where Sam had just been. And the camera zoomed in on her tired eyes—the haunting sadness there and something else. Remorse. Guilt.

The Benefactor had thought he could get through this game without caring one way or another who won his money in the end.

He'd been so wrong.

Tonight he'd sent home the guy he'd been sure was going to win it all. The guy he was rooting for in many ways. A guy with no viable family and nothing to go home to.

This was a despicable, unpredictable game. He'd been foolish to think he could control it.

July 19, 10:45 p.m.
Newport Beach, California
Cassidy McGowan

Her legs and feet ached. Running back and forth in Union Station trying to match the orange ribbons to her Rockies baseball ticket and then lugging that tray of peanuts up and down the endless stairs and aisles at Dodger Stadium had been freakin' exhausting. She was wiped. Too tired to do more than kick off her shoes and flop onto her bed.

But what felt worse was the brick that seemed to be lodged in her chest. The brick that made it hard to breathe. Hard to eat or drink. The brick that was zapping the energy she needed to cry or beat her fists against her bed or curse until her throat was hoarse and raw.

Sam was gone.

In the numb, muddied recesses of her brain, that fact was slowly taking hold. Sam was gone. Eliminated about an hour ago. Probably packing. Wondering how the hell this had happened.

Because of course, he had no clue that Cassidy was to blame. By telling Tyrell about that guy heading to Phoenix, she'd written Sam's ticket home. In Sharpie permanent ink.

The moonlight made grayish outlines in her room: her pile of unwashed clothes, her upended suitcase, the beach towel she'd flung haphazardly over her desk chair two nights ago that now fluttered a little in the breeze from the fan overhead. She heard the distant crash of waves. It was high tide. Sam had taught her how to read the changing tides and explained their mysteries. They'd talked about maybe finding some tide pools on their next day off.

She rolled to her side and clutched her stomach.

Truly, she'd only wanted to help Tyrell. He'd jumped in when that guy had been such a dick. She'd seen a side of Tyrell that was, you know, sweet. Like an older brother. So in an impulsive moment of gratitude and warmth, she'd tossed out that small bread crumb of information.

She hadn't thought about Sam. How could she have *not* thought about Sam?

Oh God. She wanted to curl up and hide. Or run far, far away and never look back. Find Sam and beg him to understand. She hadn't meant to get him eliminated. She hadn't thought it through. She hadn't thought at all.

Would she ever even see him again? It wasn't clear whether the Benefactor planned to bring back those who'd been eliminated. It was possible that Sam would be loaded onto a plane tonight and her only glimpse of him would be when she watched these episodes at home. When she would relive how she'd betrayed him. After all he had done to get her this far.

The numbness was wearing off. In its place was a throbbing ache. It started in her chest and welled up in her throat, crashing behind her eyes so that she had to squeeze them shut.

After she'd learned she was pregnant, and the father had bailed out, she'd felt pain. For days, she'd forgotten to eat, and everyday actions like showering and brushing her teeth felt like they took too much effort. So she didn't bother. Her brother later called those her "zombie days." She couldn't imagine ever feeling that much hurt, that much regret, ever again.

But this? This was different. Because mixed in with all that pain and hurt and sorrow was a new emotion. A persistent stabbing deep within that she knew wouldn't be fading anytime soon.

Guilt. She'd screwed up. And in the process lost the one guy who cared about her. Who maybe, just maybe, she was starting to care about, too.

July 19, 10:52 p.m.
Newport Beach, California
Tyrell Young

Tyrell was way too amped to sleep. He couldn't have dreamed up a more perfect ending to this beautiful game. Him and Cassidy.

He was already practicing his victory speech.

He'd loved seeing Sam's face when he'd finally shown up with his empty tray, having sold all his bags of peanuts, waving that paper in his hand. Only then did poor Sammy glance around, his eyes bugging out as he noticed Cassidy and Tyrell already chilling in the Benefactor's suite. Poor Sammy—unable to tear himself from Cassidy, who was hunched over in one of them leather armchairs, hanging her head like a lost puppy.

Man, he wished he could have hit the replay button. Watched Sam's face over and over. Disbelief. Realization. Acceptance. It had been a knockout performance—he had to give the guy props for that. He'd squeezed Cassidy's shoulder, whispered in her ear, and then pumped Tyrell's hand, good game, good luck. And then the TV had clicked on, and the Benefactor's silhouette had appeared, and it became obvious that Sam's Elimination was happening *right now.*

Sam was going home. About. Damn. Time.

The guy had been so cocky. Positive he was gonna take home the prize. And what had done him in? His own smiley-faced girlfriend and a street-smart kid from the Midwest. Tyrell smirked. Poetic freakin' justice. Served up Tyrell-style.

He pictured his dad watching this play out. He'd be slappin' backs, nodding his shiny black head with a big ol' happy grin on his lined and usually tired face.

"That's my boy," he'd say, over and over. "You see the way he took that guy out in that train station? Like it was *nothin'*! Nobody messes with my Ty. That's right."

Tyrell leaned back onto his pillows, hands folded behind his head.

That's right, he thought. *Nobody messes with Tyrell.*

'Specially not a Rasta-man from Seattle. And now—unless Cassidy was hiding some secret weapon—this scholarship was his. That old Benefactor ought to just write him the check tonight.

Save everybody a lot of trouble. *That's right.*

July 20, 6:15 a.m.
Malibu, California
The Benefactor

He sipped his coffee and debated going for a ride. He wouldn't be on this coast much longer. The final challenge was today, which meant the show would wrap up in the next day or two. Other than editing and packaging—things Yaz could take care of—it would be over. He could head back to New York and resume being the CEO of Kelly Tech, Inc.

He should have felt at least mildly triumphant. The ratings of the pilot episode had been decent, enough to make the network sit up and take notice of his little experiment. Critics and bloggers alike were already in hot debate about what this competition said about the American education system. He was fielding calls (through the show's publicist, of course, since his identity was still hush-hush) from the *New York Times* and the Huffington Post, both wanting interviews. *What motivated him to do a show like this? What statement was he trying to make about society?* He'd told the publicist to turn everything down.

Here was the truth, which he would *not* be telling journalists: He'd been motivated to do this show because the college application process was horribly outdated. He'd also wanted to do something new, something different—a challenge. Let's face it: there was an image that went along with this show that was cool and powerful and enticing. And he'd wanted to do the show because it was a final way to make amends with his father.

But here was the thing: none of that mattered. He didn't care that the ratings were good. He didn't care that eventually, when people figured out who he was, they were gonna want him on *Letterman* and *Good Morning America.* He certainly didn't care about bloggers and critics.

He wanted to know that Henry was still doing okay. Whether Allyson's mom was getting the care she needed. If Mei was pursuing her art. He wanted to know if Hiroshi had reconciled with Maggie. He wanted Lucy—proud and defiant Lucy—to quit being mad at the world and figure out how to like herself a little more.

He wanted happy endings. And yet he was slowly coming to realize that even with all his resources, he couldn't manufacture those.

Except for one of them. Tyrell or Cassidy was going to get a check by the end of the day—a big one. One that would secure his or her future for the next four years, and probably way beyond that.

His cell phone, sitting on his dresser, buzzed. He set down his coffee mug and grabbed it. Restricted number.

"Yes," the Benefactor said.

"Richard." It was a familiar voice—resonant and authoritative—but the Benefactor couldn't quite place it.

"Speaking."

"It's Chancellor Bingham." The man cleared his throat obnoxiously. "*Saturday Night Live,* Richard?"

"It hasn't even aired yet," said the Benefactor, sighing. "You have people spying for you now? On my production crew?"

"I needed to know where this game of yours was headed," the chancellor said. "I obviously didn't make myself clear the last time we talked. I don't know what you're trying to say about the institution that I'm running or the kids who attend my school—who worked hard, by the way, to be accepted here—but I'm fielding calls left and right wanting my comments on your fun little game."

The Benefactor eased himself onto the edge of his bed.

"Tell them whatever you want, Chancellor," the Benefactor said. "Tell them you disagree with my methods. Tell them I'm way off base. Tell them I'm a nut job. You're getting free publicity for your school. How is this bad?"

"My school's reputation," the chancellor spat, "is founded on principles of integrity and academic excellence, along with dedicated students and professors who hold learning in the highest regard. We're now being associated with a man who thinks that stalking a movie star for a photo op qualifies you for higher education!"

Something snapped. Something he'd been tamping down for a while.

"Says the man who recently graduated the Golden Globe–winning actress for this year's starring role in a comedy," the Benefactor retorted. "The guy who was photographed last week next to—who was it again?—oh, yes, the actor who is the top-paid guy in television. Nice photo op for you, Chancellor? Let's see, by my estimation, your school took in a whopping $5.6 million last year in endowments from Hollywood. Lots of photo ops there, I would presume?"

The Benefactor snorted, picking up steam. "You know how you got where you are, Chancellor? Sure, working hard. A solid mind, I would imagine. But you also had to network. Know the right people and know how to find others. Kind of like what I had the kids do during the *SNL* challenge. You probably had to learn some people skills, didn't you? How to motivate and lead others? Kind of like another challenge I had the kids do at the Pantages Theater. You also had to be persistent. Like another challenge they did recently in Union Station."

The Benefactor was staring out his window at the ocean. But he saw none of it.

"You want to pull your school? Do it. Do it now. I've got news for you: The kids in this competition? They could kick the asses of the kids at your school. Because they've had to figure out more than calculus and physics. They've had to figure out people and society and themselves. Most of all, themselves. If you don't want them, somebody else sure as hell will."

Silence. The Benefactor's pulse throbbed in his neck, and his breathing was nearly as heavy as if he'd climbed a monstrous hill on his bike.

"Bravo, Richard," the chancellor said, and chuckled. "Wonderful speech. Make sure you polish it up a little before you air it, though. Still seems a bit rough. Regardless, you'll be hearing from the school's lawyer. I don't believe our agreement included having the 'applicants' do meet-and-greets with celebs."

Then the silence lengthened, and he knew the chancellor had hung up. Slowly, he set his phone on the dresser. That familiar antsy feeling was building. He spun slowly toward the window.

Had he been wrong to do this in the first place? Had he concocted this game just to appease his own guilt? To send *someone* to college since he'd never gone, never wanted to go? His way of both validating and invalidating the education system, all at the same time?

His phone buzzed again. Reluctantly, he reached for it. Yaz. He hit *Ignore.*

Drained, he sank back onto his bed. Being the Benefactor suddenly seemed overwhelming. Even being Richard Kelly, CEO of Kelly Tech, wasn't all that appealing. He wanted to be Richard Kelly Jr. of Edgemere Road in Quincy. Whose mom made wicked good berry cobbler. Whose brother always beat him at basketball. Who always killed everyone at chess. Whose dad was a cop, a damn good one, good enough not to get shot during that supermarket robbery, but who came home to his stupid lopsided chair and had everyone shut their pieholes so he could watch the Red Sox.

Richard Kelly. Who could have made his dad proud by taking that scholarship to Northeastern.

If he'd just taken that scholarship. Maybe his dad wouldn't have left so pissed off. And been able to draw his weapon quickly enough, when he'd stopped for his morning coffee.

Why hadn't he just accepted the damn scholarship?

July 20, 8:15 a.m.
Newport Beach, California
Cassidy McGowan

She shoved her flip-flops in the side pocket of her suitcase and zipped it closed. This was it: her last morning in this amazing room. Nisha had told her last night to pack up everything. After the final challenge today, the winner would be announced and she'd be taken to a hotel room. Her flight home would be first thing tomorrow morning—with or without a scholarship.

Cassidy couldn't wait to see Faith. Her arms itched to squeeze that little girl tight and breathe in her milky sweet scent. She wanted to braid Faith's hair and give her the adorable pink sunglasses and matching flip-flops—both of which had tiny palm trees on them—that she'd bought at a gift shop on Balboa Island.

But leaving this house? It felt like she'd just gotten here. Barely enough time to enjoy this room. To finish off her tan. To explore Newport like she'd wanted to. With Sam.

Around every corner was a memory of Sam. Walking on the beach. Sitting on the upper deck of his house playing gin rummy. Renting a tandem bike from a place near the pier and riding up and down the bike path for hours. Making a fire one night on their day off and roasting marshmallows and hot dogs.

She blinked hard and tried to wipe away all those images. She had to focus. Today was the final challenge. Whatever was ahead, she knew she would need to use every tool at her disposal—her charm, her determination, her resourcefulness—if she had any chance at winning. Tyrell would stop at nothing.

She heaved her suitcase upright and prepared to lug it downstairs. That first night, when she'd been spared from Elimination and Lucy had been sent home, she'd thought things would be different. She'd promised herself she would play this game in a way in which she'd have no regrets. So why was she standing here again, connecting the dots of the past few days, only to see them all lead to remorse?

She rolled her suitcase out into the hall and closed her bedroom door. It was time to break the pattern. She had to start playing with her head. Because her heart sucked at this.

July 20, 9:04 a.m.
Newport Beach, California
Tyrell Young

His bag was packed. It was time. Time to show the Benefactor and Cassidy and his dad that he had what it took to be the top dog in this game. And then he was gonna get the hell out of here. That moment couldn't come soon enough.

Colin was sipping his usual English deal of tea and milk. Tyrell stuck two pieces of bread in the toaster and reached into the cupboard for a box of cereal. He wanted to eat fast and be ready.

"You good, mate?" Colin asked, lazily stirring his tea.

"Never been better."

"You ever think you'd make it this far?"

Tyrell reached in the fridge for some milk. "Never thought I wouldn't."

Colin was an all right guy, but Tyrell wasn't in the mood for twenty questions. He wanted to eat and go wherever in L.A. this challenge was gonna take place, and get it done.

"You had some tough competition," Colin said, nodding toward the toaster when the bread popped up. "You had to think maybe Sam had a shot."

Tyrell felt his jaw tense. "Sam overestimated his talents. He got cocky."

"You know, Tyrell, I've been trying to break into acting for a few years now. Tough going, acting is. Especially for a guy with a pretty good British accent, right?" Colin grinned.

"I must say, I've figured out how to spot a mate who's confident and one who's cocky. You've got to have a measure of self-assurance to make it in this biz. That's for sure. But the guy who thinks he's aces? He's usually not the guy who gets the call back."

Tyrell stopped chewing and turned a cold stare on Colin. "You tryin' to tell me I'm cocky?"

Colin shrugged. "You're here, aren't you, mate? You must be doing something right."

That's right, *mate.* He was still here. Still here and still strong. He'd gotten here by guts and determination and skills. Mad skills. It was time to finish what he'd started two weeks ago. And send that Midwestern girl with the killer smile packing.

July 20, 10:30 a.m.
Newport Beach, California
Cassidy McGowan

"They didn't say anything about when the challenge would start? Or where we're going?" Cassidy asked. She was sitting on the couch in the common room of the beach house, nervously twirling a strand of hair. Pretty much where she'd been for the last hour.

"Sorry, sweetie," Nisha answered, glancing up from her phone, where she was scrolling through something, probably Instagram or Facebook. "Just told me to have you packed and ready to move out by ten." She smiled and went back to her phone.

Cassidy could have maybe gone for another walk on the beach. But that would only pummel her with thoughts of Sam. Better to stay here. Be ready. Be focused.

Two camera guys huddled in the corner but they weren't filming. It was like they, too, had been told to show up and be ready. But nobody knew what was happening. She bit her bottom lip and twirled faster.

Nisha's phone busted out a tune by Taylor Swift. Cassidy gave her a you've-got-to-be-kidding-me look. Nisha flipped her off.

"'Lo?" she answered. She listened for a second and stood up. "Sure. No problem."

Nisha walked toward the mantel above the fireplace. She grabbed the remote to the TV and then tucked her phone into the back pocket of her shorts.

"Well, kiddo," she said, turning on the TV. "Looks like your day starts now."

Cassidy's nerves buzzed into action. "Now? Here?"

Nisha shrugged. "I'm just the messenger, but Yaz said to get the TV on because the last challenge is about to start."

Cassidy looked up at the screen. Molly was there, standing on a wide-open, vacant beach. Behind her was a white, modern-looking house that was mostly sharp edges and windows. Narrow, glass-enclosed balconies ran along each of the two floors. The roof looked like it might be a deck as well. Behind the house was a steep, rising cliff of dirt, sun-scorched shrubs, and palm trees.

Cassidy didn't know where this was. But if she ever made enough money doing movies or modeling, that is where she would choose to live. In that house. With that view of the ocean. And the beach as her front yard.

Cassidy felt Nisha's hand on her shoulder. "Hey, Cass, hon," she said softly. "Kick some butt, okay? Bring back the title for the girls' house." Then she slipped into the kitchen to watch.

Cassidy took a calming, steadying breath and faced the screen. She could do this.

"Congratulations, Cassidy and Tyrell," Molly said, as the camera zoomed in closer on her gleaming smile. Cassidy could see why she'd been chosen as host. She looked amazing on TV. In her billowing white sundress with her hair piled on her head and those large turquoise earrings, Molly looked like the girl next door meets Indian princess.

"You've overcome a lot to be sitting here. The Benefactor has been impressed with both of you. Whoever succeeds in today's challenge and walks away with a full scholarship and the education they've dreamed of has not only earned that prize but will represent themselves and the Benefactor well in the coming years."

Cassidy swallowed.

"Over the past two weeks, you've had a chance to get to know your competitors. You've hopefully learned a lot about the city of Los Angeles. And maybe you've discovered a thing or two about yourself."

Molly walked a few steps toward the house behind her and stared up at it. Then she looked back at the camera.

"But someone you probably haven't figured out yet? The Benefactor." Molly arranged her features to look conspiratorial. "Well, I'm going to let you in on a little secret," she said, tilting her head. "He's in this house. Right now. Watching me. Watching you."

Molly placed a finger to her lips, looking thoughtful. "Actually, though, the Benefactor *has* told you a little about himself." She paused and let a slow, mischievous smile spread across her face. "*If* you were paying attention."

Oh crap. Cassidy suddenly knew where this was headed, and it was like she'd just hit the 127-foot drop of the American Eagle roller coaster at Great America. Her stomach walloped her in the throat. She was screwed.

"For your last challenge, you must figure out the identity of the Benefactor. He's been dropping clues for you to follow since the very first day of this competition, since the very first challenge. In fact, some of the challenges had clues embedded in them. You just have to piece it all together and determine the name of the guy who will be signing a very large check later today. Do it first, and that check is yours."

Cassidy's brain was swirling. Muddling. Sure, there had been clues. Would she be able to remember any of them?

"How do you claim victory? Once you think you know his identity, you'll write it down on a card that your house custodian will give you. Then you'll give that card back to the house custodian, and they will place it in an envelope and seal it closed. They'll hand you that sealed envelope and a ticket. The ticket is your final clue about the Benefactor's location, since"—she glanced behind her—"he doesn't plan on staying home for long. Once you find him and are in his presence, he'll open the envelope. If he sees his name written on the card there, he'll be writing *your* name on a check. If not? You may have lost out to your competition."

Molly tilted her head and sighed lightly. "Be careful. You only get one shot. Write the wrong name, and you'll be filling out college applications this fall like every other senior in America."

The panic was rising. She could feel it speeding up her heart. Racing down her veins, making her fingers want to twirl her hair in a bad way.

"You've gotten this far, superstars," Molly said, looking straight at them through the screen. "Prove now that you are meant to have that money."

She raised her arm like she always did and dropped it. "Go," she said. And the TV went black.

Cassidy felt her legs lift her from the couch. She heard herself ask Nisha for the card and envelope. She vaguely saw Nisha hand her a pad of paper and a phone, the same phone she'd used the other day for the *SNL* challenge. And from far, far away, Nisha said, "Good luck, Cass. You got this."

But she didn't *got* this. No way did she *got* this.

She stumbled toward the dining room table, pleading with her mind to work. Begging her brain to start firing the signals she needed it to. The first challenge . . . Disneyland. What would that have to do with the Benefactor?

Oh, God. She didn't know. She didn't know! She bit down hard on her lip.

The second challenge. The bikes. Was he . . . a cyclist? What kind of cyclist would have *that* much money?

The pressure in her head. It was coming. Just like in physics. Or calculus. It wasn't that she wasn't smart. She was. She just . . . it was *so* overwhelming. She had to slow things down. Slow this down. But Tyrell wouldn't slow down. He'd be forging ahead. He probably already had a few clues.

Focus.

The third challenge. What *was* the third challenge? She couldn't remember. There'd been some time off. She'd gone to the beach with Sam. Was that before or after the third challenge?

Sam.

She dropped her head into her hands. He should have been here. Not her. *He* would've have nailed this. He was so perceptive and observant. And if she hadn't sold him out . . .

The guilt was overtaking her again. Nipping at her throat and behind her eyes. Bringing these stupid tears. And she couldn't cry. Not with the cameras on.

Focus.

The pad of paper. She'd write down what she remembered and—

The front door to the house opened, making her head snap up.

He had on his favorite Bob Marley shirt. The cut-off jeans that hugged his hips and made his thighs look even more muscled. A red, yellow, and green beanie—despite the fact that it was probably eighty-five degrees outside. And a grin that warmed her soul and instantly brought clarity to her head.

"Sam," she breathed.

He strode toward her, squeezing her shoulder as he scooted a chair next to her, pulled off his beanie, and sat down.

"So we've gotta figure out who the Benefactor is, right?" he said, turning so his eyes locked onto hers, zapping life and hope into her. "Shouldn't be too hard. I say we get you some scholarship money, Cassidy McGowan from Chicago. Are you in?"

Her heart hiccupped when he smiled. Yeah, she was in. *So* in.

July 20, 10:45 a.m.
Newport Beach, California
Tyrell Young

Hiroshi's expression was closed and unreadable when he walked through the door of the condo.

"Dude," Tyrell said, knocking his chair backward in his rush to stand. "Look, man, you have to understand . . ."

He took a step toward Hiroshi. If Hiroshi took a swing, Tyrell was going to have to be fast. Hiroshi had wings like a beast.

Hiroshi stared Tyrell down. He didn't move. He stood in front of the doorway he'd come through just a moment before, with no explanation and no warmth. Tyrell didn't know why he was there. But he had no desire to get pummeled on TV. He needed to start explaining. Beginning with why he'd betrayed their friendship during the Elimination after the Pantages Theater.

"Hiroshi," he said softly. "I know I screwed you over. But one of us was going home. I couldn't let it be me."

"I made a mistake," Hiroshi said. "I mistook an alliance for a friendship. You were playing the game. I understand that now."

Tyrell probably should have been relieved by Hiroshi's words. It was as close to redemption as he was going to get. But instead he felt a sourness low in his throat. At one point, Tyrell *had* considered Hiroshi a friend. Maybe they'd only known each other for a few days, but they'd hit it off, found common ground, had a mutual respect for each other's athleticism and work ethic.

Tyrell stared hard at the guy in front of him. Wearing a tight black T-shirt and loose basketball shorts, his arms crossed firmly over his chest and his features arranged in a do-not-mess-with-me grimace, Hiroshi was badass. But more than that, he was a classy, stand-up guy. The kind who'd have your back if things got rough. The kind who'd never in a million years sell you out.

"Man, I'm sorry," Tyrell said, and realized that he meant it. No gameplay. No agenda. "If I could do that night over again, that Elimination, I would play it differently. I know that the reason I'm here is because you're not."

Hiroshi stayed motionless. His dark eyes remained impassive. Then he nodded.

"I'm here to help you win the scholarship. And I don't intend to lose twice."

It was way more than he deserved. Tyrell reached forward for Hiroshi's hand. Like he had done on Day One of this competition, outside of Disneyland. "I'd be honored to have your help, bro," Tyrell said.

July 20, 11:22 a.m.
Newport Beach, California
Cassidy McGowan

Everything about Sam was distracting.

His smell—this intoxicating mix of tangy citrus, musky deodorant, and manly sweat. The way a sheaf of his dirty-blond hair would fall forward when he bent over the table and he'd absently tuck it behind his ear. The prickle of electricity that shot up her arm every time his skin brushed hers. She wasn't sure how she was supposed to win this challenge with him so close by. She wasn't sure how she was supposed to care.

"Disneyland stumps me a little, Cass," he said, gnawing on the eraser end of the pencil. "I'm not making the Disneyland connection so we're gonna set that one aside. Molly said something, though, right before she explained the challenge. She was talking about why the challenge was important, I think, and she said . . ."

It came back to her. "She said that he was one of the richest guys in America or something like that!"

Sam grinned. "The Forbes 400. It's a list put out every year that ranks people by how much they're worth. You know, the Bill Gateses of the world."

Cassidy grabbed the pencil from Sam's hand and slid the pad toward her. She scribbled *Forbes 400* at the top of the pad.

"Should we look it up now?" she asked, reaching for the phone.

"Naw," Sam said, grabbing the pencil again. He used his finger and the pencil to tap out a steady beat on the edge of the table. "Too many people on that list for us to know who she was talking about. Let's get a few more things hammered out. What else do we know?"

"We know he lives at the beach. In a killer house."

Sam jotted it down. "You saw the house? What did it look like?"

Cassidy described the house and the background.

Sam jammed some more on the table. "I'm thinking it can't be too far away. He'd want to be close to what's going on. Plus, it kind of sounds like maybe Santa Monica or Malibu. Definitely a northern beach. The southern beaches are all pretty crowded, and I don't think any of them have mountains right along the coast. Laguna, maybe, but again those beaches are more populated."

Cassidy jotted down the towns he'd named. "How do you know this?"

Sam shrugged. "When I knew we were coming here for this show, I did my homework. You know, learned the lay of the land?"

Cassidy studied his profile. He had a strong jawline with some rough stubble coating his chin. His nose sloped neatly downward toward full lips. She shook her head to clear it.

"Okay, so the bike-riding challenge. You think he's a cyclist?" she asked.

Sam popped the pencil against his chin. "If he is, he's recreational. Or maybe amateur. Pros don't make enough money to be a Forbes contender. My guess is that he just likes to ride." He jotted that down on the pad.

"So that bike challenge. You remember Molly saying anything before we started?" he asked.

Cassidy shook her head and chuckled. "I was pretty much in a panic about having to, you know, assemble a bike."

Sam laughed. "Yeah, that wasn't your shining moment, was it?"

Cassidy elbowed him. "Hey, I got it done, right? Not that I'll be entering a bike race any time soon."

"But you saved old Henry's ass, didn't you?"

"Yeah," she said, her smile fading. "How do you think he's doing?"

Sam shrugged. "Can't be easy. Losing your dad suddenly like that. But he'll make it. Least he's got his mom."

Sam dropped the pencil and grabbed the phone. He started to punch something in like he was going to do a search. He avoided her eyes.

Impulsively, she reached out and covered his hand with her own. He set the phone down and laced his fingers through hers. Squeezed.

"Sam," Cassidy whispered, glancing up at the cameras filming them intently. She owed him some explanations. But those explanations came with risks. And yet, thinking of how she'd felt when she'd thought she might never see him again, she realized that he might be worth those risks.

"I'm sorry," she said, looking at their hands. "That challenge in the train station. I'm the reason you went home, Sam. I told Tyrell how to find his guy. He kind of helped me out of a crappy situation, so I, you know, wanted to—"

"Cassidy." She looked up. Sam was smiling. "I know. After the challenge, our favorite camera guy told me how it went down. I know what Tyrell did and what you did. I was pissed."

Bandana. It made sense. He would've told Sam. Cassidy felt it all welling back up. The guilt.

But Sam didn't look pissed now. He looked amused. "But that's *you.* It's how you've played this whole game, right? With your heart. And why I allied with you in the first place. Plus, I'm grateful to Tyrell for being there when you needed him."

For a moment, Cassidy couldn't say anything. He'd forgiven her. So easily. It was time. Time he knew *everything.*

"There's more, Sam," she said, forcing each word from her mouth. "That night? When I pushed you away . . ."

She swallowed. *Keep going. Get it done.*

"I pushed you away because I was scared. Scared that I would lose you if you knew . . . the truth. Scared that I would look bad."

Sam turned so that his knees boxed her in. He kept his fingers threaded with hers.

"What truth, Cass?" Sam asked, searching her face.

She took a gigantic breath. She owed him this. And if she lost Alex Ginsberg . . . well, he would have found out eventually. If she lost Sam? She'd walk out of here knowing she'd stayed truthful. She glanced at the cameras again.

"The truth about me," she said. With her free hand, she cupped his chin. Pulled him forward and placed a gentle kiss on his lips. He tasted like the ocean. Her favorite place in the world.

She leaned back and locked eyes with him.

"I have a daughter," she said evenly. "She's two. Her name is Faith, and she means the world to me."

July 20, 11:34 a.m.
Newport Beach, California
Tyrell Young

They were making headway. He had to give Hiroshi a lot of credit. He had this incredibly logical, analytical mind. Tyrell wasn't sure why the Benefactor gave him this help, but it was a bonus.

"I'm not quite seeing the connection between Disneyland and cycling, but I think we have some solid stuff to go on from here," Hiroshi said, letting his eyes run down their list. "We know he's loaded, loaded enough to be named by *Forbes* as one of the four hundred richest guys around. We know he once lived in Massachusetts since Molly said something about that before the Pantages Theater challenge. And we know the business he runs has something to do with technology. That alone ought to give us enough to start a search, right?"

Tyrell reached for the phone and opened up a search engine. "So where do I begin? *Forbes*? That's a long list, dude."

Hiroshi's eyebrows furrowed. "Type in *Forbes 400* and *technology empire.* Let's start with that."

Tyrell did as Hiroshi instructed. He scanned through the list of hits. He recognized some of the names. Oprah Winfrey (though how she figured into the tech part, he wasn't sure). Bill Gates. But the other names were all new. And there were at least three more pages of names. Any one of them could be the Benefactor.

"I think we need another key piece of info," Tyrell said, turning the phone so Hiroshi could see. "We gotta narrow down the field a little."

"Okay, do we know if he's married? Has a girlfriend? Dates supermodels? Is his company in New York, or is he based in L.A.?" Hiroshi asked.

Tyrell threw up his hands. "I don't know. Molly was standing in front of his house. It was this sweet-looking place on the beach. Lots of windows and balconies. That kind of thing."

"She didn't say where it was?"

Tyrell shook his head. "Don't think so. Looked like a private beach, though. Nobody chilling on towels or anything."

Hiroshi placed his chin in his hands. "Hmm . . . upscale beach around here . . . Malibu, maybe? Or Laguna? Don't know if that helps us, though. Not like he's gonna invite us in and show us around."

Tyrell laughed. "Maybe once we win."

"Then let's win," Hiroshi said without a trace of humor.

Tyrell couldn't help but think that if the whole deal was switched up, if he was in Hiroshi's shoes? He wouldn't be as cool. He'd be holding a grudge probably. Not helping the jerk who sent him home win the grand prize.

"Why you doin' this, bro?" Tyrell asked, leaning back in the armchair. He knew they should probably be spending every minute on the task. But this was bugging him. Bugging him bad.

"Somebody from the show called. Said you were in the final two. That I needed to come back and help you with this challenge."

Tyrell felt his eyebrows arch. "You didn't have a choice?"

Hiroshi tapped the pencil on the table. "They said it was part of the contract I signed."

"But you could've been a dick when you came in here," Tyrell said softly. "I probably would've deserved that."

For a long time, Hiroshi didn't answer. Or look up from the coffee table where they'd spread their notes.

"After I was sent home," Hiroshi said, his deep voice a little rough-edged, "I had time to think about what you said during that Elimination. You were right: It was about the girl. I wanted to do this to make it right with Maggie. But you were wrong, too. I also wanted to do this to get back at my mom and dad. To punish them for doing what they thought was best for me."

He kept his head bowed.

"My dad and I talked when I got home. And it was . . . well, it cleared a few things up." He chuckled. "We're from different generations. With different ideas on what's important. But at least we kind of get that now."

He finally looked up. "I'm going to apply to a bunch of schools in the fall. Stanford even." He shrugged. "We'll see, you know. But UC San Diego is a pretty damn good school. And I can swim there."

Tyrell smiled. "Dude, you're gonna kill it, wherever you go."

"You know what I figured out during this competition?" Hiroshi said. "That I'm actually not as smart as I thought I was."

Tyrell laughed. "Yeah, I hear that."

Hiroshi offered a half grin. "When a guy like you outsmarts me during a challenge where we just have to get people into a goddamned room, I know I still got things to learn."

Tyrell laughed. A good, from-the-gut laugh—like he hadn't done since he'd set foot in California. Muscles that had been tight and guarded suddenly released, and he felt lighter.

"You get anywhere with Maggie?" Tyrell asked softly.

Hiroshi's expression darkened. He twirled the pencil absently.

"Tried calling her. She's still . . . angry. I can't blame her."

Tyrell watched Hiroshi's face change, masking all traces of emotion. It was tight again, unreadable. But Tyrell suspected that underneath all that strength was a guy who was still hurting.

"Don't quit trying. She's gonna figure it out. One day, she's gonna figure out that you're the real deal."

Hiroshi's jaw twitched.

"And here's the thing, man," Tyrell said. "We all screw up. We do stupid stuff that we think is right at the time and then realize later is jacked up. But good people—and everything you've ever said about Maggie tells me she's one of the good ones—give second chances. Keep the faith, man."

Hiroshi's head started nodding very slowly. Then he reached for the pad of paper.

"Come on," he said. "We've got work to do."

July 20, 11:34 a.m.
Newport Beach, California
Cassidy McGowan

Her eyes were glued to his face. Every muscle in her body was frozen. Her heartbeat was on hold. Her eyelids refused to blink. Her lungs had gone numb.

What would she see first? Repulsion? Outrage? Betrayal? Anger? Hurt?

Or maybe, the worst of all . . . pity?

For that moment, the competition was forgotten. The movie with Alex Ginsberg didn't matter. Scholarships and colleges seemed trivial. The cameras had faded away.

All that mattered was how Sam would feel about her. Knowing she was a mom. Knowing she'd made one huge mistake. Knowing that if he cared about her, she was a two-part deal.

"Sam . . ." she whispered.

She couldn't read his expression. His eyebrows were drawn together; his brown eyes laser-sharp on hers. His mouth was firm, set. It was like something in him had frozen solid, too.

She squeezed his hands.

"I wanted to tell you . . ." she offered, "but there were cameras, and it was complicated. I wasn't sure . . ."

Her words trailed off. What could she say really? She'd kept a huge secret from him. He'd told her how much she meant to him. And she'd still kept this hidden.

Finally, his lips parted. His eyebrows rose. His breath came out in a long, narrow stream. And he leaned back from her and pulled his hands from hers.

She felt cold.

"You have a daughter." He wasn't asking.

"Yes."

"Wow, Cass." He ran a hand through his hair. "I never thought . . . I mean, I tried to figure out . . . but this never even . . . wow."

Alarm was gathering like storm clouds. He was going to bail. Of course he was going to bail.

"I'm sorry, Sam," she said, trying not to sound like she was pleading. "I can only imagine how surprising this is. Especially right now. But please understand . . ."

And then, without warning, he was up. His chair scraping backward, his legs carrying him away from her toward the kitchen, where he leaned his elbows on the counter. She couldn't see his face. Somewhere, in a distant part of her consciousness she saw the cameras. Filming.

"A kid," he said again. "You have a kid."

"Faith," she said firmly. "She's almost two, Sam, and she's beautiful. The sweetest little girl ever. I know you'd . . ."

He kept his head down. He was talking to the kitchen counter. Not her.

"I thought maybe you had a boyfriend back home. Or maybe you had a record—you know, like a misdemeanor or something. Or maybe you'd had an issue with pills. Depression. This never occurred to me, Cass. Not once. A kid."

He turned his head. "I wish you would have told me."

She stood up and faced him. "So you could have *what*?" She kept her voice steady. "Bailed on me sooner? Looked at me with that *I'm so sorry for you* face? Maybe tried extra hard to help me out because, oh, poor Cass, she has a kid she has to support, so she needs this more than anyone?"

Her voice was rising. "I wanted to trust you, Sam. And I did. But do you get how sharing this with anyone is a huge risk? The Benefactor doesn't even know! Well, he does now, I guess; but we've pretended she's my little sister for so long . . . to everyone. My mom even moved us to a new house, a new school, so . . . so that no one would know she wasn't just my little sister. I couldn't just lean over at the beach one day and say, 'Hey, Sam, oh, by the way . . .'"

She shook her head. "I wanted to tell you. I wanted you to know and have you say, 'It's okay, Cass, I still like you.' Do you know how awesome it would have been to have someone know? To let someone in on this secret I've been carrying for *two years*?"

The stupid tears were coming. They were going to smear her mascara and give her puffy, red eyes. But maybe it was time to let it all go.

"But what if I told you and—" She felt her voice go scratchy, but she pressed on. "And you said, 'I'm done.' Come on, Sam. A seventeen-year-old girl with a kid is not a hot commodity." She laughed, a biting, knowing, disdainful laugh.

Sam straightened. "Hold on," he said, stepping toward her. "I'm not saying, 'I'm done.' I'm surprised. It's a lot to take in, okay? The girl I've fallen in love with just told me she's got a kid, and I'm not allowed to react?"

He spread his hands wide.

Cassidy's stomach roller-coastered. "What did you just say?" she whispered.

"I said I'm surprised," Sam repeated. "I had you pegged for a freakin' drug addict or criminal, not a *mother.*"

She stepped toward him, a bubbliness creeping into her belly. "No, after that."

He moved so they were inches apart. "Oh, you mean the 'girl I've fallen in love with' part?"

"Yeah, that part," she said, her voice husky, her throat tight.

He still didn't touch her, but she could feel the warmth of his body, so close. And she could smell him—that tangy, musky sweatiness. And every cell in her body was on high alert.

"This kid, this Faith?" he asked. "She look like you?"

Cassidy tamped down a smile. "Spitting image."

Sam nodded slowly. "So, I won't be embarrassed when we take her to the park or anything?"

And then it all came at once. Her laughing relief. The stupid, mascara-ruining tears. The goofy smile that she was sure made her look like a bumbling idiot.

And she cared about none of it. Because Sam reached for her waist and pulled her close. His lips touched hers, lightly but firmly, almost possessively, and the room fell away.

Sam knew about Faith. And Sam loved her.

July 20, 11:47 a.m.
Newport Beach, California
Tyrell Young

"There's this guy. Wells Lazarus. He's like number 201 on the Forbes list. He made his money in some software company, but then sold it, and now he mostly invests in real estate. He lives in northern California, though. Not sure he's our guy."

Hiroshi tapped his index finger on his jaw. "Let's write him down anyway. Can't hurt."

"Number 277 is also a software guy. But he's like sixty-two and an Indian dude. I think we would've heard the accent, don't you? Plus, I get the feeling our guy is younger."

Hiroshi nodded. "We gotta remember something else. We need more to go on."

Tyrell set down the phone. "He's rich. He likes bikes. He lives on the beach. He's from Massachusetts. He's got something to do with technology."

"What about the challenges themselves?" Hiroshi asked. "They're supposed to be clues?"

"Could be," Tyrell said. "You think he was on *SNL*? We had that challenge after you left. We had to get a pic with a cast member."

"Worth looking into." Hiroshi grabbed the phone. "He'd maybe be a guest star? Probably recent?" He began typing. "Wikipedia lists all the episodes but only gives who hosted and who was the musical guest. Unless he was the host, he's not going to be listed here."

"You think he's big enough to be a host? Like Zuckerberg?"

"I don't think even Zuckerberg's big enough to be a host," Hiroshi said, using his thumb to scroll through some pages on the phone. "The guy who played Zuckerberg in that movie, maybe, but not Zuckerberg."

"So what's the *SNL* connection?" Tyrell asked, scratching his jawline. "Not the musical guest. Maybe they did a skit about him? Maybe he did something in the news, and they were making fun of him?"

Hiroshi stared up at Tyrell while he considered this. "Maybe. But that's going to be hard to track down on the Internet."

"Maybe he dated somebody from the show?"

"Again, we're kind of grabbing at straws here," said Hiroshi. "If we could just come up with something searchable. One piece of information that would lead us right to him, you know?"

"Have we tried searching everything we know all at once just to see what comes up?" Tyrell asked.

Hiroshi shrugged. "Worth a shot, I guess. Go for it." He handed Tyrell the phone.

Tyrell opened a new browser window and began typing. *Technology, Forbes 400, Massachusetts, beach house.* At the last minute, he typed in *SNL* just to see what came up.

A whole lotta nothing. He got like two hits, and they were way off. He deleted the *SNL* part. Tried again. Hmm . . . now he had something. Some names. He started clicking links.

"Hey, write this down," he ordered. Hiroshi grabbed the pad. Tyrell started rattling off names, following each with a short bio.

"None of these guys sound like they'd do a TV show like this, though," Tyrell said after reading through a few pages.

Hiroshi stopped writing and looked up. His face spread into a wide grin—very un-Hiroshi-like.

"We're idiots."

"Speak for yourself, bro," said Tyrell. "But tell me what's going on in that genius head of yours."

"The show. Of course. It was our biggest clue all along."

Tyrell shook his head. "I don't get you, dude. How can the show . . . ?"

And then it was like a freakin' lightbulb flashed on in his brain.

"The show . . ." he said, enunciating each word like he was underwater.

Tyrell grabbed the phone and typed in *The Benefactor* and reality show. He was scrolling like a madman.

"It lists a bunch of executive producers on the website. You think he's a producer? Or this director guy?" Tyrell rattled off a bunch of names.

"None of those sound familiar from our search. Plus, he's tried to keep his identity a secret," Hiroshi said. "It's going to be less obvious than that."

Tyrell scrolled down. "Get this," he said to Tyrell. "Under 'Created By'? It just says 'The Benefactor.'"

"Damn," Hiroshi said. "He's not going to show his hand. Can you watch the first episode, though? Will it stream from the website?"

Tyrell scrolled back up and clicked on the image for the first episode that had aired a few days ago. "Yeah, man, it's here."

"Find the credits at the end and then freeze them."

He did as Hiroshi said. And felt a smile pull at his mouth.

"It's here, man," he said to Hiroshi. "For like half a second, his name shows up. You're a freakin' genius. And I might have just won this game."

July 20, 12:03 p.m.
Newport Beach, California
Cassidy McGowan

She wanted to win this thing. And she wanted it badly.

Sure, working next to Sam was incredibly distracting. Sure, she couldn't wipe what had to be the biggest, toothiest, least camera-friendly grin from her face. And sure, she was fighting the urge to stand up on the kitchen table and do an embarrassing, hip-shaking dance to show the world just how much joy she felt.

But she also wanted that scholarship.

Suddenly, it seemed more important than ever to be able to find a school near Sam, get her degree—maybe marketing, maybe communications, maybe theater, maybe some combination—and figure out how they could make this whole thing work. Without this scholarship money and the freedom to choose her school, she was stuck in Illinois.

Where she'd be texting and Skyping Sam until eventually their relationship fizzled out. She couldn't let that happen.

"Before the last challenge," she said to Sam, who was busy writing down everything they could remember, "Molly said something about a billion-dollar empire. I remember thinking, 'Wow! This dude is loaded.'"

Sam looked up. "Yeah, now that you say it, I remember, too. She said he had a tech start-up that he turned into a billion-dollar empire. Nice, Cass."

She blushed at his praise.

"What'd she say before this challenge?" he asked. "I didn't get to hear this one."

Cassidy shook her head. "I don't think there was anything. Just the house. But she did say that the challenges could kind of be a clue all by themselves."

Sam drummed the pencil on his chin. Cassidy couldn't help but grin. He had to be tapping or he couldn't think.

"Right," he said. "So bikes. The Pantages Theater. *Saturday Night Live.* Trains. The Dodgers . . ." He stopped. His eyes widened.

"Cassidy!" He jumped up.

Cassidy felt her pulse quicken. She stood up, too. "What? What is it?"

"Dodger Stadium. The suite I got eliminated in. Remember? We had to find the suite. And on every door we passed was the name of the company that owned the suite."

Cassidy's eyes grew large. "That's right! Oh my God, Sam! We were in his suite!"

"I know who he is, Cass." Sam's eyes were electric. Wired. "I know who the Benefactor is."

July 20, 12:34 p.m.
Los Angeles, California
The Benefactor

He watched the door anxiously. He'd been told that both Cassidy and Tyrell had written down their guesses and been given their tickets. Because he'd left his house, he hadn't been able to watch all of this last challenge play out. He had no idea who would come through that door first.

He took a long draw from the beer he was holding. Not his favorite—he liked darker, crisper beers—but it was a hot day and it gave him something to do, at least. Until the kids got there.

He grabbed his phone. "Yaz?" he barked. "How close?"

Maybe Yaz was rubbing off on him. Those two-word phrases.

"Just minutes."

He set down his phone. Another sip of beer. Twitchy.

There was a camera trained on him from behind, still veiling his face. In moments, his identity would be completely unearthed. Everyone would know who the Benefactor was. He'd have some explaining to do. Why this show. Why these kids. Why it mattered.

He'd told Yaz and the show's publicity people that he would do one interview. One. So they'd better make it a good one.

He wasn't sure what he'd say yet. Probably the facts and figures he'd been storing about America's education system.

He could talk about wanting to give a kid a chance. He'd probably have to field a question about why Chancellor Bingham had pulled his school's participation.

But then? Then it got personal. These kids. They were pretty damn extraordinary. Even Lucy. Henry. They'd shown measures of strength and determination that made him hopeful about this generation of young people. Mei—who didn't let a learning disability prevent her from taking risks. Allyson—who discovered that you can have faith *and* self-confidence and do some amazing things with that combination. Hiroshi—whose loyalty to an alliance cost him the game but showed a measure of character rarely seen in today's world. Sam—whose passion and confidence should have taken him to the end. And of course, Tyrell and Cassidy—tough contenders who had shown, despite the different ways they played this game, that they both deserved to be where they were.

He stood up and moved around the small room, trying to ignore the camera that followed him. There was a table of food. He wasn't hungry. He looked up at one of the many screens in the room. But had no interest in the game there.

His dad would have loved this. The whole thing. That family trip to Disneyland when Richard was nine—they'd stayed until the park closed, watching the fireworks and eating popcorn, so his dad had had to carry him back to the hotel. His dad, an avid cyclist, who'd watched every Tour de France until the day he died and taught both his sons to love the sport. A crazy guy who would drag his kids to New York—by train, of course—for the opening of a Broadway play but laugh until his sides ached watching Dana Carvey play the Church Lady on *Saturday Night Live.* These challenges. They were all a crazy but deliberate ode to his father.

And baseball. If the Red Sox were playing, he and his brother knew better than to have friends over. They knew not to interrupt him. They knew his lucky hat and beer stein better be clean and ready for him. Game days were sacred. Nothing was more important than baseball.

Unless it was making sure his boys went to college.

"You gonna throw this away, Richard?" he'd said, reaching to buckle his belt that last day. His last morning. "You get a free ride to one of the best schools around, and you're gonna throw it away? For what? Some crazy idea you cooked up on that computer of yours."

His dad had shaken his head and pointed a finger at Richard. "Not under my roof, you hear? You're going to college. You want to do your computer mumbo-jumbo afterward, you go right ahead. But you get that degree, Richard. Or you find another place to live."

As it turned out, he hadn't needed to find another place to live. Because his dad was fatally shot fifteen minutes later in a Quikee Mart down the block. And Richard's "computer mumbo-jumbo" had turned into a successful software venture which, when sold to Apple five years later, netted him a cool million and a half. That was only the beginning. He'd created apps, helped develop a social networking site for budding artists, founded his own company that worked to build the fastest processors out there, and invented a GPS device that allowed cyclists to track their data without a gigantic watch or a bulky gauge on their bikes—it actually attached to their helmets and piped stats right into their ears.

He sank back into one of the armchairs in the suite. He'd done pretty well. Pretty damn well. And yet every day of his life, he felt that sting of uncertainty. Doubt. Regret. Should he have gone to Northeastern? Would it have changed anything?

His phone vibrated. "'Lo?"

"Two minutes," Yaz said.

The Benefactor gently set the phone on the table in front of him. And took a final swig of his beer. In two minutes, the winner of this competition would be opening that door and handing him an envelope. For the first time, he'd be meeting his kids.

He fought the twitchiness. He needed to appear cool and calm. He needed to look in control. He needed to look like the damn Benefactor.

On the screen, somebody slid into home plate, and the crowd erupted. He didn't know which team it was. Wasn't even sure who was playing besides the Dodgers.

He glanced at the clock: 12:46. He looked at the door, swallowed.

The doorknob spun. He closed his eyes and breathed in a steadying breath. Then he turned to greet Tyrell and Hiroshi as they burst into the room.

July 20, 12:46 p.m.
Los Angeles, California
Tyrell Young

His stupid hand was shaking. This was it. He didn't know if he was first or last. For all he knew, Cassidy had claimed the damn prize hours ago. She could be holed up someplace in this stadium, cheering on the Dodgers, laughing it up, and knowing she was going to a kick-ass school next fall.

"Good to meet you, sir," he said, as the Benefactor rose and walked toward them.

He wasn't what Tyrell expected. But then Tyrell hadn't wasted any time Googling images of him. The Benefactor had on jeans and a black T-shirt. Tyrell figured he'd be wearing an Armani suit or at least tailored pants and a button-down. The guy's hair was an unruly, wavy, thick mess. He had deep-set brown eyes and large eyebrows. And he was thin. Like wimpy thin.

One look at him and anybody would know he spent his day with computers and not a football.

"You, too, Tyrell," the Benefactor said, offering a quick smile.

His handshake was firm, though Tyrell might have said he looked kinda nervous, too.

"You have something for me?" the Benefactor asked.

Tyrell pulled the envelope from his back pocket. "Yes. Yes, sir." He handed it over.

"You found the challenge . . . well . . . challenging?" the Benefactor asked, sliding a finger into a corner of the envelope and breaking it open.

Tyrell nodded. His heart was hammering. What if they were wrong? They'd checked and double-checked it against the other stuff they knew. Hiroshi was a genius. But what if it had been a trick . . . ?

The Benefactor pulled out the card inside. He kept it facedown in front of him.

"You want this, don't you?" he asked Tyrell.

Tyrell chuckled. "Probably more than any win for any game I've ever played. Yeah, I want this."

The Benefactor looked at the card. He looked up at Tyrell. Then he spun the card around.

"Richard Kelly Jr.," he read. And a slow smile spread across his face. "You nailed it, guys." He stuck out his hand toward Tyrell. "Congratulations."

Tyrell shook his hand, feeling a powerful wave of emotion crash over him. He'd done it. He'd won. He turned toward Hiroshi, and before the guy could stop him, he grabbed him in a one-armed hug. "Thanks, bro. I owe this to you. And I can't repay you. Ever."

Hiroshi pulled back and looked at him. Not smiling. But not glaring, either.

"Kick some ass at LSU."

"Done."

Tyrell stepped back and breathed. Breathed in the feeling of relief and victory.

The Benefactor beckoned him to some chairs, as Hiroshi was subtly led to a couch off to the side. "We've got a lot to talk about, you and I."

Tyrell sat in a chair across from him.

"I can't thank you enough, sir," he said. "This has been the most incredible few weeks. And this scholarship . . . it's going to make a huge difference."

The Benefactor nodded. "I'm glad. You've earned it. I want to hear about the competition. You've had some interesting moments."

Tyrell chuckled. "I guess you could call them interesting."

"You've also had some help," the Benefactor added, nodding toward Hiroshi.

"Yeah," Tyrell said slowly. "I have. And that's something I want to talk to you about."

July 20, 12:59 p.m.
Los Angeles, California
Cassidy McGowan

As soon as she saw Tyrell sitting in the seat across from the Benefactor, she knew. She'd lost. It was over.

She reached for Sam's hand. He squeezed her fingers hard as they entered the room. She took a deep breath and tried to remind herself how much she'd won.

Both Tyrell and the Benefactor stood up.

"Cassidy," the Benefactor said, reaching out to shake her hand. Taking her envelope. "So good to finally meet you."

She must have muttered something in return. She didn't remember. She was trying so hard not to fall apart. Not to let all her disappointment come rushing forward like the waves of Lake Michigan on a windy day.

The Benefactor opened her envelope. Read her card. Flipped it around for the room and the cameras to see.

"Richard Kelly Jr. In the flesh."

He smiled. She might have. Or maybe she just stared blankly. She wasn't sure. She'd have to watch the episode later to find out.

"Unfortunately, Mr. Young here came up with the answer a bit faster. And was able to claim the scholarship."

She clung to Sam's hand. Tried to focus on the Benefactor's words. Tried to look like she cared. When she didn't. She just wanted to get out of there. And home to Faith.

"You both deserve praise and congratulations for your efforts in this game. You've shown so many of the qualities that will no doubt bring you success in the future."

Faith. Would she remember how Cassidy always read her *The Poky Little Puppy* every night before bed? Had someone remembered to take her to her checkup last week? Cassidy had tried to reschedule the appointment, but the doctor had been booked. She'd told Justin to remind Mom.

"Cassidy, you've played this game with honesty and integrity," the Benefactor continued. Sam tightened his grip on her hand. "The depth of your character has been made evident throughout this competition, and your family, I'm sure, will be very proud."

The Benefactor gestured toward four leather chairs placed neatly around a low circular table. "Cassidy? Tyrell? Why don't you each sit for a minute? Sam and Hiroshi, would you like to wait for us over there"—he gestured toward the wide glass window where the green grass of Dodger Stadium could be seen below—"and watch the game for a moment or two?"

Numbly, Cassidy sat. She saw Sam find a stool where the Benefactor had indicated. And wished fervently that he could've stayed by her side.

"So, some quick business. Tyrell, I'll be writing a check before you leave today. This money is designated for education purposes only: tuition, room and board, books, transportation to and from school. You will be asked to provide an accounting of it, and anything that doesn't fit our qualifications, you'll be asked to repay in full."

Tyrell nodded.

"However, you and I spoke earlier—just a few minutes ago, in fact. And you've asked for one caveat to that agreement. A caveat to which I've agreed." The Benefactor nodded at Tyrell. "Do you wish to explain for Cassidy?"

Tyrell cleared his throat. He turned toward her and took a deep breath.

"Cass, I wouldn't be standing here if you hadn't helped me out in the train station. You don't even know this, but I was clueless about how to do that whole task. From watching you, I figured out that I had to read the train schedules. Then, after that guy was messing with you, you gave me exactly what I needed to know to finish the task. I'm pretty sure I'd have been out, and Sam would be standing here, if you hadn't done that."

Cassidy's brain was muddling. What was she supposed to do? Tell him *you're welcome.* Hug him. She *was* happy for him. It was great that he'd won. Now, she really wanted to go home.

"Maybe you've heard me talk about this, Cass, but I came here because I got an injury this past season that kept me from playing ball. It messed up my ACL, but mostly it messed with my head. I did all my physical therapy, and everybody said I was ready to play again, but every time I got back out there, I was freaked out that it would happen again."

Tyrell's legs started bouncing. "But here's what I figured out, being here: no risk, no reward. I'm gonna play football this year. And if I do, I'm gonna apply to LSU and try to get in on an athletic scholarship."

He looked right at Cassidy. "Which means I'd have a big old check sitting around going to waste. I just asked the Benefactor that maybe I could be allowed to, you know, pass that check along. To a really deserving second-place finisher. So she could go be with her long-haired Rasta-man up in Seattle or wherever. Though, personally, I'd tell him to drag his ass down here. You're a beach girl."

Words gummed up in her throat. Cassidy looked from Tyrell to the Benefactor. And finally to Sam sitting across the room.

Sam lifted his chin at her. "Pretty sure you're supposed to talk now, kiddo," he said. "When somebody tells you he might be giving you his scholarship, it's customary to at least say thanks."

Hearing Sam say it made it real. She smiled. And reached forward to hug Tyrell. A long, tight hug that made Sam say, "Whoa, now, I said, 'say thanks,' not accost the guy!"

Laughing, she backed up. Sam came forward and easily laid an arm across her shoulders. He reached out to shake Tyrell's hand. "You're not such a bad guy, after all," he said.

Tyrell laughed. "Didn't think I had it in me, did you?"

Sam shrugged. "Nice to see this side of you, I'll say that."

The Benefactor clapped his hands once to get their attention. "Before we wrap up, why don't all four of you grab some food and take a seat. I'd like to ask you some questions about the game. And you can take this opportunity to ask me whatever you'd like."

Sam, Tyrell, and Hiroshi headed off toward a table that was loaded with food, jostling one another like guys who'd known each other for years. Cassidy hung back, waiting until the three guys were busily heaping their plates of sandwiches and cookies.

"Did you send Alex Ginsberg?" she asked, staring down at her Converse.

"Nope," he said. "That was a surprise for me, too. But, Cassidy, be careful. Sometimes those guys will tell you what you want to hear until you aren't useful to them anymore."

She nodded. For a moment, neither of them said anything. She started to turn toward the food. To follow Sam.

"Cassidy." She turned back around. "You *are* capable. And just because you have a daughter doesn't mean you can't follow your own dreams. In fact, I think Faith should grow up knowing her mom did what she wanted to do. It might be harder, but you can set that example for your daughter."

"You knew?"

"I guessed." The Benefactor shrugged lightly. "You left clues. Your reaction to my announcement about Henry's dad's death. The way your eyes lit up with Downey Jr.'s kid. The photo in your room. The secret you were keeping from Sam. My dad was a cop. I learned to pay attention to details from him." He smiled.

"Cassidy," he continued. "When you leave here, you're going to be fielding a lot of calls. Calls from agents and casting directors and all sorts of people who want to see what you can do. You look amazing on camera, and there are going to be people who want to grab you." His intake of air was noticeable. "Make sure you have a solid support system around you to keep you grounded and help point you in the right directions."

She smiled, meeting Sam's eyes. Having loaded up his plate, he was coming back toward her. "I think I'm good there," she said with more confidence than she'd felt in a long time. About anything.

July 20, 7:34 p.m.
Malibu, California
The Benefactor

His plane left in the morning. The kids all flew out in the morning as well. They were staying at a Marriott near the airport, supervised by Nisha and Colin, but probably partying it up on his dime. The cameras were off. And they deserved to let off some steam. They'd be bombarded by media and fame and unending questions soon enough. They should enjoy their obscurity while they could.

He leaned back in his chair. He'd miss this chair. This view. His apartment in New York was smaller. Tidier. More functional. He liked functionality. But, oh, this chair. And cycling in New York sucked.

He'd been surprised by Tyrell today. Pleased, but definitely surprised. He hoped the kid made it on his own—there was something about Tyrell that made him think it would be more meaningful to him that way. Plus, it meant that Cassidy would end up with a scholarship as well. *Two birds,* his dad would have said.

Hiroshi hadn't surprised him. He had a feeling that kid was Stanford-bound—without his help. What he did hope was that there would be a pixie-haired, green-eyed girl waiting for him when he got home. He deserved that.

Cassidy and Sam had playfully argued about where she should apply to school. They'd kind of tentatively decided on UCLA or maybe UC Santa Barbara so she could be by the ocean. Sam was going to find a small apartment in North Hollywood as soon as he could, finish out high school down here, and see if he could get a gig with a local band. The Benefactor had already quietly made a few calls on Sam's behalf. In the next week, Sam was going to hear from the head of a small studio looking for a guitarist to play some backup for recording artists.

He'd miss this. Being *The Benefactor.* Pulling strings and watching the kids.

But there were board meetings to attend and prototypes to check out. E-mails to answer and ideas to invest in. And maybe this year, he'd finally find time to date.

Then next spring, he'd put it all aside again. He'd ignore the snide remarks of his board members while he waded through the files of applicants. He'd huddle with Yaz until they found their Elite Eight. Eight new kids full of hope and promise. Each with secrets to hide. Each with dreams for the future. Dreams that he, the Benefactor, could help make a reality.

ACKNOWLEDGMENTS

With the whirlwind of deadlines that came with this project, I was fortunate to have a support system of people who answered my desperate calls for help and became advisors, readers, and cheerleaders. To them, thank-yous are not sufficient; I probably owe everyone Starbucks, too.

To Jill Corcoran, Agent Superwoman, whose boundless energy is contagious and who got me this gig. I'm lucky to have you in my corner.

To Marilyn Brigham, who cuts and adds and suggests, and should definitely be given the title of Genius.

To my faithful readers, Marie Cruz, Nicole Popel, Emily Allen, Nicole Hester, and Amy Shires—you are lifesavers, friends, and the fastest readers on the West Coast.

To my father, Ron Ross, and father-in-law, Tom Fry—huge thanks for reading and commenting to the very end. (But no telling who wins!)

To Richard Johnson and Zach Fry—thank you for that walk in Central Park that produced the ideas for the last three challenges. The Benefactor would have loved you guys, and you would have taken home the scholarship money, for sure.

To Barbara Johnson—thanks for talking me through Henry's character (and breakdown) and being the most wonderful resource, sounding board, and friend I could ask for.

To Matt Elofson, for wicked good (and definitely not exaggerated) stories about Quincy, Massachusetts.

To my brother, Josh Ross, for knowing the best ways to contact *SNL* stars without ever having to look it up.

To my husband, Brad, for reading each episode hot off the press, letting me ramble about these eight kids as if they really existed, and for the clever Pantages Theater challenge.

And to my kids and Mom, for always telling me the beach was overcast and boring, so I wouldn't feel too bad about staying home to write.

About the Author

Deanna McClure/Four Eyes Photography, 2012

Growing up in the Midwest, Erin Fry was strictly a bookworm who "ran like a girl" (quoted from her brother). These days, Erin is a marathoner, a certified kickboxing instructor, and a sixth grade teacher at a middle school in southern California. She also reviews books for *Publishers Weekly* and is a co-founder of Common Core Curriculum Specialists, which creates CCSS Teachers' Guides for authors and publishers. Erin is the author of two middle grade novels: *Losing It*, which was published in 2012, and *Secrets of the Book*, which debuts in 2014. *The Benefactor* is her first novel for teens. She lives with (and frequently runs alongside) her husband, three children, and their golden retriever. Learn more: www.erinmfry.com.

Kindle Serials

This book was originally released in Episodes as a Kindle Serial. Kindle Serials launched in 2012 as a new way to experience serialized books. Kindle Serials allow readers to enjoy the story as the author creates it, purchasing once and receiving all existing Episodes immediately, followed by future Episodes as they are published. To find out more about Kindle Serials and to see the current selection of Serials titles, visit www.amazon.com/kindleserials.